LIN FINITY
AND HER
MAYHEM RISING

Other Books by Edward Allen Karr
* * * * *

SERIES: Fringes of Infinity
(Contemporary Fantasy Fiction)
Lin Finity in Holding On – Novella
Lin Finity and the Words Unspoken – Book Two
Lin Finity and the Islands of Time – Book Three
Lin Finity and the Flights to Forever – Book Four
Tayo Tersoo and the Hunter of Souls – Book Five
* * * * *

SERIES: Thrills N Kills in the Hills
(Racy, Comical Horror in Beverly Hills)
Dayzee Dazzle and the Kildare Killers – Book One
Dayzee Dazzle and her Manic Mansion – Book Two
Dayzee Dazzle and the On-Set Onslaught – Book Three
Dayzee Dazzle and the Cadaver Collectors – Book Four
* * * * *

SERIES: Risk and the Killers
(Sequel Series to Thrills N Kills in the Hills)
Below the Bay – Book One
Dying to be Widow – Book Two (Coming in 2025)
* * * * *

SERIES: Socrates Lewis Stories
(Psychological/Religious Fiction)
Crosswinds – Book One
Crossovers – Book Two
* * * * *

SERIES: A World So Close
(Middle-grade Fantasy Adventure & Coming of Age)
Jayden Blue and the Gift to Imagine – Prequel
Jayden Blue and the Sword in his Shadow – Book One
Jayden Blue and the Call of the Wings – Book Two
Jayden Blue and the Lair of the Iron Lions – Book Three
Jayden Blue and the Journey to Val ka'Yoom – Book Four
Jayden Blue and the Forest of Night Fallen – Book Five
Jayden Blue and the Wait of the Sun – Book Six

* * * * *

LIN FINITY
AND HER
MAYHEM RISING

Fringes of Infinity
Book One

Edward Allen Karr

Lakeside Letters, LLC
30628 Detroit Road, #247
Westlake, OH 44145

This is a work of fiction. Names, characters, businesses, events, and incidents are the products of the author's imagination. Any resemblance to actual persons, living or dead, or actual events is purely coincidental. Certain long-standing institutions are mentioned, but the characters are imaginary. The opinions expressed are those of the characters and should not be confused with those of the author.

Lin Finity and her Mayhem Rising
Fringes of Infinity Book One
©2019 Edward Sechkar.   All rights reserved.

No part of this book may be reproduced in any form, stored in any retrieval system, or transmitted in any form by any means—electronic, mechanical, photocopy, recording, or otherwise—without prior written permission of the copyright holder, except as provided by United States of America copyright law. For permission requests, submit a written request to the publisher at the address shown.

First Edition, 2019
www.LakesideLetters.com

Cover design by JD Smith Design
Front Cover Model: Kim Hendrickson as Lin Finity

ISBN-13: 978-1-950886-00-5

Dedication

This work is dedicated to all who have left,
and any who might yet leave,
a trace of their magic on my soul.

"And even if I told you about those guys, I wouldn't have any chance at explaining to you what happened. How crazy it felt. How I felt crazy. No, Jack, you just think of me as Pussy May—"

She sat up quickly, casting the heavy coverings aside as her breaths suddenly realized it was time for some serious activity.

"Mayhem? Pussy Mayhem? Oh, God, Jack. That explains it as well as anything."

The fan waited for more, not quite understanding her point.

"That's what the hell is going on with me. It's mayhem!"

From Chapter 8 – Mayhem Within

Table of Contents

xi

Chapter 1 – Lin & Gabby

"Broken hearts or broken bones . . ."

Lin parted her red lips only enough for the words to escape.

"Does it really have to be one or the other?"

"Yes, Gabby, it does. Every time."

Lin grasped the wheel more tightly and repositioned herself in the black leather seat. Beneath the hem of her short black skirt, bare thighs led to shapely calves that ended with her favorite heels.

She stepped down hard on the gas, demanding more performance from the Temt8tion's big engine. Signs dotting the edge of I-79's surface streaked past. She kept her car rocketing through a tunnel carved out between hard pavement and low clouds.

"I'm exaggerating, of course. I've never broken anyone's bones."

"Hearts, though."

"Oh, yeah."

Lin laughed lightly and relaxed her hold, and her eyes never left the road rushing toward her.

But the smile withered and was gone, and Lin groaned while trying to pull her short skirt down to cover more of her thighs. There just wasn't enough fabric to maintain any real modesty.

"Do you enjoy dressing like this? There's been a big change in your clothing the last couple of months."

"Yeah, I like it. This feels like the new me. Or, I should say, the real me. I've had enough of downplaying myself. Why hide it?"

"You definitely have a style now. Very memorable."

"You get the credit, Gabby. About a year ago, you made a comment about my unimaginative outfit. I forget which one. You weren't being mean—I can't imagine you ever would—but it hit a nerve somehow. Starting then, I became more and more tired of the old look."

"Perhaps it was just time for you to make such a change. Your new style is quite striking. Have you stopped with the chocolate bars too?"

"Yeah. I can't keep gobbling those forever."

She gave her skirt a rest and resumed strangling the steering wheel, staring straight ahead as the big motor hummed.

"It might go easy this time, Lin. Maybe no one needs to get hurt. Hearts *or* bones."

She nodded, never looked over, and said, "Well, let's hope. I just need to get this assignment wrapped up, then I'll slack off for a while. I need some easy times in the sunshine after I get through this."

"Do you really need this part-time job of yours?"

"Gabby, I like working at the vet's office, but it doesn't cover everything. So, this is what I do, along with an acting gig when I can get one. You know I don't have a flashy lifestyle."

"Except for your car?"

"Yeah, it isn't cheap. But a girl's got to have some fun too."

Lin watched the road vanish beneath the leading edge of the hood, and the steering wheel patiently tolerated the incessant throttling she was administering.

"Maybe I'm getting too old for this, Gabby. Or too tired."

As she took one hand off of the wheel to shake the tension out of it, she said, "We'll be there soon, and remember, I'd rather you not be in the line of fire. Well, so to speak—I don't expect any violence. I'll meet up with you when it's over, okay?"

"Sure, Lin. Just remember, I'm here to help. I can do more than just keep you company."

"I know, Gabby. God, what a friend you've been. A real angel. I don't know where I'd be without you."

Lin returned her hand to the steering wheel and shook the other.

"I think that's your exit there," said Gabby, "with the sign—"

"Route 5 west. Yeah. I see it."

She gunned the engine and cut over, earning a blaring horn and the obscene gesture that matched it.

"I know you don't need—"

"No, Gabby. No. I don't need a copilot."

A few seconds passed with nothing but a rumbling engine while Lin glanced at the approaching storm coming in off of Lake Erie.

"Gabby, sorry. I told you I was tense."

"You never have to apologize to me, Lin. You know that."

"Yeah, I know."

She scanned both sides of the street as she idled into town, an area wearing even more darkness with the swollen black clouds above them about to unload.

"Think you can find something to do in this dump?"

"I'll be fine, Lin. Just pull over wherever you need to."

Under her breath, mostly to herself, Lin said, "By the ocean. That's where I need to pull over."

But she postponed murdering the steering wheel just long enough to fling back her long blond hair on each side. And she confirmed, with a quick gaze at the green eyes in the mirror, that she'd managed to impose on herself the necessary level of determination for whatever would come next.

Chapter 2 – Sweet Talker

A short drive brought Lin to the hotel where she expected her target would be hiding, just a few miles off of 79. Ancient buildings populated the streets in the almost forgotten area of town. Most were vacant, some seemed to lean and tempt gravity, and others waited only for a match to mercifully finish them off. The hotel's aged brick front featured metal grills over the first-floor windows and a flickering neon sign advertising hourly rates. Its harsh light only deepened the darkness inside pressing against the glass.

Lin pulled up along the curb and scoped the place out from a block away.

"I'll leave you to it, then, Lin."

Never looking over, Lin said, "Okay. Talk to you soon."

A minute later, she saw her mark leaving the hotel on foot. The Temt8tion's low growl echoed off of the crumbling walls as she idled her way along the street, trailing him.

After a block of slow pursuit, the man ducked into a bar, and Lin watched the incoming storm's winds catch the door, forcing him to fight for a hold on it, then slam it.

With the car in park, Lin killed the engine, checked her looks in the mirror, then focused on the bar as she popped open her door.

She swung her legs out, finding small areas of unbroken asphalt for her heels, and she stood and attempted to pull down her skirt.

"What are you staring at?" she said to a shabby man frozen across the street, gawking at her.

"No, I, uh—nothing."

He looked down, then away, and he hurried along.

"Can't blame him, I suppose," she said as she tried to tug down her skirt. "Dressing like this."

The impatient storm crept closer, pushing cold air that swirled around her legs and stirred aromas of garbage and rot. She stood outside the pub's dented metal door and looked up and down the street before she kicked loose a sheet of newsprint from around her ankle and pulled the door open. Damp, smoky air greeted her.

She strutted into the dank air of the dive, past losers and drunks, ignoring comments and soft, appreciative whistles, and took a place standing at the bar. On a Monday afternoon, only the serious drinkers had begun downing shots and beers between those dark walls.

She took a moment to view up and down the bar, then leaned forward on the bar when the barkeep approached.

"Whiskey on the rocks," she said.

"You got it."

"Always like this on a Monday?"

"These folks are pros, lady. They don't take a day off."

As the tattooed bartender shuffled away for her drink, Lin stayed bent against the bar, giving her skirt time to stay high and flash her legs for all to see. She gave that a minute, sometimes swaying her hips to the juke box tunes, then straightened up and gave the room another study.

No face got any of her attention except for her target, sitting in the shadows but with enough neon light to identify him. She held his gaze for a second before she turned back to offer a smile as the barkeep wiped up a spill and set down her glass.

She didn't look toward her quarry again and in less than a minute, he stood beside her.

"Another one for the lady," he said, waving for the barkeep, who rolled his eyes like he'd seen that act too many times.

Lin turned to him and gave him a smile.

"Well, hello, handsome. Are you here to rescue me from the high price of liquor?"

"Lady, I'd rescue you from anything at all. You new in town?"

"As a matter of fact, I am. How did you know?"

"Your style. You got more class than everyone in here combined. I like that style a lot. How can I get to know you better?"

"I'd say you're off to a good start, sweet talker."

Still smiling, Lin finished her first drink and swayed with the music as her next one was set in front of her.

"Are you a model or something?"

"Oh, I'm something, that's for sure. How about you . . . new in town?"

"No, I'm from around here, but I'm heading out real goddamn quick. Maybe out west. Who knows? What's your story? What brings you here?"

"Oh, just looking for some company. So, local boy, know where I can find some?"

"I have a room right down the street. Come back with me, and we can drink in private. I promise, I'll be a perfect gentleman."

Lin laughed just enough for him to hear, then said, "Eh. Gentlemen are overrated. Free drinks, though? Hmm."

She tipped her head back to finish her drink, but her eyes stayed on him as he chugged the last of his and set down the glass.

The man dug out his wallet and threw a few bills on the bar. Lin popped open her small purse and smirked at the sight of a fat roll of large bills crammed in at the top.

"Dammit. Here," she said to the bartender and held out a credit card.

While the card slipped out from her fingertips, she saw her suitor writing on a cocktail napkin.

"I'm going to head over and straighten it out a bit. Can't wait till you get there."

He slid the note to her, then spun off of his stool and walked quickly toward the exit.

"Well?" she said to the bartender, who was still standing over her, holding her card.

"Oh. Yeah. I'll cash you out."

Lin snapped another look at the door, then read the note aloud.

"How far away is that?"

"Not far. A block or two."

The bar door slammed shut, Lin gave it a glance, then turned to stare at the bartender.

"Hey, buddy, how about hurrying it up a little?"

"Sure. I'm on it."

He shuffled toward the cash register, got himself involved with a ringing phone, then lazily punched a couple of keys and swiped her card.

After slamming down the receiver and finishing his own cocktail, sucking it through the thin straw, he sauntered back and handed Lin her card.

"Sorry it took so long, sweetie. Here's one from a secret admirer," he said and poured another shot, then tipped his head toward the end of the bar.

"I don't have time for that."

But she held it up, toasted the stranger holding up his own drink, then downed it.

"Another fan," said the bartender. "Imagine that."

"Just what I need," she said, then swiveled around and strutted toward the door.

A hard shove of the door delivered her onto the windy sidewalk, where the storm's first raindrops evaded her outstretched hand as she looked toward his hotel.

*　　*　　*

Lin ventured inside the hotel and looked around the cramped, dim lobby. A seedy young clerk huddled beneath the weak light of a desk lamp, flipping pages of a magazine. He looked up and belched as he watched her stride toward the stairs with her heels clicking on the bare wood floor.

A second look at his note, then a soft knock on her target's door caused it to swing in a few inches with a low squeal. Silence and the smell of unwashed sheets oozed into the hall.

Lin winced at the sight and smell and pulled back her hand, then groaned softly as she looked toward the stairs.

But she dug into her purse, found her pepper spray, and held it behind her. She gave her wristwatch a quick study.

With a sigh and shaking head to send her mane out of the way and back over her shoulders, she reached again for the door.

A slow push earned her another protracted squeal, and she took one step through the doorway and stopped.

"Hello?"

Without a sound, the worn wooden door swung toward her and cracked into her head. Lin stumbled back, the pepper spray fell to the floor, and her eyes were wincing shut as a cold hand covered her mouth.

Her scream stayed muffled tight as he kicked the door shut and dragged her toward the bed, where he forced her onto her back and held her by her arms.

"Hey, don't even think of it, you damn creep! Let me up!"

"You goddamn tease. You wanted to turn me on, huh? Well, you did it. Get ready for your goddamn prize."

"You don't know who you're—hey!"

Laughing, he started fighting to get a knee between Lin's legs, and she kicked around enough that her skirt was shimmying up over her hips and winding tight around her waist.

"I don't need to know who you are, though," he said, laughing and wrestling to get between her legs. "You're damn hot, and you're getting just exactly what you wanted."

"Last chance, dammit. Get the hell off me!"

"Go ahead and yell, girl. I like screamers."

"You're a piece of shit. Get off me right now!"

"Uh . . . no. Not just yet."

"What are you doing? Since when are you a rapist?"

He froze, leaning his head as he stared down at her.

"What?"

"Nothing. I only—"

"What the hell do you know about me?"

"Nothing, I just met you. Now, get the hell off me!"

He continued the battle, eyes fixed on all that he'd uncovered.

Lin tilted back her head and watched the metal headboard beat against the plain white wall with every savage attack to get her legs apart. The randomness of the pounding became ordered, a steady rhythm.

Like a heartbeat.

Watching and listening, her arms stopped straining against his grip. Her legs stopped kicking.

And the beating heart in the quiet hotel room amplified, became a steady booming.

One arm was released, and a momentary zipper unzipping added to the noise.

"There you go, now. Don't fight it, sweetheart."

The heartbeat quickened.

"You wanted it . . . I know you still want it . . ."

Lin groaned as her eyes batted, then started to close.

"Not now," she whispered. "Oh, God, not now."

She barely heard him say, "Right now, baby. Right now."

To the unrelenting sound like her own heart trying to escape that room without her, everything went black.

*   *   *

Lin awoke to a silent room, lying on her back on the hotel bed and staring up at the ceiling. She lifted her left arm, let it drop, then lifted her right. She kicked each leg.

"No broken bones, at least."

She lifted her head enough to see her skirt still bunched up around her waist and one shoe missing. Laying her head back down, she scoffed as she wiggled her skirt back down with both hands.

9

Covered again, she looked to the right and saw only a packed bag and a clock on a dusty dresser, which told her that only a minute had passed.

Lin looked to the left and gasped.

"Oh, what the hell?"

The man had squatted himself down against the wall in the corner, and an occasional tremor rocked his body. His pants had dropped to his ankles. One white-knuckled hand clutched the floor-length curtain, which he'd pulled up against his head. His other hand covered his eyes, and she could see several trails where tears had streamed down his face. He sat in his own puddle on the linoleum.

With her heart racing, Lin scrambled from the bed and toward the door, where she grabbed her pepper spray off of the floor and turned to face him.

The man looked up at the sound, shuddered when he saw her between his shaking fingers, then covered his eyes again.

Keeping her eyes mostly on the man in the corner, Lin rushed over to her purse and found her cuffs. A few quick awkward steps on one heel and she stood over him, where she paused a second as fresh tears coursed down his cheeks.

"Look at me."

Hiding his eyes behind both hands, he sobbed and shook his head.

"Loser."

Her hands shook as she snapped the cuffs tight onto his wrists. He couldn't push himself far enough into the corner. He didn't speak, didn't resist, and never looked up at her.

Lin got her clothes straightened, slipped on the lost heel, and checked herself in the mirror. Two eyes struggling to hold in tears stared back. She brushed her hair over her shoulders and turned to look at the chained man cowering and hiding his eyes.

"What's the matter, tough guy?"

No reaction.

Lin stepped closer and without a word, grabbed the man's shoulder.

He recoiled and knocked his head against the wall, but still he said nothing. His quiet sobbing continued.

"Yeah, you're a real badass, aren't you?"

She let him go. And she stood and looked down on the once talkative man who had just tried to rape her. She shook her head a couple of times and shrugged.

"Okay, crybaby . . . on your feet. It's payday."

Chapter 3 – Ben & Luanne

Their house crouched uneasily atop a low rise, leaning drunkenly downwind, and the area surrounding it was clear of junk and natural life. It appeared that the Earth all around had gradually nudged all of their belongings up to a high spot, where the next big wind could sweep the hill clean and restore dignity to the land.

Through the red mud and scattering chickens and cats strode Benjamin Barlow, his heavy black boots kicking what tried to get out of the way and stomping on what wouldn't move.

He cussed under his breath, muttering about not taking any more, about fixing things once and for all, as he punched open the dented door.

Just what he needed—a deep gash on the big knuckle of his right fist, same place as last time. He vowed he'd destroy that door later. But not now. This business couldn't wait.

He stood for a moment in the open doorway and bellowed, "What the hell, woman, you cheatin' on me now? Where were you this afternoon?"

Through the doorway, clouds of flies charged inside with him, some orbiting his pale shaved head and more clinging to his sunburned neck.

Luanne's face sagged as she turned to face him. She leaned her head to one side, and she'd already begun to wince. But she seemed determined to answer his question.

Before she could speak, a rough shove sent her flailing toward a kitchen counter crowded with empty beer bottles and dishes and mugs that no longer knew any other place to be. Her curly blond hair swept over her face, and the clutter flew in all directions as she hit the counter hard. Fresh shards of flea market china shined brightly against the grease spots decorating the shack's floor.

Her face betrayed a weariness from another round of the usual drama, and it was immediately greeted by the blur of Ben's backhand. Drops of her blood splashed onto the growing artwork beneath her bare feet.

"Damn, I was nowhere, Binge. Just shopping in town. Why . . . what are you talking about?"

She wiped the blood from her mouth with her left hand while the right attempted to straighten out her knee-length garage sale dress.

"Don't gimme your shit, dammit. Jimmy said he saw you coming out of a bar, laughing and talking with some dude. What the hell were you up to?"

A single throbbing vein had appeared on Ben's forehead. Luanne stopped nervously fussing with her dress and cowered even further.

"Honey, I just went in to say hi to Carla. She said it gets so slow in the afternoon sometimes. I don't know that guy, and he just said something about the hot weather in Georgia, that's all."

He got a strong grip on her hair and forced her to her knees, grinding one into a sharp chip of china. More of her blood made it onto the floor. Her mouth opened for a scream, but she made no sound.

"I've about had it with you, bitch. Why do I even keep your cheating ass around? Why shouldn't I end you right now, huh? Right now!"

He twisted her around, streaking the blood across the floor.

Luanne closed her mouth and allowed her head to be supported by Ben's grasp of her hair. It had been a long while since she'd dared to protect herself, and her eyes, watery and pointed down, said that she'd reached a limit.

"You know, you weren't always like this, Ben."

"Don't call me that. Don't ever."

"Binge. Okay, Binge."

"I wasn't always what? What the hell you talking about, woman?"

"When we were fifteen, Ben. That day with the big truck. You changed after that. I know it's still you in there. You don't have to be this way."

She'd managed to chase away his perpetual scowl, if only briefly, leaving him stupefied. But it didn't last.

"You're a senseless bitch, that's all I know. Keep your dumbass thoughts to yourself, unless you want me to really get mad. And you don't want that, dammit."

Still twisting blond hair in a clenched fist, he looked up at the cracked ceiling, shuddered, then shook her head around like an unwanted doll.

"Dammit. Damn you."

He let her go and quickly gave her head a shove, then spun around and brutalized the door on the way out.

Luanne sobbed quietly as the flies found her to be just as enjoyable as Ben.

*   *   *

The pickup truck had been wearing down from Ben's constant abuse, and it seemed to shrink back as he approached. Countless dents that matched well the size and shape of his boots adorned every side of the vehicle, attesting to their strained relationship.

"Damn Luanne."

He gave the door a solid kick, climbed in, and added more mud, gravel, and a bottle cap to the field of trash beneath the pedals.

With the tall exhaust pipes behind the cab billowing black smoke and hot cigarette smoke snorting from his nose, Ben headed north. All four tires dug into Shotgun Road, squealing and spraying loose stones as he cussed under his breath.

After a skidding turn on Route 29 and a stretch of driving with flagrant disregard for the speed limit, he rattled his truck to a stop at his favorite watering hole.

Ben had some thinking to do.

And drinking. He planned on mostly drinking.

Chapter 4 – Something Inside

The sign flying past on the right said that they were barreling south toward Pittsburgh on 79. The cold rain fighting to reach the back window said that the storm was in hot pursuit.

Over the engine's content rumbling, Lin heard Gabby.

"Do you want to talk about it?"

Lin continued looking straight ahead, repositioned her tight grip on the wheel, and said nothing. But only for a moment.

"The fugitive's in custody, there's cash in my purse, and we're heading south . . . what else is there?"

The sliver of clear sky ahead lured her onward. Lin answered the call by boosting the speed.

"You just seem like you have something on your mind, that's all."

"Listen, Gabby, you worry too much."

After more silence, Lin relaxed her hold on the wheel and sighed.

"It's probably nothing big. I don't want to make a big deal about it. Something weird happened when I was apprehending him. Actually, it was when I was in some serious trouble."

"What kind of trouble?"

"He attacked me. Tried to rape me."

"Tried? Meaning he didn't do it?"

"That's right. Something stopped him. I don't know what. I blacked out."

"Oh, you blacked out. Did that mess up the arrest?"

"No, it didn't cause any problems at all. I mean, I don't know. I don't know exactly what did happen. But something happened, something that shook that loser up. Made it easy to cuff him. He started with way more fight than I expected. Then, he was broken. A scared, broken man."

"You didn't hurt him, though, did you, Lin? No 'broken bones?'"

"No. I don't think so—that's not what I meant. At least, he never complained. I sure wanted to break some bones, though. It was really strange how it happened—I didn't just black out. The feeling is hard to describe—it doesn't make sense."

"How did it happen? What did it feel like?"

Lin frowned, staring ahead, and gave the engine more gas.

"I can't explain, Gabby. It's insane. God, I thought that was all behind me. It's been so long."

"So, this isn't the first time. Do you remember when it first happened?"

"Of course. Years ago. I was young. About the time my troubles finally stopped. I met you shortly after that. It's just not a time in my life I like to look at too closely."

"Yeah, I can imagine. But maybe you can't hide from it forever. Maybe you need to face it like you've faced so much in your life. Figure it out."

"I'd rather not. All I did was black out. It's probably nothing. I shouldn't even have brought it up."

"What if it's not 'nothing?'"

Lin's manicured fingers wrapped around the wheel, strangling it and keeping the car speeding south.

"You're probably right, Gabby. I probably have a lot to figure out. But that, that blacking out, that's . . . I don't know. It scares me. And I know it sounds weird, but I'm fascinated by it too."

Checking the mirror, seeing the black skies chasing her, Lin gave the accelerator an extra stomp, rounding a line of traffic and opening up a clear lane.

"You really like this car, don't you?"

Lin managed a weak smile.

"Oh, yeah. It's not cheap, but it's worth every penny. Fast is good, Gabby, and this car is crazy fast. I have to have eight cylinders. And I like the line of little lights down the hood. The more of them that light up, the faster I'm accelerating."

"Don't people wonder how you can afford it? Nobody knows you're a bounty hunter, do they?"

"Just Jones. And you, of course. It's better if nobody knows. I disappear once in a while, and I'm back before anyone notices. The story I give, if anyone pushes the issue, is that when my folks died, I inherited some money. Which is true. I got enough to pay off their house from the life insurance. That's their own fault if they imagine it was much more."

"Well, that's good—at least you're not lying. Not technically."

"And in case you're wondering, I still haven't told anyone about my daughter's problems either."

"Perhaps that's not really their business anyway."

"Nope."

She drove in silence, except for the engine's steady hum, and only occasionally checked that the storm behind her had conceded its inability to catch her. Through the windshield, the patch of blue sky expanded as she sped up to evade the outermost edge of the bloated black cloud cover.

"How's work going? Your day job?"

"Oh, just the usual. I don't think I ever told you, but I'm starting to suspect that Dr. Grayson has kind of a crush on me. It started a while ago, but I think it's getting stronger."

"Is that because of how you're dressing now?"

"No, can't be. He never sees me like this. The crush started years ago, but it was a lot less noticeable at first. Lately, though, I don't know. It's like he's having a hard time hiding it. I like working there, but I have to be really careful. He's a married man, you know."

"You must know the tight skirts and heels are going to turn heads."

"Know? Oh yeah, I'm well aware. It comes in handy most of the time."

"Not always, though."

"No. It can attract a lot of undesirable crap sometimes too. But you know . . . this is who I am."

Never looking to her right, still monitoring the road ahead, she made an effort to stretch her skirt farther down along her thighs.

"How's Jack?"

"Jack's fine. He's good company when I need it."

"I bet he wants more than that. Did he want to head south with you?"

"Yeah, he does want more. And he probably wanted to go, but he didn't ask. I have a life to live. Jack knows that."

The storm had all but stopped in its tracks, bidding her a safe journey, and the windows had dried. Only the engine's deep rumble could be heard.

"How's Nomad?"

"Oh, Nomad. My God, what a character. He loves me. And I can't help but hug him whenever I see him. He's really something."

"Miss him when you're gone?"

"Of course. Who wouldn't? Look, I appreciate you making small talk, Gabby, but I know you really want to talk about me blacking out. I just can't right now. All I can say is that it wasn't a simple blackout. I don't know how to explain it, but it felt like something from deep inside me built up and came to the surface.

"I think maybe I'm losing my mind. Let's just get to the airport."

Chapter 5 – Rough Talker

"How much longer to the airport, Lin?"

"Less than an hour. But the signs said there are construction zones up ahead. The traffic's already slowing."

"Can you get around it?"

"Yeah, I'll try heading west on 80, then I can take 376 right to the airport. Good idea, Gabby. We have time but still, who wants to sit in gridlock?"

"Nobody."

"Right."

She raced ahead, wove through a slow-moving line of cars, then zipped onto the exit ramp.

"Besides, seeing some Pennsylvania countryside sounds pretty good right now. Hope you don't mind."

"I never do."

She steered her car onto I-376 and headed south on Route 422, then took some smaller roads, at one point heading west under 376.

"This will definitely take us around it."

"I never get lost, Gabby. And look—the scenery is already so much better. We'll get back on the highway in no time."

*　　*　　*

Ten minutes later, a small pond appeared off to the right, calm and murky in the dwindling light. Silent train tracks seemed to float above the water on the far side.

Lin slowed and cruised along the shore until she'd found what she wanted: a small parking area off of the road. Only one other car was there, and she pulled in two spots over and killed the engine.

"There's no rush, Gabby. I just need to sit for a few minutes. That thing back in Erie has me kind of rattled."

"Just take your time, Lin. Sitting here should help."

Lin stared out over the water and brushed her hair back over both shoulders.

"I know. It's just because—"

A rapping on her window interrupted the talk, and Lin looked through the tinted glass to see a man in a white shirt looking in on her. She powered the glass down a few inches, and the man leaned to look in.

"Well, hello there," he said, speaking as if his lips were too swollen and wet to form the words. "I was wondering if you could help me out. I pulled in a few minutes ago, and now that rotten car won't start. I think it's out of gas."

Lin gazed at the grinning man and shook her head.

"I don't have any gas. Have you called roadside assistance or anything?"

"Yeah, I tried. But there's no reception here."

"Well, I can't help you. Good luck."

She hit the window button, but the man had quickly jammed his travel mug in the gap.

"Mister, get that crap out of my window."

With the window stuck, the man peered inside and got a good look at Lin's legs barely covered by her short skirt. A smile lit up his unshaven face.

"I will. Of course, I will."

He paused and sucked at his teeth, scrunching up his face.

"I didn't mean to be rude. It's just that I could use some company until I figure something out. Why don't you stick around a while? We could pass some time and maybe get to know each other better."

"I'm not interested. You need to get back to your car. I'm in no mood for this."

"Sure. I can do that. But I want you to stick around. Come on. Get out of the car for a while."

He licked all around his lips, then grinned.

Lin reached for her pepper spray just as he pried the mug from the window and took a step back. She immediately shut the window and hit the start button. Her Temt8tion roared to life but before she could back out, he'd hurried to her rear bumper and stood blocking her retreat.

She revved the engine high while still in park, then she put it in reverse and inched the car backwards. The man never moved.

"You can't just run him down, Lin."

"He's either fearless or stupid. Gabby, what the hell am I supposed to do?"

She could see the man in her rearview, mouthing words and laughing.

"Call the police?"

Lin checked her phone and tossed it back down.

"No bars."

"What if he had a bounty on his head? What would you do?"

"He'd be facedown, cuffed, and eating gravel. That's what I'd do."

"Well, no need for 'broken bones,' Lin. But you'd handle it, right?"

Lin looked down from the mirror, grabbed her pepper spray and cuffs, and sighed deeply.

"Gabby . . ."

"I'm sure you'll be fine, Lin."

Under her breath, she said, "Why do I attract all the crazies . . ."

She cracked the door and stepped out. The gravel grabbed at her sharp heels as she slammed the door and locked it.

"Yes! I knew you'd come around!"

He started walking around the car.

"Stop. Not another step."

Lin raised her spray and aimed. He stopped.

"Whoa, whoa, whoa, little lady. No need to be nasty."

He held his hands up as if he were under arrest, which made his bloated belly more obvious as it sagged over his belt and stretched his white dress shirt along with it.

Lin scoffed at the sight and said, "You haven't begun to see nasty."

She swiveled her head to look when two doors of his car opened, and two more men stepped out, one from the passenger side and another from the rear door.

She fanned her spray at all of them.

"Not another step, any of you. You two, stay right there by the car. You, mister, step away from *my* car, or this won't go well for you."

"You're not leaving, lady. John, Tommy, get over here," he yelled at them, clapping his hands. "Don't listen to her. She's probably afraid to spray that shit anyway."

He resumed a steady clapping of his hands as the two men took tentative steps toward her.

"She's going to keep us company," he said, almost singing the words along with his clapping rhythm.

"No, I'm not. I'm leaving. I have a plane to catch. Right after I make you regret this."

His clapping took on an urgent, relentless beat.

"She's not going anywhere . . ."

He began a slow walk toward her, and Lin pointed the spray at him, her finger on the trigger.

But it could have been her heart beating with every clap of the man's hands.

"She's my new best friend . . ."

It was only her heart beating, loud and strong.

She blinked, and her head tipped from side to side. Her arm slowly lowered, aiming her defense at the gravel.

"She's *our* new best friend . . ."

The forceful drumming of her heartbeat continued.

And everything went black.

*   *   *

Lin slowly opened her eyes and gazed straight ahead. The silence was broken occasionally by random gusts of wind rattling the dry weed stalks near the pond.

The clapping had stopped, and her heartbeat had calmed.

She looked to her left and locked eyes with John, standing nearby and grinning. She looked to her right and saw Tommy looking up at her. He stood way too close with a big smile and rapidly bounced his head up and down while pointing at the ground before her.

Lin clenched her jaw tight and looked down.

She let out a short scream and pointed her pepper spray. The man lay facedown in the gravel with arms bent in front of him and hands and sleeves covered in dust. His head rested on his chin, which was pressed into a mound sloped up to his mouth. His eyes were locked open, and he'd jammed his mouth full of gravel, all red and shiny wet in the weak sunlight. His ripped and bloody fingertips showed the effort he'd expended in working to fill his mouth with the jagged stones.

He lay there like a man who'd died too quickly to think of closing his eyes. Only a thin stream of blood coursing down his chin gave any life to the scene.

She took quick looks at John and Tommy and saw that they were still grinning insanely at her and not even looking down at their friend.

She stepped close to nudge him with her shoe, but she jumped back just as he had a violent spasm and began struggling to breathe through his rock-filled mouth.

Lin lowered her spray and watched as tears streamed down his dusty cheeks and thickened into a paste.

John and Tommy sat the man up and began plucking the gravel out piece by piece, all the while smiling up at her. Their bloody fingers fumbled about without eyes to guide them.

"Are you worried about him, lady? We can help him if you want," said John.

"Yeah, yeah, we can help him. If you want us to," Tommy said while laughing. "I think you do want us to!"

The man sat there shaking and wheezing air between the stones. Blood and small specks of rock were splattered across his white shirt. The garbled sounds coming through the packed-in shards could have been from some small savage animal that he'd tried to swallow.

When his eyes drifted aimlessly then fixed on Lin, the sobbing became muffled screaming.

Lin took a step back and looked away from the man's terrified eyes. John and Tommy continued to smile at her.

She shook her head and backed away with her heels stabbing into the gravel. She chirped her remote, swung open the door, and got in.

Through the glass, she watched John and Tommy looking more at her than the man they were trying to help. Their mouths moved as they were calling out to her, but only their crazed laughter made it inside the car.

She started the Temt8tion, carefully backed out, and drove past the three men on the side of the road. One sat on the ground, gagging on gravel. The other two watched her drive past, waved to her, and smiled like not a thing in the world was wrong.

"Don't even ask, Gabby . . ."

Chapter 6 – Changed World

Lin's eyes drilled through the windshield, and her body shook weakly. Her hands choked the steering wheel as she piloted the car back to 376, aiming it south. The highway ahead gave her a clear path, leading her on with the promise of sunshine.

"I know you don't want to talk about it, Lin, but maybe you should."

"You're right—I don't."

The engine's deep roar filled the otherwise silent car.

"I blacked out. Again."

"Yes, I know. The second time today. But that's not all that happened, is it?"

She continued to watch the river of pavement flow under the hood.

"Just let it go, Gabby. Not now, okay?"

After half a minute without speaking, she scoffed and half turned to speak to her right.

"I wouldn't know what to say. It's weird. Whatever it is, it's powerful."

"Yeah, I'd agree with that. What does it feel like?"

Lin watched the road, listening to the engine's rumble, and said, "I don't want to talk about it. I know you're a good friend, but I think maybe I'm just insane."

"Are you afraid to talk about it?"

"No. Well, maybe a little. Fine, Gabby, I'll give it a try."

She cleared her throat and began.

"Back in Erie, and just now by the pond, I had a feeling almost like panic but not quite. There was anger too. A feeling that what's happening isn't fair . . . isn't right. And it's even more complicated than that. Both times—in Erie and again just now—I felt that I got myself into trouble from looking good. Maybe too good. Like I caused it. So, maybe there's some guilt there too? I don't know, but it kind of felt like the guilt was holding back my anger and keeping it from spiraling out of control."

"That doesn't sound too strange, Lin. It's understandable. But what about when you black out? What's that all about?"

"Well, that's where things get really weird. All jumbled up. It's hard to describe. It's like my senses are getting confused. Overlapping, somehow. Like I can see sounds . . . smells have colors . . . things like that. It takes over. I can't seem to stop it. And it gets mixed with the anger and other feelings, and it's overwhelming, Gabby, and I know I'm in trouble and have to do something, and it all swirls together, building bigger and bigger, and I can't hang on. I can't. I just black out."

Lin's breaths had become fast and strong.

"Maybe I'm just losing my mind?"

"Oh, I don't think so, Lin. There's something going on, but I don't think it's a mental health issue. But it sure is hard to understand, isn't it? This is a good start. We should talk more often. I think it would help. Let's give it a break for now."

*　*　*

"What'll it be, Binge?" said Duke, the barkeep and owner of the place.

"Whiskey. And don't say a goddamn word about what I already owe you."

"Sure thing, Binge. No worries."

He reached back for a bottle, angled it over a shot glass, then slid it up close to Ben.

"Good start. Keep the damn bottle uncapped."

Ben sparked a lighter to a cigarette, dragged on it, then let it cloud up the ceiling.

"Sign says no smoking, Ben."

Ben scoffed, downed the shot, and said, "You know better than that, Duke. I'll fold you in two like a greasy napkin."

The whiskey bottle rattled a few times as Duke set it down.

"Yeah. Sorry. Thought I owned the place there for a second."

Ben snorted a dry laugh and pushed the glass toward him.

"No one needs you to think. Pour."

Duke poured.

"Problems?"

"Luanne."

"What about her?"

"Nothing. It isn't about her."

"Uh, okay. Maybe another shot, then."

Ben lifted it, sent it down after the first one, then clinked the glass back down.

"That's two," said Duke. "Maybe you'll be—"

"You'd better not keep counting, dammit."

"Yeah. I mean, no, I wasn't. Here. Have another."

He poured, shaking the bottle some but getting most of it inside.

"You having a bad day, Binge?"

"Today's fine. It's . . . no, I'm not even looking at that."

The third shot vanished. The empty glass clinked.

He belched, then turned his eyes over to hold Duke's gaze.

"Better?"

"Enough. It was a long goddamn time ago. Back when I was Ben."

"What was?"

Ben shrugged and began studying the dusty bottles lined up below the mirror dead ahead of him.

"You don't remember?"

"I remember, goddammit."

Duke hurried another full shot glass, then took a step back. From there, he watched as a thick tear jerked its way down Ben's cheek, pasting itself up with dust on the way.

"I remember. I remember the pain and the fear."

He turned to catch Duke's worried gaze, then got his own eyes back to the bottles.

"And the goddamn humiliation."

The fourth shot was history, and Ben slid the glass to Duke without bothering to look. Duke snagged it, filled it, and sent it back.

Ben, still looking straight ahead, wiped at his pasty tear.

"And Duke?"

"Yeah, Binge?"

Ben swirled the whiskey around before gulping it down to join the rest. And the drained glass stayed close to his lips.

"I can't forget the absolute fucking wonder of it all."

*　　*　　*

Lin approached the airport hotel desk in Pittsburgh and said, "Finnerty. I have a reservation."

In the room, after locking and latching the door, Lin let an exaggerated sigh bleed out.

"How about no bounty hunting for a while?"

Wine glass in hand, she propped herself up on a stack of pillows, clicked the remote, and got the TV to illuminate the room. The wine got a healthy hit before she could even scoff at the start of questioning.

"I know you're tired, Lin, but can I ask you something? Can you tell me about the first time you blacked out like that? What led up to it?"

"Oh, I don't know if I want to go there. That was easily the worst time of my life. Back then, I didn't think I'd make it."

"It might help to talk about it, though."

She kept her head from shaking only long enough to finish off the glass.

"Okay, I guess I can try. I remember it like yesterday."

She tried to sip out the last few drops and continued to stare at the TV.

"Gabby, it's best left in the past. I don't think I'll black out again."

"Yes, you might not. But I'd still like to hear about when it started."

"Okay, what the hell. But this is only for you. I don't need to think about it.

"It started the day after my twelfth birthday. I was so sad because I got only a box of crayons and some coloring books. My dad had lost his job months before, and they were struggling to make ends meet. They hid it well, and the only reason I knew there was a problem was because they explained why my uncle, my dad's brother, came to live with us.

"Something about him bothered me, but I didn't know what until one day about a month after that when he was home with me alone. My mom was in the hospital, and Dad was visiting her. My uncle Ray, he . . . oh, Gabby, he molested me right there in my own house. He just took complete control of me like I was a toy. In a soothing voice, he told me I had to be a good girl and do as he said because otherwise, no one would pay my mom's hospital bills, or the rent, or my school, or anything else. He said he was the only thing keeping us together as a family. He told me if I said one word to anyone, it would be me that had destroyed my own family."

Lin paused and wiped at her eyes.

"Uncle Ray worked a night shift somewhere, and he made good money. So, when my parents both finally got jobs, which weren't very well-paying either, and they were out of the house every day, he was always there to 'watch' me when I got home from school. Gabby, you could never understand how this tore me apart."

"Maybe I could . . ."

Lin continued. "But somewhere in my twelve-year-old mind, I knew that even though I couldn't stop it, I shouldn't hide from it either. After it had happened several times, I sort of saw a place where I could hide— somewhere inside. Like a box. I knew I could crawl in there and not even know what was happening to me.

"But that seemed wrong. I couldn't let myself do it. I believed I could do better than that. I knew if I hid, I wouldn't get any stronger. I kept believing that I was getting stronger, every time, and one day, I'd be strong enough.

"I didn't even know what that meant, Gabby. Really, how could I have ever gotten stronger than him? But I believed it. I *felt* it.

"So, I faced it every time, building an anger, a monumental desire that I could stop him. Make him want to stop. We're talking a few years, Gabby. I had nowhere to go. No one to confide in. It was me against him every time.

"God, listen to me. I'm ranting."

She took another moment for her breathing to slow. When it had, she reached over for the bottle and refilled her glass.

"One day when I was fifteen, after years of this, something inside me felt strange. It wasn't like I was in a dream, but the world around me somehow seemed different. Even as I opened the front door and walked into the house, I felt it. I knew it would be different that time.

"Uncle Ray was waiting and was genuinely happy to see me. Of course, he was, the evil pervert. As he walked toward me with his boots clicking on the wood floor, the room seemed to rush at me. Like I was falling into it. The last I remember was the look in his eyes, a look I'd never seen before. No living thing should ever look that terrified. Then, it all went black.

"When I woke up, my world had changed. Ray had changed. Ray never bothered me again."

Lin emptied her glass, poured another, and stared at the TV without saying another word.

*   *   *

Hours later, Ben snorted in his sleep, waking him on the cot in Duke's backroom.

"Damn Duke," he said, slurring the words. "Forcing all that goddamn whiskey on me."

He was close enough, so he kicked the door shut, giving the juke box music a slab of rotting plywood to filter through.

"Dammit, I can't hide anymore. There's only one way to fix this. And dammit, I'm sure as hell going to fix it."

*　　*　　*

The flight took off on schedule and after a short time in the air, it touched down for a brief layover at Dulles. Lin sipped her coffee while reading a magazine, occasionally watching the travelers hurrying in every direction.

"Did you do something to Uncle Ray?"

"Gabby, you just never let anything go, do you?"

"No. I can't."

"Alright, fine. I blacked out, Gabby. But no, I never touched the man. He did it all himself. Or at least, that's what I was told later."

"Did all of what?"

"He . . . um . . . fixed himself. So he could never do again to anyone what he did to me."

"How did he fix himself?"

Lin closed the magazine on her lap and raised the coffee, inhaled its strong scent, and downed a large gulp. She let out a deep sigh.

"I was unconscious for maybe ten minutes. Or at least, it seemed like that, but it might have been more. When I woke up, my dad was there. Actually, he's the one that woke me up. He was saying my name over and over, telling me everything was okay, but I could tell not a damn thing was okay. Somehow, I felt safe and warm and didn't bother to answer him. He seemed to be miles away.

"I could hear my mom crying hysterically in the kitchen but trying to keep it low so I couldn't hear. My mom had bad bouts of depression—that's why she was hospitalized earlier. That whole thing hit her hard. She was never the same after that. I heard sirens too. Getting louder.

"The cops showed up, and I remember a detective, he was wearing a nice suit, and he mostly just looked me over. He took my hands and rotated them around, looking closely. I know now that he was looking for blood. He tried to ask me things, too, but I don't remember answering him.

"I had to go to the hospital for a while, but I don't remember any of that. They didn't bring me back to my house. I stayed at a friend's place for a while. Mom and Dad saw me all the time and called me often, but they were really preoccupied with something. I could tell.

"Months later, I found out that my dad had come home, found me unconscious, looked for Ray, and found him standing in the kitchen. They say he mutilated himself. With a steak knife, which was still in his hand, dripping. I heard it was a bloody mess, Gabby. And that thing about him I hated the most, that was on the kitchen floor."

Lin paused until her breathing had slowed.

"Ray never lived with us again. I was told only that he moved out. My parents somehow managed to keep paying their bills, and no one ever spoke of him again.

"But Ray had really been locked up in a psych ward. My friend Luanne's older sister worked at the hospital, and she told Luanne that Ray was the most timid, quiet person she'd ever seen. All the life was drained out of him. He was like a ghost. He never spoke of what happened that day. In fact, he never spoke to anyone there.

"He hanged himself three months later."

*   *   *

Ben groaned and pried his eyes open, and he snarled at the smell of urine heavy in the air.

He sniffed around a few times and laughed when he said, "Deal with it, Duke."

He rubbed his face and bald head a few times, then hammered the side of his head with a balled-up fist.

"Shit. Goddamn whiskey."

He started to get up, then fell right back again and sat frowning until the door creaked open and Duke leaned in.

"You gonna make it, Binge?"

"How much did I tell you when you were dumping all that whiskey down my throat?"

"I was, um, what? What did—"

"Just screwing with you. I don't need any help with that."

"You, uh, didn't say much. Just some fucked up memories is all."

Ben stood, towering over the spindly bar owner.

"Forget I said anything at all to you."

"Sure, Binge. You know I will. You heading out?"

"Yeah. To St. Simons Island."

"Huh?"

"No, forget that. She probably isn't there anymore."

"Who?"

"No one you know. Run on ahead and get a shot poured. I got time."

"Sure, Binge. I'll get right to it."

Duke backed away, and the sound of his boots scuffing along dwindled quickly.

"If I did go there, I'd probably see her witch ass hiking down Mallery."

*   *   *

Lin tested her rental car's guts, gunning the engine to get started the drive up from Jacksonville to St. Simons Island, and her scowl showed her disappointment. It took longer to get it up to her usual cruising speed but when it got there, her arm hanging out the window, feeling the warm air rushing past, made it somewhat acceptable.

Even with unbroken blue skies wrapped all around her, she still checked the rearview for storm clouds or any other dark things that might be hounding her.

"Gabby, I trust you more than anyone. You've been a Godsend to me. But I've never told you about my nightmares."

"Nightmares? No, you haven't. What kinds of nightmares?"

"They're like everything else, Gabby—confusing, terrifying, and in a weird way, exhilarating too. I don't know what you'd think of me if I told you about them."

"I promise you, I'm always on your side. It's like a job for me. What are they like?"

She gave Gabby a very brief outline of the first one she'd ever had.

"That's awful, Lin. It sounds like you're in some way reliving that horrible experience, when your uncle—"

"No. That's not it, Gabby. That's not it at all."

Chapter 7 – For Taylor

It wasn't her usual fast car, but Lin still got it to speed and weave through traffic as she cruised over the bridge leading into Glynne Avenue. After battling lines of slow-moving vehicles, she finally made the turn onto the Causeway, a four-mile stretch of easy traveling that offered the only real access to the Island, and she let herself sigh and even smile.

"Mm, just seeing those marshes again. The smells, Gabby. God, this brings back some memories."

"I bet it does, Lin. I hope they're good memories."

"Most of them. Not all. There are some really bad ones festering around here."

"You'll sort them out, Lin. You weren't born here, were you?"

"No. Pennsylvania. My folks were having a rough time there and thought a fresh start here would help. Well, it didn't help much. Still, the memories are mostly good. All except for that bastard, Ray."

"That's understandable. Can you just drop me in the Village? I feel like wandering around and mingling with the crowds."

"You're such a free spirit."

"I've been called worse."

They shared a comfortable laugh.

"Sure, Gabby."

Lin pulled to the side, waited patiently, then angled the car back into traffic on Mallery.

Before checking into her hotel, she whipped her car into a bank parking lot and shut down the engine.

"Money matters first," she said while getting out of the car.

She slammed the door and added, "Broken hearts and broken bones later."

Inside the bank, she handed an envelope stuffed with bills to the young teller.

"Yes, all of it. And if you could print out the new balance, I'd appreciate it."

The young man struggled to not look Lin over, then got himself busy typing and staring at his screen. A minute passed, and he gave her the bad news.

"Ms. Finnerty, your deposit *is* the new balance. There was a recent draw that took it down to zero."

Lin stared at him for a second, mouth moving but not speaking.

"Would you like me to print out that transaction?"

"No, I know exactly where the money went."

"The withdrawal was only a few days ago."

"Happens all the time. I shouldn't be surprised it got cleaned out. That's for my daughter. She's got, uh, problems. It isn't cheap."

"Oh, I'm sorry to hear that. This deposit should help."

"It will, and it's fine," Lin said and forced a calm smile. "We'll figure it out."

"I hope so. Have a good day, ma'am."

"Thanks. That's why I'm here."

She wiped at an eye, turned quickly, then made a straight line toward the exit. A quick walk across the lot delivered her to her car.

Seated inside, she roared the engine to life and set the air conditioning on high. The unbroken canopy of the live oaks held the sun's rays back, but the air swelled with water and clung to every surface.

All the vents on the dash were tipped toward her, and the cool blast managed even to lift her hair and flutter a few strands.

"Oh, Taylor, Honey. I'm trying, baby."

*   *   *

Lin shifted into reverse, then quickly put the car back in park. "Dammit."

She gave the steering wheel one last strangle.

"It's for you, Taylor."

She got out, and walked to a nearby pay phone. She dug a scrap of paper out of her purse, dialed the phone, and looked around her former hometown while waiting.

"This is Arnie."

"Hello, Arnie. I was given your name by Jones in PA. He said you're the guy I should see."

"Sure, I remember Jones. Is he doing alright?"

"Yeah, things are good. Look, I'm in the South Georgia area for the next couple of days. I was wondering . . . do you have any fugitives here that I could round up for you?"

"Lord, yeah, I always have a few. You have a preference? We got all kinds of criminals around here that think they can just slip away."

"I was thinking someone with a high bounty. Maybe not your usual lightweight type."

"Not a flabby white collar crime kind of guy, you mean?"

"That's exactly what I mean. Got anything a little more, uh, profitable?"

"Well, I do have one. But he's bad news."

"Um, how bad?"

"Bad as in violent. He jumped bail on assault and arson charges, and he's also suspected in a murder, but there's no solid evidence yet. High payoff, though. Sure that's what you want?"

She hesitated, shook her head, then took a good breath before answering.

"I can handle it. Jones gave me your address—are you still in that office in Brunswick? When can I stop by?"

"Yep, I'm still here. Lovely part of Brunswick too. Why don't you swing by Friday? We'll get you set up."

"Great. I'll see you then. I just need to polish up those cuffs."

She lost her grin as seconds went by in silence.

"It's a joke."

"Okay. Yeah, that's pretty good. This guy really is a handful, though."

"I can joke and still do my job. See you Friday."

*　*　*

The sunlight invaded through every window on the cruise to her hotel, almost laughing at the air conditioning's sad attempts at scaring it away. But the sights and sounds were familiar, even after so many years, as she crossed Mallery and continued on Ocean Boulevard.

"Polish the cuffs. Arnie's right not to laugh at that."

She wrestled with the wheel when the hotel parking lot entrance appeared off to the right. Slowing to turn in, she shivered once as if the car's air had found some reserve strength.

"Don't worry, Taylor. I'll be fine."

Chapter 8 – Mayhem Within

Lin's bulky travel bag tried slipping down over her shoulder when she swiped her hotel room key, and her quick reaction tipped a thin stream of hot coffee onto the hallway carpet.

"Oops."

She bumped the door with her hip, rolled herself inside, and leaned to close it while scanning around the room.

The dresser was closest, so she tossed her luggage there, never slowing as the sight of the ocean through the sliding glass doors called her closer.

On the way, she dug out her phone, held it up with a finger ready to tap some numbers, then shook her head and tossed it onto the bed.

"Just you wait," she said, pointing past the small balcony and addressing the sea directly.

The room phone was near, so she held the receiver to her ear while still studying the playful blue waves.

"The salmon would be fine. Oh, hey, a bottle of Pinot Noir, too, okay? Thanks."

The glass door slid easily, and she kicked off her heels before stepping out onto the warm concrete. She held the top rail and gazed out at two shades of blue separated by only a thin line that bounced gently but still kept them apart. A warm wind lifted her hair and brought the scent of the sea and an occasional squeal from a child playing in the sand.

She let a deep breath out steadily, controlled, and said, "Fugitives in Erie hotels. Rude slobs eating gravel. None of you can find me here."

The deep blue kissing up at the lighter blue sky kept her almost hypnotized until a rapid knocking on her door, followed by someone calling out, "Room service!" shattered her reverie.

Lin hurried over and swung in the door.

"Your order, ma'am."

"Ooh, it looks so good."

"We apologize for the Pinot Noir being room temperature. We had to replenish the supply, and that was just minutes before your order."

"It'll be fine. You can make up for that by uncorking it, okay?"

"Alright! Yes, I certainly will!"

She handed him a generous tip and returned to the balcony to savor the salmon, Brussels sprouts, and wild rice. And with only an infinite field of water for company, one spilled there for her alone, her dinner and wine slowly, each bite and each sip, convinced her to sink deeper into the cushions of her sun-warmed chaise.

*   *   *

Her plates and silverware had been picked so clean that they didn't appear used, and Lin stacked them neatly on the small dining table. The half-full bottle of wine complied and gave up more of itself, filling a glass, which Lin carried, sipping, into the bath.

With hot water filling the tub, Lin traded wine glass for phone and gave it a few taps. She sampled more wine while waiting for Jack Madison to pick up.

"Lin?"

"It's me, Cowboy. How are you?"

"Oh hey, Cowgirl, doing fine. Great to hear from you. How's life treating you?"

"Oh, you know. Usual ups and downs. Nothing I can't handle. I'm mostly caught up on stuff, and I thought I'd give you a call."

"I'm glad you did. It's always good to hear from you. I'm thinking of making it a long weekend. I'd love it if we could get together."

"Yes, of course. But this weekend isn't good. You forgot that I'm in St. Simons for my thirtieth high school reunion?"

"Oh. Yeah. I remember now."

"And I won't get home until late Sunday. When I get back to PA, we can definitely work something out."

"That still seems odd to me—a reunion in November. Whose brilliant idea was that?"

"Oh yeah, that doesn't sound like it makes much sense. But during our senior year, we lost four members of our football team in a bus crash. Whoever organized this thing thought it would be a nice tribute."

"That does make sense. Cool move, actually. I hope it doesn't drag the party down."

"It should be fine. Heck, Jack, that was years ago. This isn't some thrilling event, but it's an excuse for me to get away for a few days and feel some sunshine again."

"Yeah, I get that. Hey, I officially miss you."

"I like that. How about my mayhem? You miss that?"

"Oh, hell yes! I still can't believe you used that name online—Pussy Mayhem. That name and photos of you hooked me right away but I have to say, it's who you are that keeps my attention. *Can* keep my attention forever."

"Careful, Jack. Forever's a long time."

"Right. I do know that," he said, laughing at himself.

Smiling, she said, "Well, you called yourself Cowboy Jack. What the heck—you're a carpenter. You wouldn't know a horse if it kicked you."

"No, I probably wouldn't. But having a Cowgirl in my life is all I need. However much."

"You're sweet, Cowboy."

"So are you."

"Maybe a little, but you don't know everything about me."

Lin had finished undressing and stood naked next to the tub filling with hot water. With the phone to her ear, she let her other hand shake a bottle under the stream, causing a billowing cloud of sparkling bubbles to erupt from the churning water.

"Someday you can show me—um, I mean *tell* me."

"It's a date. Both show *and* tell. By the way, I'm just getting into a hot, soapy bath. Wish you were here?"

"Damn, you drive me crazy. Yes! Yes, I wish I was there."

"I wish you were here too. There are some places that need extra attention. And you know I like to be squeaky clean all over."

"Mm . . . you can be so dirty when you're clean."

"You won't have to wait too long, sweetheart. I should be back in PA like normal by Monday. Think you can find some time for me?"

"Nothing could stop me."

"Perfect. I'll see you soon. But it's late, and I have to soak a while and get some sleep. Goodnight, Jack."

"Goodnight, Lin. Goodnight to all of those hot, soapy bubbles too."

"You're jealous of the bubbles?"

"Damn right. Oh, yeah."

"You're silly. Goodnight, Jack."

"Bye."

Lin cranked the water off and watched the mound of bubbles level out, covering the water completely like a soft, soapy patch of carpeting.

"Oh, Jack," she said while setting the phone on the counter. "You really don't know everything about me. That part-time job of mine. All the horrible secrets from my past."

Satisfied that the bubble carpet would wait for her and didn't need her constant attention, she spun enough to snag the wine glass, raise it quickly, and down it all.

"But you do know that you love me."

She raised the glass higher and let the last few drops trickle through the air and into her waiting mouth, then she set the glass back down.

"But you probably don't know . . . that I love you too."

* * *

The room's air conditioning unit hummed a steady tune, keeping the nearly lightless room cool and blending any prying outside sounds into a calming oblivion. The only light source, the modest numbers of a digital clock on the nightstand, strained to cause even a weak sparkle on the empty wine bottle beside it.

A few ambitious bits of its light ventured higher, up above the bed, and toyed with the lazy fan blades revolving and sending cool air down to a traveler from Pennsylvania, a part-time bounty hunter struggling to pay her ill daughter's medical bills.

That blonde in St. Simons mostly for a high school reunion kept the thick quilt pulled high, almost high enough to cover green eyes that gazed up at the dutiful fan blades tirelessly working for her.

"Sure, Jack. You know my alias—Pussy Mayhem—but there's so much more."

The fan didn't disagree. It seemed to urge her to continue.

"The bounty hunting. Even that I have a daughter. You don't know any of it."

She paused, and the slow spinning above her in the dark asked for more details.

"I could have—maybe almost did—just kill two guys on the trip here. Nothing to it, Jack. Easy for me."

The blades kept spinning.

"And even if I told you about those guys, I wouldn't have any chance at explaining to you what happened. How crazy it felt. How I felt crazy. No, Jack, you just think of me as Pussy May—"

She sat up quickly, casting the heavy coverings aside as her breaths suddenly realized it was time for some serious activity.

"Mayhem? Pussy Mayhem? Oh, God, Jack. That explains it as well as anything."

The fan waited for more, not quite understanding her point.

"That's what the hell is going on with me. It's mayhem!"

Chapter 9 – Vastness Below

A quaint café on Mallery Street in the Village was a hub of swarming locals and tourists, mostly all dressed in shorts and sneakers, t-shirts and ball caps. Their chatter sometimes rose above the incessant sounds of cars and trucks parading past, some of them offering a quick horn toot or an impatient brake squeal.

Lin, though, seated at one of the café's small tables near the sidewalk, didn't play along with any of that. Her bare legs were on full display, stretching from the bottom hem of a short beach cover-up to her sandals. Her swimsuit was obvious beneath the thin cloth and though she didn't look eager to venture into the ocean, she'd laid a plush beach towel over the back of her chair.

She tipped up the brim of her hat and lowered her sunglasses, smiling at the sight of such busyness while she had nothing but time for sunshine and humid South Georgia air.

Her scoff at all of them was her way of telling them to carry on, and she fished out her phone, tapped it a few times, then gave it a few seconds of study, her eyes scanning the lines of the message.

"Good job, Jones," she said, mumbling to herself. "Yeah, I know that motel—that seedy dump off Glynn."

She stowed the phone at a pleasant voice nearby saying, "May I take your order, miss?"

Lin looked up and offered a smile to the young local.

"Sure. How about blueberry hotcakes, bacon and grits, and coffee. Oh, and a small orange juice too. Thanks."

"No problem. I'll get the drinks right over first."

Lin watched the server walk toward the restaurant's door, then disappear around the large potted shrubs framing the entrance. She was still watching that entrance when another voice, a very familiar one, got her attention.

"I told you, Lin, that I'm never far away."

"You never are, Gabby. Have a seat. I already ordered."

"Nothing for me, Lin. Except to hear what's on your mind."

"Gabby, I don't want to deal with any of it. But I need to own this. All of it. Those weird encounters in Erie and with that guy and his gravel, even back to all that shit as a kid. It's all connected somehow. Maybe I'm insane. Or maybe I have some kind of power."

After a short pause, she added, "Maybe I'm evil."

"No, you're not evil, Lin—you do so much good in the world. It's obvious how much you love your daughter and the hard life you live to help take care of her. And Nomad . . . where would he be without you? And would Jack love an evil woman? You must know that he loves you."

Lin tilted her head back to look at the clear sky, and she let out a heavy sigh.

"Yeah. I know all that. But still."

"You've never intended to hurt anyone, have you? And you're definitely not insane. What you call a power . . . maybe it's more of a gift?"

Lin bit her lip as the drinks were set on the table. When the server had retreated once more, she shook her head and scoffed loud enough that it could have been a snort.

"Oh, come on. That 'gift' mutilated Ray, messed up some kid in high school, and almost hurt that guy in Erie—that could have turned out horribly too. And that 'gift' force fed gravel to that punk in PA. Some gift.

"At least, I think I'm responsible for all that. God, I don't really know."

"I know that you didn't look for trouble with your Uncle Ray. There truly is evil walking the Earth. That man was evil.

"And those two guys in PA—they *did* look for trouble with you. As for high school, you've never told me about that."

"Oh. That turned out so bad, Gabby. I teased him way back when we were fifteen. Humiliated him in front of our friends. I didn't need to do that. So many guys deserve it, but he probably didn't.

"It was right after that whole ordeal with Ray. I think I was out of control. I felt crazy inside, like something was itching to get out. It scared me, and acting reckless seemed to help."

"Did you keep feeling that way, Lin? Have you felt that way ever since?"

"No. God, no. I never would have made it this far. I somehow got control of it. Locked it down. I don't know what 'it' is, but it's never coming back out."

Lin coughed and looked up at the sound of footsteps, and she waited as the server placed a steaming plate in front of her.

"Anything else, miss? Ketchup or anything?"

"No, this is fine. It looks so good. Thanks."

"You're very welcome."

She let the footsteps retreat without watching, and she showed no desire to continue any discussions with Gabby. No, the hot breakfast couldn't wait. And it didn't have to. Mixed in with sips of hot coffee, it all vanished quickly.

While dabbing around with a napkin, she looked up and across the table again.

"Maybe I just need some alone time for some rest, and I can put it all behind me. I have nothing scheduled for the rest of the day. I'm just going to wander around, shop a little, and sit in the park to catch some sunshine."

"That should help, Lin. I'm going to head out and do some wandering of my own."

"Great plan, Gabby. I hope you'll join me here at breakfast tomorrow."

"I'm almost certain I will."

"Yes. You really never are very far away."

Lin Finity and her Mayhem Rising

*　　*　　*

With the breakfast bill paid and goodbyes to Gabby given, Lin began a leisurely walk along Mallery, and she stopped after only a few steps at a walk-up window for coffee and all sorts of delicious snacks.

"Just a coffee, please. No cream or sugar."

She paid, resumed her walk, and only marginally noticed the foot traffic passing her in each direction as she hiked as directly as she could toward the pier. Some shop windows called out for her attention, and a few them even had enough substance to make her stop, survey the items for sale, then resume her trek.

And a block later, Lin had reached the pier, a reliable structure reaching out mostly southward toward Jekyll Island but not ambitious enough to lay itself over much of the Sound.

Even on a Wednesday morning, she noticed, the pier had attracted a lot of visitors. She looked for a place to be alone, but no private spaces remained. So, she took the closest empty spot along the rail.

The blue of the ocean quickly captivated her, and she stopped noticing the chattering around her. Within seconds, she was alone with the sea.

Compared to the bustle of the Village, the waves were subdued, almost shy, and barely showed themselves. Several times, she fixed on one in the crowd of them and watched as it almost immediately retreated back into the Sound's depths.

Each wave that she singled out for inspection rose up, seemed to look around but only for a second, then sank back into the vastness.

If they tired of having an identity of their own, they could just give it back. Her study revealed that not a single one of them was ever truly alone.

Lines of onlookers on each side of her could have stopped and listened, and she wouldn't have noticed.

"Oh, you're so vast, aren't you?"

She didn't hear their conversations or their laughter.

47

"Maybe me too. We both have our mysteries."

She did hear the nearest conversations cease, though, and looked each way. Staring eyes looked back.

Giving her eyes back to the bouncing water, shimmering its way across the sound to a strip of land on the horizon, Lin shook her head and sighed.

Then, she turned and left behind her the pier and its feeble attempts at intruding any solid shapes into the water's vastness.

Chapter 10 – Binge Warning

A stubborn fly seemed to be playing a game: landing on Ben's nose, timing it just right to get him to swat at it, then buzzing happily away as the drunk man on the couch slapped himself and cussed.

After three good hits while sitting on his ratty couch in his run-down house, Ben focused on the fly, watching it loop around over the coffee table that was missing a leg and relying on bricks and a whiskey bottle to stay somewhat level.

And that fly, perhaps wanting to help out the sot after having had his share of fun, landed on a stack of mail that no one had had the ambition to pick up and put in the trash. The third envelope down, angled out just right, showed a return address somewhere in St. Simons Island.

"No way. What the hell?"

He swept the top layers to the floor and held up the letter, the envelope already torn open sloppily. The fly waited only a second before landing itself on the top edge of the letter as Ben held it up and scrutinized it.

"Luanne! Get your ass in here!"

"One beer or—"

"Just get your ass in here. Uh, bring two."

She hiked in with two sweating cans and wedged them into the slop on the table. Ben snarled and held the paper up for her to see.

"You knew about this?"

She squinted and leaned toward it, then straightened herself back up.

"Uh, yeah, Binge. High school stuff. So?"

"At St. Simons?"

She almost laughed, but a glance at his fists squeezed tight, ready, gave her a more survivable thought.

"Well, yeah. Where we went to high school."

"Smart ass bitch. Stay."

He stomped straight to the kitchen and aimed for the coffee can. With all the clattering on the counter, cans and bottles hitting the floor, and a constant stream of cussing, Ben didn't hear Luanne walk over and watch him from the doorway to their tiny living room.

"Just how much drinking do you need to do, Binge?"

"This ain't for drinking. I need this. I'm going away for a few days."

"That money's for fixing the house, Binge. You know the wind's been working this place apart bit by bit. If you gotta go, just go. But do it on the cheap, alright?"

"Dammit, Luanne. Where I'm going, I can't just sleep under a bridge. Why don't you just shut up and get back to your damn soap operas?"

"Just where are you going? Don't tell me you're—"

"Damn right. And so help me God, if you try to stop me, I'll take *you* apart bit by bit."

His big boots crunched a beer can as he walked over and stood glaring down at her. She looked down and winced behind her curly hair, but she managed a reply.

"Like I could ever stop you. That reunion?"

"Yeah."

She looked up with wide eyes.

"You haven't been back there in thirty years! But you're going back because of that stupid thing?"

Ben's fists were clenching. Arm muscles were flexing.

"I don't give a shit about the reunion. It's who might be there. I got some business that needs fixing."

"Like what? You got no business in St. Simons anymore!"

"Luanne, I got to fix this. The only way is straight through that witch, Lin. I should have done this years ago."

"Oh God, Binge, what are you gonna do?"

"She ruined my life. Now, I'm gonna ruin hers if she can't explain it. Maybe even if she does explain it. And if you say one word of this to anyone, anyone by God, you're next. You got that?"

"Yeah. Sure, Binge. But please don't do this. She didn't mean anything by it."

"Like you would know. You were kissing up to her like a fly on hog shit after that."

"Don't go, Binge. Just let it go. Stay, okay?"

"Just get the hell out of my way," he said and shoved her aside.

A hard pull slammed the door back against the wall, deepening the knob-shaped crater, and Ben was gone.

*   *   *

Luanne stared at the not quite rectangular door that closed as well as it could behind him. Seconds later, after the squawking and screeching of chickens and cats had died down, she heard the truck's engine fire up.

She fell back into the sagging couch cushions and listened until the squealing tires told her that he and his truck were gone.

"Dammit. He's right, though. That was one fucked up day."

She'd just clicked on the TV, then sat straight up with her eyes bugging out. On the small table next to the couch, she began digging, tossing all kinds of things to the floor. After scraping bottom, seeing the scratched and dented wood surface, she leaned and looked under, and the phone, upside down amid bottles and cans, waited patiently.

She snatched it up. Dialed it. Waited, humming to the wait music.

"Dr. Grayson's Sweet Pets. How can I help you?"

"Uh, hello. I'm a friend of Lin's. I'm trying to get a hold of her. Does she still work there?"

"Yes, she does, but she's not in the office today. In fact, she won't be back in until Monday. May I take a message?"

"No, no. This is kind of urgent. I need to talk to her. Can I have her number? Please?"

"I'm sorry, but we can't give out her number like that. But if you give me your name and number, I'll try to reach her, and she can call you back. Does that sound okay?"

"Uh, okay. I guess I have no choice, huh?"

She gave the receptionist a number for Lin to call, then set the phone neatly on the tabletop that she'd cleared.

Sinking back into ripped fabric coughing up bits of stuffing, Luanne focused on the TV. And two cats, sitting on it, focused on her.

"What? Nosy cats."

Chapter 11 – Cowboy Poet

Lin bumped closed her hotel room door, but she gave the slide latch only a glance as her arms were loaded with packages. The names of shops on the bags were testament to her travels all over in the Village, and the coffee cup clutched in one hand advertised her thirst while traipsing around near Neptune Park.

After dumping it all on the bed and setting the coffee next to a fresh wine bottle, delivered during her absence, she decisively changed her preferred drink and poured a full glass.

She'd barely taken the first swig when her phone chimed. A couple of taps revealed the poem from Jack, offered with no other message.

A quick look in the mirror above the dresser didn't show a blushing blonde looking back, but she still grinned and tapped out a call to him.

"Oh, Cowboy. You're such a goofball. Very sweet but a goofball."

"Just trying to make you smile, sweet Cowgirl."

"You did, and I'm still smiling. Do you ever get tired of writing me poetry?"

"Nope. Never. And you can believe that everything I write is the truth."

"It's just another reason why I'm looking forward to seeing you again. It'll be soon. Maybe even Sunday late."

"I hope so. Hey, I've got those numbers for you too. I don't know why that can't wait until you're back, but I guess it must be pretty dang important."

"Yes, Jack, it really is. You don't need to understand it. It's something I need to stay on top of."

"Alright, alright. What do you do with all that information anyway?"

"I keep it in a spreadsheet. I can look back and see how it went months ago and if anything is changing, I'll know right away. It matters."

"But why does it matter so much? Why not just let him do what he wants and not worry about it?"

"Jack, don't give me a bad time about this. I don't need you to understand, okay?"

"Alright, I get it. It's important to you. That's all I need to know. I let myself into your house and found the notes your dog-sitter has been keeping. No, I didn't crawl into your bed either. Wanted to, though."

On the balcony again, she squirmed around more than needed as she sat in the patio's flimsy chair.

"Next time, Jack. And I'll be in the bed. Doesn't that sound better?"

"Hell yes. Soon."

Lin's phone rang with another incoming call.

"Jack, there's another call coming in."

"Ah, let it go, Lin. If it's important, they'll leave a message."

"Okay, it's probably nothing anyway."

Jack said, "Wouldn't you rather I texted these numbers to you?"

"No, it's easier for me this way. It's just better when I'm entering the numbers if I have it written in front of me."

"Sure, I get it. Let me know when you're ready, alright?"

"Hang on . . ."

She rummaged around in her travel bag and smirked at pulling an empty hand back out. A bit more digging produced a take-out menu, folded up and stained. She shook her head and smoothed it out on the nightstand.

"Okay, Jack. Let's have it."

He read through the list of dates, times, and weights. She clicked the pen after writing it all out, then let out a big sigh.

"Great. Got it. Thanks, Jack."

"Where did you ever find a dog bowl with a digital scale built into it? Not exactly the kind of thing you find at the pet store."

"Oh, that. I had it custom made by one of the companies we order lab equipment from. I don't know what I'd do without it. Keeping track would be impossible."

"Yeah, no doubt. He's lucky you care so much about him. I'm a little jealous."

"Jack, don't be silly. Of course, I care about you. I just have no desire to control how much you're eating."

"Yes, please don't even try!"

"I won't. Promise. That was quite a poem, Jack. I'm pretty sure you meant the last line . . ."

"Oh, hell yeah."

". . . but that thing about the stars . . . you really meant that too?"

Lin squirmed again and reached for her wine.

"I do." He paused. "Wow, I like those two words."

"Settle down, Jack. We're miles apart, remember?"

She took another big swallow.

"I do. Oops. I mean, yes, I know you're far away. And I can't wait to see you again."

"Me too. So, tell me about the house you're working on now."

After she'd finished the list, she set it on the nightstand. The ceiling fan kept blowing the menu down to the floor, so she absentmindedly folded it and tucked it under the alarm clock.

She'd just finished the last few drops of wine, and her eyes were telling her that she needed sleep more than talk with a carpenter poet.

"Jack, I'm sorry, but I should probably get some sleep. The last couple of days have been tiring."

"Alright, I should probably sleep too. Lots of building planned for tomorrow. Have a good night, alright?"

"You too."

Lin almost set down her phone, then scrolled around until she could again read Jack's poem to her:

> "You're such a sweet thing, I wish I could sing,
> A love song straight to your heart...

I'd croon each line, a thousand times,
Stopping would be the hardest part.

I'd make you mine, till the end of time,
Till the stars have all burned away…
Cuz you're a beautiful queen, like the world's never seen,
Oh yeah, and you're a damn good lay!"

"Damn, Jack. Give up that carpentry nonsense, okay?"
She set her phone on the charger and let the night take her.

Chapter 12 – Ben Again

"What the hell do you want?"

Ben glared through the windshield of his old red truck, its cracked and dented grill pointed toward St. Simons Island and trailing behind it a hot mix of black exhaust smoke and twangy country music.

"Binge, I'm just worried that—"

"Dammit, Luanne, I hate goddamn phones. You know that!"

"I know, but dammit, Binge, just listen! Don't go doing anything stupid if you find Lin, alright?"

"Here's an idea for your dizzy blond head: maybe I'll just have a polite conversation with her, huh?"

"Sure, Binge. Uh-huh. Like you—hey, can you turn down the goddamn music for a minute?"

He held the phone between his bared teeth and hammered the dashboard with a massive fist, changing the tunes to static. Another hit silenced it altogether.

"There? How's that?"

"You could have just used the switch. Dammit, Binge."

"You wanted no goddamn music? You got it! Remember this next time I tell you to shut your trap! Now, what the hell are you talking about?"

"I was saying, don't have a 'conversation' with her like you did with that boy back in school. You remember him?"

Ben snarled, stared ahead, and let the truck's rattling fill a few seconds of time.

"Yeah. I remember. That fucker."

"Ben, you almost—"

"It's Binge, dammit."

"Not then, it wasn't! You were Ben, and you almost killed him! It's why your family had to pack up and get the hell out of town!"

"Goddammit, Luanne. He had it coming. Laughing at my shirt. Then, he thought he'd—"

"It wasn't a very nice shirt, Ben."

"Don't try to make me laugh, dammit. No. It was a piece of shit, like everything else I had. But that son of a bitch called me a pussy, Luanne. He must have thought—"

"I know. I know. He was a lot bigger than you, and he figured he could—"

"He fell pretty damn quick. One good punch. They all fall quick, Luanne. And I'm not anyone named Ben anymore. That ended. It ended that day."

"That day with the big truck, Ben. One of those boys called you a pussy then too. I know. That's why it bothered you so much."

"Stop trying to be so goddamn understanding. Dammit, Luanne."

"Sorry. I didn't mean anything."

The big man coughed out the window, then wiped under each eye.

"Dammit, Luanne, why do you keep trying with me? It's only going to get worse. When I find that goddamn witch, you can't imagine how much I'm—"

"Don't, Ben. You get your ass thrown in prison again, and I won't be waiting for you. Not again."

"Why the hell not?"

"Because when this goddamn shack collapses, it should be on both of us."

"That's actually funny. Good one."

"That's all the romance I get. Just don't kill her, alright?"

He laughed, then said, "Luanne, there aren't any laws against killing a witch. Saves them the cost of a stack of firewood and some matches."

"That's funny, Ben. Just talk to her if you have to, alright? Maybe you can clear up all that bullshit from the past and go back to being Ben again?"

"Never. Nobody was afraid of Ben. Binge, though. Binge doesn't take any shit."

He listened, and Luanne didn't have an immediate comeback.

"Not even from you."

He tossed the phone to the seat beside him, then tried turning up the volume. Nothing happened, so he spent a half-mile beating on it and weaving along the country road leading toward the Island.

*　　*　　*

He'd rattled and rumbled his old truck over the Causeway, cussed to himself most of time while cruising along King's Way, and savaged the steering wheel while waiting for the red light at Mallery Street.

"It's goddamn fate," he said, laughing and watching as Lin strutted across King's Way.

Watching the wind bounce around her long blond hair, sometimes glancing up at the light, he revved the engine gradually and got ready to pop the clutch.

Then, he noticed her walk. An effortless strut on heels like he'd never seen Luanne wear.

Legs. Bare and toned and built for the sunshine beating down, even in November.

One hand holding a coffee cup, the other taming the wide brim of her hat as the ocean breezes flooded in.

And he let the motor calm back to a patient idle.

"No," he said, shaking his head. "Too easy. Too easy for a goddamn witch."

She'd crossed King's Way and turned enough to face across Mallery, giving him a perfect view of a perfect ass in a perfectly tight skirt.

"It isn't right. No witch should look that good."

She began her walk, and he never looked up at the light, just idled his way after her, responding to honking horns and yelling with a raised finger out the window, rarely looking away from the blond witch.

Until she turned on the walkway leading to a hotel entrance. He laughed at finding a space to park in the road right there, and he almost forgot to switch off the engine as he rushed out of his truck and followed up behind her.

She entered and so did he. Almost step for step, he tailed her, eyes on her hips swaying and ears tuned to the sound of her heels on the cool tile floor.

Ben laughed quietly and mumbled to himself, "Another dizzy blond," when he saw Lin taking the stairs.

He crept quietly behind, following her all the way to her door.

* * *

At her room door, Lin tucked her newspaper under her left arm, passed the coffee to that hand, then swiped her room key. She'd just started pushing in the door, when she stopped herself suddenly.

And Ben, close behind her and snarling without a sound, held his breath.

She leaned into the door to hold it open, then fumbled around for her phone, tapped it a few times, then scoffed.

"Huh. Forgot all about that call."

She leaned harder, swinging in the door, and took a few steps into the room. So did Ben, who held the door and guided it to close slowly and quietly.

But it should have latched itself closed more quickly, and Lin spun around, dropping the coffee and paper at seeing a giant man in dirty clothes, with a shaved head and a snarling face that seemed familiar, blocking her exit.

He clicked the door shut behind him, never taking his eyes off of her. As he reached behind to chain the door, Lin pointed at his face.

"Ben!"

"It's Binge now. Get it right—you don't have much time left. Trust me."

As he stomped heavily toward her, Lin took quick steps back until she'd reached the bed, and she fell back to sit, causing her hat to slip off behind her. He towered over her, snarling.

"What . . . what are you doing here? I haven't seen you in forever."

"Did that make it easier for you? You didn't have to see the wreck you left behind?"

"Are you talking about that day with the truck?"

"Look how damn fast you remember that."

"Well, it was kind of—"

"Damn right, it's about that truck. It's all clear to me now, Lin. You've wrecked so many years of my life. Now, it's your turn. Do you even have any idea what you did to me?"

Lin looked away from his eyes to focus briefly on the size of his fist as he clenched it by his side.

"Uh, that was so long ago, and . . . um . . ."

Without taking her eyes off of him, she reached down reflexively and searched for her purse and the pepper spray. But she found nothing.

"Yeah, plenty of time for you to forget. How nice for you."

She scoffed at the sight of her purse lying near the door with the paper and spilled coffee.

"Ben, I mean Binge, I'm so sorry I teased you. I shouldn't have, and I've felt bad about that ever since. Maybe it was the beer? We were all just having so much fun, and it kind of got out of control."

"I don't give a shit about the teasing. I know that's what kids do. I'm talking about what you did after that. What exactly did you do to me? What the hell was that?"

"Nothing, Binge. I didn't do anything. I blacked out, remember?"

"Bullshit. I watched you staring at me and when your eyes started closing . . . shit, I can't even describe it."

He winced but never took his eyes off of her.

"You didn't just pass out. Quit bullshitting me. You're some kind of witch or something. Tell me what you did!"

She glanced down to see both of his fists balled up tight, the knuckles big and white. And they were shaking more noticeably. She looked back up into his glaring eyes.

"How did you get a name like Binge anyway?"

"I drink. I drink a lot. Now, answer me, bitch. What the hell did you do?"

"I can tell you what I remember, but it's not much. Maybe we can figure this out together, okay?"

"Go ahead. Explain it like your goddamn life depends on it."

"Okay, um, when you grabbed my shoulders, I remembered mostly being scared. We were friends, and I'd never seen you act like that. It scared me a lot. Even back then, you were so big and strong. And now, you're even bigger and stronger. I bet not much scares you, does it?"

"Hell, no. Nothing."

"I didn't think so. That's why I stopped fighting you back then. It was hopeless. I knew I couldn't hurt you or even get away. Just like now . . . do you see me trying to get away?"

"Like I'm gonna let you out of here anyway."

"I just want us to understand what happened. And I hope you can understand that I didn't do anything to you. I don't know what happened. When I woke up, I wasn't even close to you, but I didn't remember how I got there."

"You woke up, huh? I never blacked out. I felt the whole goddamn thing. Every second of it. It's made me crazy ever since trying to block it out. But I can't go on like this. I gotta deal with it. You got nowhere to go, so stop the goddamn bullshit. What was that? What *are* you?"

Lin's right hand went up to cover her heart, which she felt beating a strong rhythm, and she looked at each of his fists again before looking back up at his eyes. He stared, waiting for an explanation.

But Lin only rolled her eyes, scoffed, and shook her head. She cleared her throat with a short cough and spoke calmly.

"I've told you all I know, Ben. There's nothing more to say."

She stared at him, struggling as her breaths got more strained and choppy.

"It's been quite a surprise to see you but now, you need to get out of my room."

"Oh, sure. I'll leave, but only after you've suffered like I have."

He was rocking back and forth, flexing both fists.

"Um, Ben. I can understand how that could have bothered you because—"

A lightning fast backhand snapped Lin's head to the side, and she spun around and collapsed onto the bed with her nose bleeding into the blanket. Covering it with her hand, she turned her head up, facing him again.

"How dare you come in here and think—"

"Enough talk, bitch. Who's got the power this time, huh? Time for you to learn your lesson."

He wrapped a meaty hand around her arm above her elbow, squeezing it hard and making her wince. As he pulled her roughly up off of the bed, he laughed.

"Not such a tough goddamn witch now, are you?"

He held her by both arms, glaring into her face and ready to strike again. But his snarl weakened when his eyes were drawn to her chest, where her heavy breathing kept her breasts moving toward him, then back, then toward him again.

"Damn. Never knew a witch could look so damn good."

"Don't you even try hitting me again, dammit."

"Hit you? No, witch. I want a piece of that fine ass. Never had witch ass before."

She didn't speak as she fought for every breath, bouncing her chest and giving him something to grin at.

He laughed and said, "Damn sexy witch. Yeah."

Still holding both of her arms, he shook her like a limp doll, laughing, and said, "Sexy witch."

She barely noticed his grip, or the scowl on his face, or the beer on his breath as he was forced to hold up more and more of her weight.

And when he kept repeating, "Sexy witch," Lin let her eyes start to close, and his words became chanting.

Then, not even words.
Just pounding, incessant pounding like a heartbeat.
And all of St. Simons was lost in the blackness that swallowed her.

Chapter 13 – Witch Hunt

When Lin's eyes opened, they were aimed through the sliding glass doors, over the beach, and far out over the water. The morning had been sunny, with patchy white clouds, but the clouds had won the battle. They'd become dark and thick and seemed pressed down upon from above. A wind from the south swept across her balcony, occasionally vibrating the lightweight chairs.

A leisurely wipe across her cheek left wet red streaks across the shaking hand that she held up to see. She took a deep breath before looking down.

At her feet, curled and crumpled and unconscious yet somehow still menacing, Ben lay still with only an occasional twitch. There wasn't a mark on him, but he resembled a marionette that had been tossed from a roof and not at all like a man who'd decided to lie down on plush hotel carpeting.

There was blood on the back of his right hand too.

She watched him just long enough to see a distinct spasm—sign enough that he was still alive—before hurrying to pick up her purse and take out her phone.

Before keying any numbers, she paused and studied the man she'd leveled with the mayhem.

"Shit. They'd probably send that same detective."

She jabbed the phone back into her purse, kicked the newspaper and dripping paper cup off toward the wall, and took the few steps needed to get to her travel bag. Hardly anything had been unpacked, and those few items got stuffed back in, then she slung it up over a shoulder.

Then, Ben groaned and stretched out, facedown and mumbling.

"Dammit. Don't wake up, Ben."

His eyes were still closed, and he was muttering more, sometimes slurring the word "witch."

"Dammit, I'm not a witch. Be a good boy and sleep until I'm long gone, alright?"

She'd just started stepping around him to get to the door, and the groggy man with Lin's blood on his hand shifted around, with no real control over his arms and legs, and tried to get up onto his hands and knees.

"Oh, goddammit!"

He'd managed to get all the way up, but his head was still hanging, lips barely moving as he cursed and wheezed. Lin gave his ass a gentle kick, and he crawled one step toward the door. Shaking her head, almost laughing at her new plan, she gave him a push, careful to not stick him with a pointy heel.

He moved closer to the door.

Lin leaned ahead, grabbed the door, and held it open.

"Witch," he said, then shook his head. "Son of a—"

"Dammit, Ben," she said, then gave him a hard push, driving him through the doorway and into the hall.

Ben's eyes were blinking, not quite staying open, and he groaned and reached for his head with one hand.

Looking up at Lin, perplexed and wincing, he said, "What . . . what are you—"

Lin stepped closer, gave him a soft kick then a shove, lunged back into her room, and set the lock. It was only seconds before she heard a brutal banging on the door.

She took a step forward and peered through the peep hole, only to see a gigantic bloodshot eye staring through. She backed away, kept watching the door, and fumbled around for her pepper spray.

The door groaned from another attack, and Lin heard, through the door, "Lin!"

He pounded more, some hits sounding like fists and others like kicks with heavy boots. The door shook with every impact, and Lin retreated farther into her room.

"Sir," Lin heard through the door, "can I help you? Are you locked out?"

"Leave me the hell alone."

After more pounding, Ben screamed, "Lin, open the goddamn door. What did you just do? You never touched me! What the hell are you?"

"I don't know!" she said only for herself.

His feverish onslaught continued, stopping only at the sound of a polite but stern voice.

"Sir, don't make me call security."

The strikes against the door halted, and Lin heard a dull thud, then the sound of a cart falling against the wall and crashing onto the floor.

The door beating resumed.

"Open this goddamn door, Lin!"

She held her pepper spray up and aimed toward the door.

"Goddammit, Ben, just go away!"

She heard a fresh voice through the door.

"Sir, step away from the door. Now. I'm calling for backup."

"Shut the hell up."

More pounding.

"Lin!"

"Alright, come with me—"

Another dull thud and a groan as a second body hit the floor.

"This ain't over, witch!"

The hallway had gone silent.

Lin backed farther from the door, never looking away, and she reached behind her to find the sliding glass. She turned and stepped out just far enough to peek over the edge. There was only the sand and sea and the supposed safety of a second-floor room.

Holding the railing, Lin watched the waves and forced her breaths to calm. Only then did she turn, fix her eyes on her travel bag, then scoff.

"Right. Like he won't be waiting. Dammit."

She tried to laugh about it until she heard a car alarm screaming from the front of the hotel.

"Oh, what now?"

She gave the sea no attention as she again held the railing and looked left, then right at the building's corners.

Seconds later, the end of a long, silver ladder emerged around the right corner of the building with a bungee cord still attached, followed a second later by Ben.

"Dammit, Ben. No!"

She backed into the room before Ben looked up, and she made a move toward her bag before stopping.

"No. Not yet."

She walked back out and leaned over the rail at a man with bloodshot eyes looking up at her, snarling.

"You goddamn witch," he said as he planted the ladder's legs in the soft soil of the landscaping.

"Dammit, Ben, I'm not a witch!"

He took one step, and that side of the ladder sank, so he stepped back onto the ground and repositioned it. Again, he took a step, only to have it sink once more.

Lin looked down one last time at his snarling, frustrated face, and she turned and hurried through the room, grabbing her things. She pulled the door in and saw dents, with thin red trails below them, and two unconscious men and scattered room service trays.

She eased the door closed without any sound, ran down the hall and stairs, and walked casually out into the Georgia heat.

Passing the desk in the lobby without slowing, Lin exited the building and forced a slow, calm walk to her rental car.

Inside, concealed behind the tinted glass, she started the engine and piloted the vehicle to the neighboring hotel's lot, allowing herself a view of her hotel's entrance.

And she waited there. Watching and shaking quietly.

*   *   *

Ben raged at the ladder, picked it up, and stabbed both legs deep into the ground. A slow climb, with the ladder rocking to each side with every step and nearly dumping him, brought him to the balcony. He stepped over the railing and walked into the room, looking for the witch with big fists clenching.

He hurried to the door, pried it open enough to see what he'd done and laugh about it, then latched it.

A careful study of the room revealed that everything of Lin's had been cleaned out.

"Just like a witch. Smart and sneaky."

He reached for the door again, then stopped.

After a deep, slow breath, he stretched his arms out, then let them drop and turned himself around. A short walk got him to the bed.

Sitting on the end of it and looking around, he saw nothing of any use—she'd taken everything of hers.

"Dammit. Think, Binge."

He closed his eyes for several seconds then opened them slowly.

"Oh, shit. The reunion."

He laughed as he laid himself back and looked up, then snorted in a few sharp breaths. Rolling to his side, he buried his nose in the quilt and inhaled a truly deep breath.

"Mm. Witch. She smells good."

Grinning, he sat up and took a last look around, and his eyes rested on the alarm clock on the nightstand. Not the clock. Just the corner of a piece of paper sticking out from under it.

He looked over the menu and frowned at all of the scribbling around the edges. Just a bunch of dates and numbers that made no sense. Unfolding it, then tapping it with a thick finger, his smile reappeared.

"Huh. Allentown. Gotcha, you goddamn witch."

His relaxing came to an abrupt end as he jumped to his feet, wobbled, then steadied.

Holding his head, he said, "Goddamn witches and their spells."

He wadded up the paper and stuffed it into a pocket before heading out into the hallway. He laughed out loud at the two he'd knocked out just minutes before and stepped around them.

A cold bagel leaned up against the wall, tempting him. He laughed again as he picked it up and kept moving.

A slow walk brought him to the front door, and he stepped far enough out to stand in the hot sun. With the sound of approaching sirens, his smile turned to a scowl. While wiping his fingers on his jeans, he began a slow hike to his truck.

Chapter 14 – Sun Watch

Lin slumped into her seat and held her breath as she watched Ben stomp out of the hotel. Only minutes had passed—barely enough time for her to make her hasty retreat. She flexed her legs to stop their shaking and tugged at her skirt, but it refused to stay down.

She scoffed at the sight of Ben tracking his boots through the landscaping and across the lot to a run-down pickup rusting in the sun. He kicked the passenger side door before jerking it open, then poked around inside while standing at the end of a trail of mud and mulch. Straightening up, he kneed the door closed, then scanned the surrounding area.

Lin looked where he was looking and saw only the tasteful scenery and locals and visitors dressed in casual clothing, all talking and laughing. And her head shook on its own when she again focused on Ben, who had started a determined march toward the Village.

His heavy boots pounded the pavement hard. His jeans were greasy and sagged, even with his chain belt. His ragged black t-shirt showed a skull and crossbones on the back. And he was a big man: at least six-foot-four and thick but not flabby. And his perpetual scowl just didn't fit well with the happy tourists milling about.

He looked like a man who'd reached his limit. Desperate. Angry. And kind of scared too.

As Ben continued toward Mallery Street, Lin gasped at seeing that he'd pass near her car. She ducked down even farther and turned her face away.

After he'd passed, she got out and followed a block behind him, scrutinizing him like any other fugitive she'd pursue.

He never looked behind him as he walked, like he never thought he might be followed or just didn't care.

He made no effort to blend in. His pace was direct, and he had a sense of purpose, while everyone around him looked relaxed and taking their time.

The nearest bar got his attention, and he pulled open the thick wood door. The cool air washing classic rock from the bar unrolled like a thick, syrupy liquid out into the late-morning heat. The darkness of the lounge swallowed him up, and she was left standing and staring as bodies chattered their way past her.

Scoffing toward the bar, Lin began a brisk walk back to the parking lot of her abandoned hotel, where she saw two police cars parked near the entrance, and an ambulance had just pulled in. Several officers and hotel employees were standing around talking.

"See? Always use an alias."

She groaned as she checked her pockets and wrestled a hand around in her purse.

"Oh, shit. No, he didn't find that. He was just looking for someone to kill."

She once again hiked toward the bar, this time continuing past it on the opposite side of Mallery.

A few more steps brought her to an outdoor café that had an adequate view of the bar that Ben had entered. She walked through the wrought iron gate and found a seat where she could surveil his hideout, but it would be difficult for Ben to see her. The tree branches near the sidewalk draped low and swayed in the light breezes.

Lin felt her legs still shaking, but she was hungry, too, and she picked up the paper menu that was held tight to the tabletop by her crossed arms. She was about to call a server over when Gabby appeared and joined her.

"Gabby, God, it's good that you're here. I've had an incredible morning already."

"Hi, Lin. I'm happy to be here. Why don't you tell me all about it over lunch?"

"I'd love to."

Lin stood and stretched her arms to each side while looking for a waitress. Though her legs still trembled, she smiled at the heads turning. She gestured to a young girl, who came over to take the order.

*   *   *

"This is all just a bit much. I know I've acted like Monday was no big deal, but it shook me up. I don't remember much of what happened either time, in Erie or by that pond. I just know that something happened—something bad. Or maybe not bad, but crazy. God, I don't know. And I was trying to put that all behind me, and then today happened."

Lin paused only long enough suck in a deep breath and let it rush back out.

"Do you remember what I told you about that boy from high school, the one that I teased and it went bad? His name's Ben. Gabby, he attacked me. He followed me into my hotel room, angry as hell. I tried talking to him. I tried ordering him out of the room. I tried everything I could think of, but nothing worked. Out of nowhere, he struck me—see?—and that's when it began again. The mayhem. I felt it start up and when I woke up, he was out cold. He didn't appear injured, though, thank God, except for my blood on his hand. I can't keep hurting people."

"The what began again?"

"The mayhem. That's what I call it now. Really, it's the right name for it.

"It took a lot to get away from him. He beat on the door, he got a ladder . . . oh, never mind. It's too much to explain. That was just minutes ago. I'm still kind of shaking from it."

"What's that about a ladder?"

"Nothing. It doesn't matter. Right now, he's drinking in that bar."

Lin pointed in the bar's direction. The window's smiling neon sun belied the presence of the homicidal man inside.

"I'm glad you're okay, Lin. Did anyone get hurt?"

"Yeah, a couple of hotel employees. And Ben's knuckles. Gabby, he punched dents in the metal door! He's like some kind of—"

"What do you plan to do now?"

"I'll watch him and see what he does. My hope is that he'll take his crappy truck and go back home. I might have scared him with the mayhem, but I don't think it was enough. He blames me for all the shit in his life. I know he's kind of scared, but I don't think that'll stop him if he wants to come at me again."

"If he leaves, you'll let it go at that?"

"Hell, yeah. I have enough other problems right now. Ben's the biggest problem, though. I have the sickening feeling that he'll come after me again. Maybe I should run. He'll never find me in PA. My house is owned by my trust, and my name isn't on public record."

"Running isn't your style, Lin. What else is going on?"

Lin took a moment to let her breathing slow down. After letting out a deep breath, she continued.

"Gabby, this mayhem! What exactly is that? I need to get that under control even if I still don't understand it. I can't go through life like this—not knowing when I'm going to black out and what damage that might do. Most of the time, I think it's some kind of mental illness and I should get help."

"You'll figure it out, Lin. I have no doubt. I'll help you if I can."

"Thanks, I know you will. And there's another thing. I took on another case. A dangerous one. This guy has probably already killed someone. I've got tabs on him—Jones has some amazing connections—and I think I know where he'll be. I plan to grab him Sunday."

"Maybe you already have enough to deal with. You can pass on that assignment, can't you? Why not try to enjoy what time you have here?"

Lin stretched back in her wicker chair, arching her back, with her white tank top straining. She managed a weak grin at seeing the heads turning.

"Taylor will be starting a new treatment soon. It's expensive. This fugitive is worth a lot because he's dangerous. This is for my daughter. It's on me. There's no one else."

"Let's hope Ben leaves town, then. That'll be one problem gone. As for the mayhem, I'm sure we'll figure that out. And that fugitive Sunday? Just be careful, okay?"

"I will, Gabby. Broken hearts or broken bones, remember?" Lin said and forced a smile.

"Not your heart and not your bones, okay? And hopefully, no one else's bones either. But I think you'll never stop breaking hearts."

And then, Gabby was gone.

*　　*　　*

"Oh, shit . . ."

Lin jerked her phone out of her purse and hit a couple of numbers while keeping her eyes on Ben's bar.

"Hello, Lin," she heard. "This is Gina at Sweet Pets. I got a strange call here just a moment ago from someone that says she was a friend from a long time ago. She wanted your number but of course, I didn't give it to her. But maybe you should call her? She sounded pretty worried. Her name was Luanne. Call me back if you need her number, but maybe you already have it. Hope you're enjoying your trip. See you Monday!"

"Luanne? Why?"

She hadn't had any contact with Luanne for more than a decade. And even then, it was only to tell her that one of their high school friends died in a car wreck. They both said that they'd stay in touch, but there wasn't any reason, so they didn't.

She searched her contacts list and was surprised to find that she still had her number. She hesitated, ready to call, then scoffed at the sight of the bar and tapped to make the call.

"Hello, Luanne. This is Lin. How have you been?"

"Lin! Where are you? Are you okay?"

"Yeah, I'm fine. Why? What's wrong?"

"Where are you? Please tell me you're in Pennsylvania!"

"No, I'm not. I'm back in St. Simons for the thirty-year reunion. Why? What's bothering you?"

"Oh, Lin, Ben and I, we—"

"Let me guess: you two are still together?"

"Shit. If you can call it that. Ruts are easier to dig your ass into than to crawl out of. We had a big fight, the usual bullshit, and I probably shouldn't have said anything, but I told him he changed that day, that day with the truck. You must remember that, right? I told him he didn't have to be like that. He could have had a better life. And that rattled him. He stormed off to drink and the next day, he was in a rotten mood. But I've never seen him so determined like that. He left to even the score with you, Lin. Just please, get out of there. Go back home. I don't think he knows where you live now."

"It's too late, Luanne. I've already seen him."

"You what? Are you okay?"

"Yes, I'm fine. But you're right, he definitely wanted to even the score. Maybe he still does. But I hope not."

"Well, what are you going to do? You're going to leave, right? Just get your shit and go—forget that stupid-ass reunion!"

"It's under control. Don't worry. He blew off some steam, and he's in a bar drinking right now. My guess is that he'll head for home soon."

"I hope you're right, Lin. He's a dangerous man. I doubt you could stop him if he really came at you."

Lin smiled, covered the phone, and said, "That mayhem sure stopped him."

She held it up again to speak.

"What do you remember about that day, Luanne?"

"I remember that day like it was yesterday. I've never talked about it, though. Not to anyone. I bet you remember it well too."

"Actually, I only remember up to the point when I blacked out. I've since had dreams—at least I think they're dreams, more like nightmares, really—about what happened. But I don't know how much of that is real and how much is my imagination."

"I'll tell you what I remember. It was your idea to sneak into that construction company's yard and hang out. You even brought two six-packs of your daddy's beer. That's probably what got things going out of control. It got crazy when you decided to take that dump truck for a joy ride. We thought you were nuts, but you said the key was right there in the ignition like a damn invitation."

"I said 'damn?'"

"Uh, no. I just added that. Sorry, I'm scared for you! Anyway, it was fine for a few minutes, you driving slow around the yard, the rest of us on the seat next to you or standing on the running boards and hanging onto the mirrors. We thought you were really some kind of badass! I think it was me that started calling you Ms. Mayhem. You probably don't remember, but 'mayhem' was one of our vocabulary words back then."

"Yeah, I do remember that. And I liked being called Ms. Mayhem."

"But then, the shit got serious when you stopped the truck, we all got out, and you said it was Ben's turn to drive. Oh, the look on his face. Damn, he was basically a good kid back then. I know he was scared because of his dad. I think he got his ass beat a lot those days. He still won't talk about it. Well, he wouldn't drive. He wouldn't even sit behind the wheel. And then, you teased him. You pushed him."

"I remember that too. I feel terrible about that. I didn't mean anything by it."

"Hey, don't feel bad. We were just kids. So, then one of the other boys decided to jump in on teasing him too. He called Ben a pussy. Ben ignored it, but then the rest of us—not you, though—started calling him that. He broke after a while. It was too much for him. He grabbed you and pushed you up against a stack of lumber and said you were nothing but a tease, that *you* were the pussy, and you should prove yourself right then by doing something to him, something I ain't gonna repeat even now."

"Oh, I remember that. God, we were just kids!"

"Yeah. Well, like I said, he kind of went crazy. Him saying that scared us a little, but we were dumb kids, and we made it even worse. After he called you the pussy, one of the boys said you were Pussy Mayhem. We all started chanting, 'Pussy Mayhem, Pussy Mayhem!'"

"I loved that name! But I was terrified of Ben. He was big, even back then."

"Oh, he's much bigger now. And mean like nobody's business."

"I know. God, I know."

"We were all scared, but I was pulling on Ben's arm and trying to get him to let you go. Then, all of a sudden, you stopped fighting, and you were looking him right in the eye. Your eyes started to close real slow. I felt some kind of tingly feeling, which actually felt pretty awesome, and then Ben's arms were down. I didn't even see them move. They were just down, and he collapsed. We could all smell that he'd lost it in his pants. All of it.

"Your eyes opened all the way, and you started walking away real slow. I ran over to you and asked you what the hell you just did. I was amazed, and I know I wanted nothing more than to be around you. I felt like giggling just looking at you. You said nothing happened, you kind of blacked out, and you said it looked like Ben got sick or something."

"That's what I remember, too, Luanne. I blacked out and when I woke up, Ben was on the ground."

"Ben was never right after that. Do you remember how he kept away from all of us? And then, he got in serious trouble, and his family moved away. But after high school, after you and your folks moved, I thought about what Ben used to be like. Before that day. I went and found him. We've been together ever since. It hasn't been a joyride, I can tell you that much."

"I can only imagine."

"No, Lin, you really can't. If his stupid bullshit gets him a prison cell, you won't see me crying over it. I'm not sure I can take his shit anymore."

Chapter 15 – John & Tommy

Lin set down her phone just as the server walked up with her plate.

"Here you go, ma'am. Any ketchup with that?"

"No, this is fine. Thanks."

Lin stared up at the girl leaning, inspecting her.

"Um, you need some kind of bandage or something?"

Lin grabbed at her cheek and said, "Oh, no, it's nothing. It's fine."

Lin studied the girl walking away for only a second, then gave another second to the cheeseburger and fries, then looked across Mallery at the bar while fumbling for a fistful of fries.

The neon sun in the bar's window continued to grin. She scoffed at its smile, then gave her attention to picking up the hot sandwich.

Holding it up but before taking the first bite, she said to herself, "My hometown. The best food on this side and violent attackers right across the street."

She chomped down, wiped some mess off of her lips with the napkin, and chewed while diverting her eyes back to Ben's adopted lair.

And she saw a sight that got her jaw to freeze up, even with cheeks packed: across the street, near the bar entrance, stood John and Tommy.

"What the hell?" she said, garbled as the words got filtered through a mouthful of food.

They both looked as if they'd just tumbled off of a rolling train. Dirty, wrinkled clothes. Unshaven, and probably without a shower since she'd first seen them. They were even wearing the same clothes as Monday—business casual—except coated with enough gravel dust to be visible even from Lin's seat across Mallery.

She sank slowly into her chair with her legs pushing out the other side of the small glass-top table.

"No, no, no. This can't be happening."

Even low in her seat, a warm breeze was able to fluff out her hair and without thinking and immediately regretting it, Lin gave her mane a strong fling back over her bare shoulder.

Tommy's diligent scanning of every face he could see came to an abrupt end. He spun around to look her way, recognized her, and launched a smile so big that it looked like he was stretching his mouth open manually.

Without taking his eyes off of her, he grabbed John's sleeve and started tugging it downward while pointing in her direction. John's smile grew almost as wide as Tommy's, and they scurried over, completely mindless of the traffic. Amid squealing tires and honking horns, they somehow made it across Mallery.

*　　*　　*

Their excited voices carried above the din of traffic long before they got to Lin's table. Tommy pointed at Lin's face and giggled, and John, though he grinned insanely, elbowed him and whispered, in a strained way, "Settle down!"

They struggled to remain still as they stood next to Lin, smiling down at her like clowns. She didn't get up or say a word. She only stared at one, then the other.

"I knew we'd find you. I knew it. I knew it!" said Tommy.

"It's our lucky day!" said John.

Tommy continued. "We've been looking for you for days now. You're amazing! I'm so glad we found you. Did I say we've been looking for days?"

"Yes," said John, "you said that. Settle yourself, Tommy. Lady, we can't get over Monday by that pond. It was the most amazing thing. You're amazing! We had to find you. We had to."

"And we did find you. We did!" said Tommy, rocking to either side and peeking over his clapping hands. "Here we are! We're here to see you!"

"Easy, Tommy. Let the lady have a chance to speak, alright?"

Lin looked from one to the other several times, and she started speaking several times, only to stop and give each another stare.

John was taller, and his wire-frame glasses and short black hair made him look more serious than Tommy, who was chubby and short and nearly bald. Both wore toothy grins and were straining to show Lin as much of them as they could.

John stood perfectly still, with eyes wide, like he'd spied a bag of gold coins and was too shocked to pick it up. Tommy was agitated, gleeful even, with eyes blinking rapidly and occasionally looking upward, as if thanking God for his great fortune.

"You two. From Pennsylvania. What are you doing here? How did you find me?"

Tommy said, "There's nowhere else we wanna be! With you, that's where we wanna be. And here we are. With you. Here. We're here with you—"

"Tommy, cool it. Lady, what you did in PA was astounding. It made me tingle all over just watching. Tommy too. We had to find you."

"You're talking nonsense. I didn't do anything. And just how did you find me?"

"Oh, that was easy," said John. "I have a friend at the airport, and you said you had a jet to catch. So, we got the inside scoop. In Jacksonville, we bribed a guy at the rental desk—took the last of our cash. But it was worth it. He dialed in the GPS, and guess what we saw: St. Simons Island. So, here we are!"

"Boys, I don't know what you think this is all about, but you should just go back home. This isn't just a vacation for me. I have serious work to do. It was a strange surprise seeing you, but really, go back home."

"I have nothing to go back to," said John. "I phoned in and quit my job. There's nothing for me back in Cleveland. This is where I belong."

"Me too, me too, me too," said Tommy. "I phoned my family and quit that too. Gone, just like that. It's a new life for me. With you. Here. We're all—"

"Tommy!"

"Guys! Just stop, you're making a scene."

They fell silent, but their insane grins never faded.

"Okay, if you're not leaving, sit down. Both of you."

John and Tommy grabbed the chairs but their eyes never left Lin. They banged them together, scraped them all around, then finally sat. But then, they both sat quietly across from Lin, silver dollar eyes staring at her, looking like they were about to leap from their seats.

"You two, I don't know what you think about what happened Monday evening. But I never meant your friend any harm."

"He wasn't our friend. We were at a convention in Pittsburgh together, and we decided to all share a ride back. I never knew Tommy before that either."

"Okay, but I didn't do anything to that guy. He attacked me, remember? I just wanted to leave."

"Yeah, he was a bastard, a real bastard," said Tommy. "He got what he deserved. He should have got more! How dare he bother you, you of all people? More, more, he shoulda got—"

"Tommy!" said John through a strained smile.

"Look, you two can believe what you want. I don't care. What are you doing here?"

"There's no place else for us now," John said as he offered a genuine smile and no hint that he was being overly dramatic.

Lin's mouth hung open as she looked from one to the other several times. She started to laugh, then stopped, tipped her head, and stared over at John, who only grinned back.

Wincing at him for a second, then turning her head to check Tommy, she found that he was grinning too. And nodding.

"You're like . . . what? A fan club?"

"Okay!" said John.

"Yeah, yeah, yeah! We—"

"No, I didn't mean—"
Silly grins froze in place, and eyes like strange bugs stared at her.
"Unbelievable."

*　*　*

A crack opened to reveal the dark world of the bar, and out strode Ben. He stood for a moment, blocking the window's sun, then he began a slow, confident walk back toward his truck. He appeared to have submerged most of his rage in alcohol.

Lin took only the second bite of her sandwich and stood up.

"Okay, guys. It's been fun, but I have to go. Here's for your lunch too—on me."

She threw down two twenties before finishing her coffee.

"We're not hungry. Not at all. Nope. Not even a little. I might not eat again—"

"Tommy!" said John. "Thanks, lady, you're very kind too. Not just amazing."

They both got up and stepped away from their chairs.

"Sit down, boys. I really need to go."

And with that, Lin began a brisk walk back to her rental car, lagging behind Ben but always keeping him in view from across the street. He was an unyielding force stomping along, never moving for anyone and never once looking back.

Erratic footsteps and snickering caused Lin to glance over her shoulder, and John and Tommy were only a few paces behind with their unblinking eyes focused on her.

She stopped and turned to face them. They stopped too.

"Stop. Go back. Now!"

She turned to keep walking. They continued to march behind her, giggling and elbowing each other.

Lin made it to her car and through thin shrubbery, she saw that Ben had reached his truck. She watched as he got in and started the engine.

With her eyes fixed on Ben, she unlocked her car and got in.

And they got in too. Both in the back seat.

"Get out now!"

"We want to be with you," said John.

"Yeah, with you, we wanna be with you, we—"

Lin raised her hand, silencing him, replacing his rant with cussing under her breath. She started the motor and slowly rolled out to the street, falling in a block behind Ben.

"Just keep your heads down back there."

*　　*　　*

Ben's truck traveled much like Ben on foot: rolling directly through traffic and pedestrians, ignoring signs and lights, offering a very unmistakable gesture if a horn was sounded or even if it wasn't. Lin followed closely with John and Tommy content in the back seat.

"Where are we going?"

"Don't worry about it, John. No one told you to stow yourselves back there."

"I'm stowed back here," said Tommy. "Stowed away. A stowaway. I'm—"

"Quiet, Tommy. Lady, we don't care where you take us. As long as you take us."

"You guys. Just look out the windows. Enjoy the marshes."

They left the bustle of the Village and cruised over the Causeway, following Ben into the heart of Brunswick. Up ahead, he pulled to the curb, and Lin slowed then stopped.

He got out and walked into a quiet brick building, so Lin idled past, then paused alongside his truck.

"Wonderful," she said, leaning to look out through the passenger side window.

"What, lady? That truck?"

"No. That sign. It's a pawn shop."

"Why is that wonderful?" said Tommy. "We know why you're wonderful, but why that place?"

"Sarcasm, boys. Ben isn't planning to play nice."

85

Chapter 16 – Pawn Shopper

Lin had continued past Ben's truck and parked at the curb half a block away. In the rearview mirror, she kept a dedicated watch over the pawn shop's entrance.

"Listen, you two. There's some serious shit going on. I want you to sit quietly. Don't distract me. And if I tell you to get down, you get down as fast and low as you can. Got that?"

"We'll do whatever you want. Just tell us," said John.

"Right. Right. I can get so low that you'll think I'm a floor mat. So low you'll think—"

"Lady, we'll behave. Promise. What should we call you?"

Lin stared through the windshield at the heat rising from the road.

"You two? You can call me . . ."

She paused for a quick scoff, then shook her head and smiled.

"Lin. Just call me Lin."

She glanced up at the rearview.

"Hi, Lin. I'm John."

"Hi, Lin. I'm Tommy. Just Tommy. Tommy without a family. Tommy that is happy right here, getting so low on the floor that—"

Lin heard the smack, and Tommy quieted down.

"He wasn't like this before, Lin. Not before that day."

Lin let out a deep groan and stared into the mirror, looking past her new companions at the pawn shop.

They weren't in a bustling center of town. The Georgia heat weighed more heavily in Brunswick, which didn't share the cool ocean breezes of the Island. The few trickles of sunlight seemed to be struggling to squeeze between the deserted buildings crowding both sides of the street. The old structures looked tired and leaning out over the road as if pleading for the sweet relief of the wrecking ball.

There were a few stragglers wandering around, mostly without any urgent destination. A few sloppy locals paused to bend over and gawk at them, but the tinted windows didn't reveal much.

The pawn shop door swung open. A large shape appeared.

"Down! Get down!"

"We're down, we're down, we're so low—"

"Shut up!"

Ben stepped out of the building and stood just outside the door. He looked both ways, then he reached behind to the small of his back to rearrange something.

"Oh, that's nice. You just bought one, didn't you?"

"Just bought what?"

"Shh!"

Before he took another step, he took a piece of paper out of his pocket and studied it, scratching under his chin. After shoving it roughly back into the pocket, he turned abruptly to walk the opposite way, away from Lin and back to his truck.

That direction was blocked by a rough-looking man even bigger than Ben. They collided hard, with the other man being knocked back a few feet. Ben stood his ground.

The man walked up to Ben and got right up in his face, waving his arms all around, sometimes pointing and almost poking Ben's face, and sometimes holding a fist close, ready to strike.

With no warning, Ben punched the man's gut hard, doubling him over. A brutal knee to his face put him on his back. Ben leaned over and with one hand holding the man's shirt and lifting him up off of the pavement, he proceeded to punch and punch until even from her car, Lin could see light reflecting off of the spreading pool.

The man hadn't quite lost consciousness yet. One hand reached up feebly, and he looked to be begging for his life. Ben reached around his back and grabbed a pistol out of his waistband. The barrel met the man's face, and it looked like Ben told the bloody man something. But he didn't shoot.

At least, no one in the stakeout car heard a gunshot.

Ben looked at the gun, allowed the man to drop to the concrete, and took a few steps back to examine his weapon.

He dug into a front pocket of his jeans and came out with a small box. Casually, not even looking around, he proceeded to load the revolver.

"No. Really, Ben? Right there on the sidewalk?"

Lin held her breath when the gun loading was done, but Ben walked around the man and his blood like it was all just more trash on the sidewalk. He spat on the trash as he walked past.

"Maybe he's just saving his ammo."

"What, Lin? What about ammo?"

"Nothing, John. I hope."

*   *   *

"Stay down, you two."

Lin stared into the mirror, put the car in gear, then waited and watched as Ben squealed his truck in a quick U-turn and sped away.

"We're down, Lin."

She put the car back in park and said, "That helps, John."

"I'm helping too. Helping. I'm—"

"Yeah, you are. Thanks, Tommy."

Lin turned and looked over the seat at her fan club, still huddling out of sight, and said, "Boys, you can sit up. The scary man is gone."

"I'm not scared of him. And Halloween was only a few days ago, Lin," said Tommy. "I didn't wear a costume. I like these clothes—I wear them all the time. But if you want me to wear a costume, I will. I can dress like—"

"You already look like a hobo, Tommy. *That's* your costume, alright?" John said before smiling at Lin and bouncing his eyebrows robotically.

Lin spun herself back around and grabbed the wheel with both hands.

"I should buy one too."

She tugged at her short skirt, then checked all around the waistband.

"Buy what, Lin?"

"Nothing, John. No room. Not the way I dress."

"Buy new clothes!"

"Thanks, Tommy. Good advice. But no thanks."

She let out a deep breath and turned the mirror back to look at her two new friends. Their eyes were huge and their smiles wide.

"You boys must be hungry. Let's go eat and see if we can figure out some of this nonsense."

"Scary men aren't nonsense," said John. "Uh-uh."

"You,"—she pointed at each of them a few times—"are the nonsense."

Chapter 17 – Lookout Lunch

Lin turned off of the Causeway partway back to the Island and idled around the marina restaurant's parking lot, then swung her car into a space near the entrance. She put it in park and before cracking open her door, she turned enough to face her companions.

"Just what am I supposed to do with you two?"

"Anything," said John. "I just want to follow you . . . help you if I can with whatever you're doing."

"Me too," said Tommy. "No place else I wanna be."

"But I don't need your help. I work alone. We're not forming some kind of posse here."

"A posse sounds great! I wanna be in your posse! Wherever you go, I go, and where I go, you—"

"Enough, Tommy. I think she gets the idea."

"Look, we need to eat, and we can talk about this over lunch. But after lunch, I want you two gone. I'll give you bus fare to get back to Cleveland. John, you can get your job back. Just tell them you were in an accident on the road back in Pennsylvania or something. Tommy, you need to go back to your family. Beg them to take you back if you have to.

"Not another word. We're going inside, and you two had better behave."

*   *   *

The restaurant's floor-to-ceiling windows allowed Lin and the rest of the diners a clear view of the Causeway leading to the Island. The generous windows on the dining room's other side boasted an enviable view of the marina where boats sat completely still, baking in the sun.

Lin gave the Causeway a thorough scan, then turned just enough to match the gaze from John and Tommy. Across the table, they remained rigid like mannequins, silly grins stretched wide and eyes big and rarely blinking.

She raised a hand toward them and snapped a finger, and scoffed at seeing no reaction from them.

"John. Tommy. I don't know what to tell you guys. So, why don't you start. Why did you follow me to St. Simons Island? What do you want with me? John, you start. Tommy, you just wait, and you'll get a turn."

"I can't explain it, Lin. Something in me changed," he said, shaking his head, "and now, I can't imagine being anywhere else than with you."

"In Georgia?"

"Anywhere. Mars."

"But why, John? Do you think there's something special about me?"

"Oh my God, yeah. You're special. I can feel it. I felt it right away."

"You felt what right away?"

"You're so special I felt it—a tingle. Right there by the pond, when that punk we were with tried to hurt you."

"Exactly when did you feel this tingle?"

"As soon as your eyes started to close. I know because I was looking right at you. Right then, a tingle shot through me all over."

"Me too, me too," said Tommy. "Like he said, with your eyes, then the tingle, something magic, magic in your eyes."

"It wasn't your turn to talk yet, Tommy."

He grinned and nodded, and Lin shook her head and scoffed.

"Look into my eyes, both of you."

They never stopped their loony smiles, but they leaned each way and did as she'd told them. The seconds dragged on.

"Okay, that's enough. Do you see anything magic? Are you feeling any tingling?"

"Well, no," said John. "No tingling, but I still know you're special. I'll never forget."

"You too, Tommy? Is that how you feel?"

Tommy launched his head into vigorous nodding with a huge smile on his face.

Lin squinted at him, waiting for an answer, but he didn't say a word. He just kept nodding until Lin pointed at him.

John looked at him in surprise, then he looked back at Lin and shrugged.

"A tingle, huh?"

Both nodded.

"Huh. Luanne said something about that too. From way back when."

"Who's Luanne?"

"Just a friend, John."

The server approached the table and fought hard to not stare at the two disheveled men sitting with the fabulously dressed woman. She professionally asked if she could take their orders.

"Are you Luanne?"

"John, no," said Lin. "Luanne isn't anywhere around here."

"Is she going to get Luanne, then—"

"Tommy. No. No Luanne, okay?"

John and Tommy abandoned all interest in the server that wasn't Luanne, giving Lin their full, big-eyed attention.

"Guys, she's ready to take your orders. Just tell her what you want— it's on me."

"I don't care about food anymore, Lin."

"Me neither. I don't care about nothing."

John said, "Double negative, Tommy."

"She knows what I mean. I think she knows everything."

Lin sighed, looked up, and said, "They'll each have a burger, medium well, with everything. And a draft for each of them."

"And for you?"

"Lobster. And a gin and tonic."

"Okay, I'll get this going."

She left for the kitchen, and Lin turned to glare at the two grinning men.

"Okay, I don't know what to tell you about some kind of tingle that you think you felt. But I can assure you, I didn't tingle either of you.

"John, what did you see? I blacked out, so I really don't know what happened."

"It was amazing, Lin. Kind of in a scary way, though. I didn't see you do anything. Nothing at all."

He stared at Lin while straining to enlarge his smile.

Lin stared back and leaned toward him, her elbows on the table.

"Okay, so what *did* you see?"

"I saw Davey. He looked like a puppet. He really messed himself up. Just as he started walking toward you, he stopped."

"That's when your eyes started to close. I felt the tingle!" said Tommy.

"Yeah, that's right. He's right, Lin. Right then! So, Davey froze. I mean, his arms just hung there. His eyes were open but really, he wasn't there. When the tingle stopped, I can't understand how, but Davey was down in the gravel. He wasn't moving. He was a bloody mess. But you were amazing, and I walked right over to you."

"Yeah, amazing!" said Tommy.

"We walked over to be near you. Then, you opened your magic eyes all the way, and you looked straight ahead. You looked over at me next, and I knew right then that all I wanted was to be with you."

"And you looked down at me, and I felt like I could jump twenty feet straight up, and I was so happy, and I pointed at Davey. Man, he was messed up!"

"But that wasn't my—"

Lin snapped her eyes away from the pond stories from the two men upon hearing the distinctive rumbling and rattling of Ben's truck. She scoffed at the sight of it passing traffic on the Causeway en route to St. Simons Island.

"What's wrong, Lin? Was that the bad man's truck?"

"Yeah, John. I'm afraid so."

"Don't be afraid," said Tommy. "We'll protect you. I'd die for you without a second thought."

"He's right. We both would. We—"

"Hold it. Both of you. Nobody's dying."

"We don't die if you don't want us to, Lin."

"John, that's a dumb thing to say."

"It really is!" said Tommy.

Lin scoffed and was close to chiding them more, but they all looked up at the sound of footsteps.

The server placed plates for all of them, and the boys practically vacuumed up their meals. Their burgers might as well have been tossed into a wood chipper, and they both chugged their beers noisily.

"Guys, slow down."

They stopped.

"I didn't say to stop. Just eat like normal people."

They started and kept a normal pace.

"Better."

She shook her head before sipping her cocktail, letting her eyes linger on each of the men forcing themselves to eat at a normal pace.

Only because she'd told them to.

Chapter 18 – Cowboy Jack

Jack wedged himself deeper into his worn vinyl couch, keeping his phone pressed to an ear.

"Just get those supplies delivered before Monday, alright? The garage will be unlocked, so just pile it up in there. And stop calling me a carpenter."

He waited, grinning and listening.

"Lin can call me that or anything else she wants. Not you. How do you know she does that anyway?"

Another pause.

"Right. I remember bringing her out to pick out flooring at your shop. Yeah. Don't remember her calling me a carpenter, though."

He sat up and stretched, gave his watch a glance.

"Well, she's got an eye for color, stuff like that. I can build anything, but colors? Eh. Not so much."

He gave his watch another look.

"Okay, look, I really have to go. I got another call to make, then I'm writing a poem."

He grinned, listening.

"For Lin, of course. Hey, I've learned a lot of new things since we were in high school. So did you. You didn't know shit about flooring back then. Look, I really have to go. Try to get that stuff delivered, alright?"

Jack listened for another second, then tapped his phone and set it aside. A good stretching of his arms, straight out to his sides, evoked a single laugh, then he reached for the phone.

He mumbled to himself, "Didn't know I wrote poetry. Well, who does?"

He typed for a minute, smiling at his work, then hovered a finger over the phone for a moment.

"Hell, yeah. Send."

He gave it another tap, then tossed his phone back onto the cushion beside him.

His smile faded quickly, and he tipped his head, looking around the room. And he grabbed for his phone again.

"Dammit, I'm doing it. She likes surprises."

He tapped a few keys, then waited.

"Uh, I hope she does."

He had time to scoff only once.

"Hi. I'd like to book a flight to St. Simons Island in Georgia. I guess I'll have to fly in to Brunswick? No? Okay, that'll do. I'll need a car too. Yes, I can wait."

*　*　*

Lin had set down her drink and had just stabbed a chuck of lobster when her phone chimed. She took it, tapped a few times, and smiled.

"John, Tommy, I need to make a call."

"Is it Luanne?"

"Tommy, no.

"I'm going to step out into the lobby right over there. You don't need to come with me. You can see me right through the glass doors. I won't be long. Stay."

Tommy barked, then panted.

"Did you just bark?"

Her squinting eyes got pulled to John's when he said, "You're training us, Lin. We can be your dogs. We can even—"

Tommy barked again.

"Tommy. No barking in the restaurant."

He stayed quiet but panted, and Lin leaned forward to get a better look at the bit of drool working its way out.

"You guys. I want you both to—"

"Stay," said John.

"And don't bark!" said Tommy.

"We won't bark, Lin. Um, unless you want us to."

"Tell us to!" said Tommy. "Just tell us!"

"Oh, my," she said as she scooted her chair back and stood.

She backed away from the table, maintaining eye contact with them, and sometimes raising a finger and pointing at them.

Softly, too low for anyone but her to hear, she said, "Just be good dogs. Good dogs, please."

All of the people in the restaurant were enjoying their meals, talking, and viewing the scenery. Not John and Tommy. They were faced directly at Lin, and they never turned their heads. Tommy's arms were up, hands dangling, looking like paws.

Lin squeezed through past the door, her eyes on the boys at the table, then let the door close as she raised up her phone and called Jack.

"Jack, another nice poem. You'll get tired of writing those someday."

"You're seldom wrong, dear Cowgirl, but on that count, yeah, you're completely wrong. How's life in Georgia?"

"I wouldn't know where to begin. It's probably best if I don't. No, I don't want you to think it's that bad. Just a lot of weird issues I'm dealing with. It'll be great to be back home and spend some quality time with you, sipping whiskey after we, um, *see* each other."

"Can't wait. What kinds of issues are you dealing with? Do you feel alright?"

"Yeah, I feel fine. Just lately, my life seems so much more complicated. I mean, in ways,"—she frowned and pointed at John and Tommy—"like you'd never imagine. It's like things are catching up with me."

"Things from your past? Anything you can tell me about? You know, I'd do whatever I could to help you, even if that meant just giving you a big, long hug."

"Ah, nobody gives better hugs than you, dear Cowboy. But there are things in my past that I've kept to myself. Not just from you—from everyone. And for some reason, they're starting to hit me in the head. I'll be fine, but spending time with you sounds like more of a vacation than being here in St. Simons."

"Your secrets probably aren't so bad. You know you can tell me anything, don't you?"

"I know, but I don't think talking is going to fix any of this. There are things I need to work through. So, enough of that. How's work on that old house coming along?"

"Ugh . . . that old house is taking forever. I just uncovered more damage to part of the foundation, and I need to figure out what to do about that. But like usual, there's no rush. It'll get done. That flooring that you helped pick out should get dropped soon. Hey, did you get all that info into your spreadsheet?"

"Oh, those numbers. Um, I haven't been able to, uh, look at that yet, Jack. Maybe soon. It's just been so nice to enjoy the warm weather and relax. I don't relax enough. Neither do you."

"Yeah, that's true. Way too much work for me. But not this weekend. I'm definitely taking a break for a long weekend."

"It's about time you took a few days off. You work way too much. Do you have any special plans?"

"I don't have any details worked out, no. I wish you were back. I'd spend the whole time in bed with you."

"That sounds heavenly, Jack. But I won't be back for a couple more days."

"I know, but I miss you. Wouldn't it be nice if we could get together sooner?"

"Well, yeah, of course. Hey, here's something crazy for you to think about—why don't you fly down here and hang out with me Friday and Saturday? You're not working anyway, so why not? We both need a little vacation like that, but I know there's no way you could swing that."

"You really want me to drop whatever I'm doing and climb on a jet just to come see you for a couple of days?"

Lin grimaced through the glass at the sight of John pawing at Tommy, who was barking silently up at the ceiling.

"Oh, boy."

"Huh?"

"Oh, nothing. I mean, uh, yeah, drop everything. I know you can't Jack, because you have so much—"

"I already bought the ticket. I'll be there Friday afternoon, staying at a place on Beachview."

Both of them were barking up at the ceiling.

"Seriously?"

"Yes, seriously. I'll text you when I'm in town. I can't wait to see you."

"Yeah, Jack. Yeah. Me too."

The boys had stopped their barking and both stared at her, panting, paws raised.

"But I really need to get going. See you soon."

Chapter 19 – Lost Puppies

Lin gave the two at the table an angry gesture through the plate glass, and they shrank back, almost groveling. She'd just begun sliding her phone into her purse, but she scoffed and took it out again.

"Gabby, do you have any time to chat?"

"Of course, Lin. I'm always around for you. What's going on?"

"There's enough to make a list. It's just one thing after another, then another comes along, and—"

"Lin. Just pick one."

"Okay. Fine. That kid from high school, Ben, just bought a gun, and I saw his junk trunk cruising the Causeway. He's not leaving. Oh, no, he's staying right here on the Island."

"Can you leave too?"

"What? Run? Not my style, Gabby. Besides, now Jack is coming to spend a couple of days here too. I can't just pick up and get out of town."

"He's always good company, isn't he?"

"Yes, Gabby, but not with bullets flying!"

"That's true. You might have to keep a low profile, Lin, until you can get back to Pennsylvania."

"Right. Uh-huh. How do I do that with two yapping dogs following me around?"

"You adopted two dogs? Why?"

"No, they adopted me! Oh, I can't explain right now. There are just too many moving parts in my life these days."

"Sometimes, every part just needs to find its place, Lin. It'll work out."

Lin winced at the sight of John and Tommy swiping paws at each other and sometimes leaning over their plates, biting at what was left.

"Oh, boy. I have to go, Gabby. I hope to see you soon."

"I'm really never far away, Lin."

She looked at her phone, then stowed it away.

After rapping on the glass, settling both of them, she grabbed her hair with both hands and pulled it back, letting it fall past her shoulders, tugged her skirt down a bit, and walked back to the table.

*   *   *

"John, Tommy, how was your dinner? Do you feel better now?"

"I'm fine, Lin. The food was good, but I was fine anyway. We don't care. What's next?" said John.

"Next, you guys take a train or a bus and get back to your lives."

"Can't do that. Nope, can't do that, Lin. We're here, we're staying here, we have nowhere—"

"Lin, we just want to help you in any way we can. We really don't have any lives to get back to," said John.

"You both know you're making a huge mistake, don't you? I have a life to lead, and it doesn't involve you two hanging around me all the time."

She paused to look at the sadness in their eyes.

"And acting like dogs. Don't be dogs, alright?"

"Okay, then we can stay with you! I'm not a dog anymore!" said Tommy, causing John to only grin at Lin, shaking his head, until he spoke.

"We won't be dogs if you don't want us to. We know you have a life. We just want to be part of it."

"Yes, part of your life, Lin. You and John and me, we can all do everything together."

"We're not getting on a train. Or a bus," John said as he stared calmly into her eyes.

She studied them for a moment and saw that, despite their unkempt clothes and lack of hygiene the last few days, they were completely happy to be there at that table with her. They really did seem like lost puppies that had nowhere else to go.

They were her lost puppy posse.

"Okay, boys. Here's what we're going to do. I have a lot of things to take care of in the next few days and as much as I enjoy your company, these are things I need to do alone."

"We won't bark."

"That's wonderful, Tommy, but I still need to be alone for this.

"Let's find you a nice hotel where you can clean up and get some rest. You'll need to rest because I'll need your help with something on Saturday. Does that sound okay?"

"We'll help you with anything, Lin," said John.

"Yep, anything you need, we're there, we're there and helping and not being dogs, we're—"

"Tommy, that's quite enough. Thanks, guys. This is what I need you to do. Besides not being dogs, this is how you can help me, okay? You both need to rest and get cleaned up. I'll give you some money for food and some more comfortable clothes. And a laundromat. Very important—get those clothes cleaned, okay?"

"Are you sure there's nothing else, Lin? We can help with whatever you're doing. I know we can."

"I'm sure you can, John, but there are things I need to do alone. Just remember that I'll need you to be somewhere for me on Saturday. Very important."

*　*　*

Lin had kept her eyes only on the road ahead on the drive away from lunch at the marina. Behind her, despite the car's air conditioning on high, John and Tommy had their windows down and their heads out to catch the wind.

She pulled into a hotel on Demere and parked, but she kept the motor running.

"Boys, roll up your windows."

Tommy barked softly, but they both complied.

"Here," she said, handing a thin stack of bills over her shoulder. "For the room, food, clothes, laundry, and whatever else. There's extra there for bus fare too. That would be the best, then you can pocket the rest."

"No buses for us, Lin. Nope."

"How about a plane ticket, then, John?"

"We'd have to be in crates in the cargo room," Tommy said, and Lin tipped the mirror enough to see his gigantic grin.

"You guys."

"He's not really a dog, Lin."

"Thanks, John. That's helpful."

With the cool air rushing from the vent, tossing wisps of her blond mane around, Lin dug through her purse and closed it with a scoff.

"I'll have to get the address to you later. Just remember that you have to be there Saturday at 5:00, okay?"

"Okay, okay, Lin," said Tommy. "Are you sure they'll let—"

John's elbow caught him in his ribs, forcing a gasp, then a laugh.

"He's only having fun, Lin. He knows he's not really a dog."

With a long, slow sigh, Lin studied them in the mirror.

"Okay, good to know. Guys, get going, alright?"

She watched. They stayed.

Seconds crawled past, and their grins only got bigger.

"Go!"

Giggling, they popped open their doors, got out, and kept snickering and elbowing each other as they walked away.

Chapter 20 – Only Dreams

After dropping John and Tommy at their own hotel, Lin drove back up to Ocean Drive, but she found a new hotel and didn't return to the scene of Ben's attack.

She let the motor hum and kept the cool air blasting. Only a moment passed before Gabby joined her.

"I knew you'd find me."

"I always do."

"Gabby, I'm in the mood to tell you about my nightmares. Up until now, I've tried to keep them buried—just keep them to myself. But with all the mayhem erupting lately, it's probably best if I try to work through it. At least get some idea of what's going on. You're always a big help. I'm glad you're here."

"I'm never far away, Lin. When you need me, you know I'll find a way to get to you."

"I wonder sometimes if maybe I shouldn't even dwell on these dreams, though. Maybe it's all just a bunch of nonsense. Just my imagination."

She paused.

"You know, I had to say that, but I don't believe they're nonsense."

"Why don't we talk about them and see where we end up?"

"Okay, sure. How about the first one?"

Lin paused and cleared her throat.

"I open my eyes, and it takes a moment to figure out where I am. I feel myself breathing. I'm standing, and I feel weak, like I got heavier and it takes more effort to hold my body up. Then, I see that I'm in my kitchen at home. I scan along the counter until I see what I'm looking for. I take it in my right hand and hold it in front of my eyes.

"That's when the sound of silent crying begins. No sound, really, but I kind of hear it anyway. As I begin to move the knife down, the silent crying becomes silent shrieking. Trust me, Gabby, you don't ever want to hear silent shrieking. It hits you inside, in a place you didn't know existed, and your mind can't process it.

"I can never remember any details after that. The nightmare ends, and I wake up sweating with the hairs on my neck standing up."

"And you still don't think that's your way of reliving that event with Ray, of dealing with the trauma?"

"No, and I'll tell you how I know. The first time I had that nightmare? It was before anyone told me anything about what had happened to Ray."

Gabby had nothing to say for a long moment.

"Lin, whatever happened to Ray, and however it happened, it was justified. He was definitely an evil man. And we have to stop evil whenever we can."

"But Gabby, did I somehow do that to him? How? How could I have seen it through his eyes? How did I hear his shrieking? He didn't want that to happen. He was forced. And God, he was terrified."

"I think the important thing for you to remember is that he was evil and deserved it. No one should ever treat anyone that way, especially a child. Try not to be too hard on yourself. What about your other nightmares?"

Lin leaned her seat back and tried to stretch her legs. Without the heels, there would have been enough room. She hung her arm out the window and waved it lazily, letting the ocean breezes brush her from different angles.

"Maybe that's enough for now. They're just stupid nonsense, Gabby."

"Perhaps. Why don't we try to get through more, though?"

"Okay. Fine. That jumper in Erie should have gone easy. He had no history of violence. But Gabby, maybe I pushed him over some kind of edge. You know how I've been dressing lately. I was really strutting it in that bar, hoping he'd notice me. He did, and I reeled him in. The guy probably would have felt dumb if he didn't ask me to go back to his room.

"But he was clever. He set it up with the bartender, I think. I've thought about it, and I think I understand what he did. He didn't want to be seen leaving with me, and he didn't want the desk clerk to see us together. He had it all planned out, and the bartender helped.

"Anyway, none of that's important now. What matters is that he attacked me as soon as I got to his room. I was helpless from then on."

"Except somehow, you weren't helpless."

"Okay, yeah, maybe in some strange way. I detested that man for attacking me like that. He seemed like a decent guy, and I never expected him to get violent. I wanted him off of me, maybe even hurt, but I felt in a way like I'd kind of brought it on myself.

"The nightmare starts with me on my back and him on top of me, and we're fighting. The headboard is banging on the wall, and it's all I can think of. It takes on a life of its own. I know I'm in trouble, and I'm still thrashing around like a wild animal, but the sound's affecting me more than the struggle I'm in. The sounds are sharp and loud. Over and over, I hear the separate sounds and the spaces in between, each sound seeming to be preparing for the next. Separate but connected. Like links of a chain. The sounds become a dark gray chain. The chain keeps moving toward me as his body wrestles against mine. As the chain moves past me, I feel I can grab it and hold it still. I can almost feel my hands wrapping around that chain. I want to take that chain and beat him senseless.

"And that's the last I remember. That's the nightmare."

"That sure is weird. And tell me again how he looked when you woke up?"

"He was huddled in the corner with one hand holding the drapes up against his head. Oh, Gabby, if there had been a chain or anything else dangerous in the room . . ."

"How about the next time you felt dizzy, by the pond on the way to Pittsburgh? That whole thing seemed to upset you a lot. You didn't want to talk about it then. Maybe now?"

"Sure, why not. Let's cover them all.

"After that hotel room in Erie, I was tired and stressed out. And confused from what had just happened. And how I must have done something to the guy. I wasn't looking for trouble, but that Davey character pushed me too far.

"And I don't know, maybe I kind of brought that on myself too. My skirt was way up high and not hiding much. When he got a look at me through the window, he seemed to decide right then what an asshole he was going to be. When I finally got out of the car, he looked me up and down and for him, there was no turning back.

"That guy really pissed me off. It all started up quickly. I couldn't remember the details right after, on the drive to Pittsburgh. Well, it's all come back to me since. Again, it was the sounds. And this time, smells too. All jumbled up until I blacked out.

"He had this annoying way of talking. His lips would smack together—before he spoke, after he spoke, even in between words. He sucked his teeth constantly. He was about to attack me, and I tried to focus on the danger I was in. But I couldn't get past the image of his wet lips and tongue sticking together, then pulling apart and making those nauseating sounds. I started to feel faint, and I could see the sounds. They were loose and seemed to drip as they moved out in all directions. They had a pale yellow color, like some kind of mucus. They wobbled and expanded and broke into smaller pieces as they moved away. The smaller pieces merged with brown streaks, which I think now were the smell of the pond mud, and they were all coated with a slimy residue, probably the smell of his cologne. It was all I could see. It sounded like he was chanting, and the sound of that somehow turned into a loud heartbeat inside me. The world around me was fading fast.

"My eyes began to close, and I felt my arms spread wide, like a net, gathering up the disgusting collection of slimy blobs. They felt warm and wet, and they stuck together as I swept them toward me. I thought about his mouth, that sickening mouth, and I kept pulling it all in, as much as my net could carry. Anger was the last thing I remember.

"It sounds like I've lost my mind, I know. That's why I call it 'mayhem.'"

"You're not insane, if that's what you mean. Did you want to hurt him?"

"Yeah, I think I did want to. And I think I did hurt him. There was a lot of blood."

"But you didn't kill him, did you?"

"No."

"Why not?"

"I don't know. I felt like something held me back. Like I held myself back, maybe."

"I'm glad you did, Lin. You're not a murderer."

"Well, I don't think I am. But the anger sometimes . . ."

"Okay, what about Ben? What happened with him?"

"Like I started telling you before, a bunch of us were messing around where we shouldn't have been. We were drinking, and I teased him. No, actually, I cornered him. I don't know why I pushed him like that. I think it was because it was right after what happened with Ray. I was like a raw nerve. I felt insane, like I'd better find a way to put myself back together. The other kids were laughing at him, and he broke. He came at me, and the mayhem came back at him.

"I had to do something, Gabby. But the mayhem—I have no control of it. It's never intentional. I have a nightmare about that time too.

"The short story is that he was physically threatening me, and I had no escape. The laughter from the other kids kept getting louder and louder. He had me by my shoulders, pressing me up against something. My eyes started to close. As my mind started to drift, each sound of laughter became a disk, soft and flexible. I felt like I was seeing them. All of those disks were floating past me. Ben stood right in front of me with all those disks of laughter floating around. I could feel his fear, but he was still attacking me. I felt a little faint as I started grabbing all the disks. It became obvious how scared he was. And sad too. I felt the disks would help, so I started laying them on him. They were just pieces of laughter, you know?

"There were as many disks as I could grab, and I stuck them to him and wrapped him in them. But those pieces of laughter didn't help him—he was more scared than ever. I felt frustrated, like maybe they weren't on him tight enough. So, I tried to tighten them up a little. It didn't help at all, and I felt really bad. That's all I remember.

"When I woke up, I was standing a few steps away, and he was on the ground. He smelled terrible, but I found out later that was his own fault. Um, sort of. Luanne was right next to me, and she looked excited by the whole thing. I felt horrible.

"That's what I do. That's what the mayhem does."

"But Lin, in all these cases, weren't you defending yourself? You might have teased Ben, but did that justify him attacking you?"

"No, I guess not, but I don't want to hurt people, Gabby. At least, most of the time. I hate to admit it, but I was happy about that guy by the pond. He was a bastard and deserved more than that. And the guy in Erie too. What a piece of crap. If I had a chance to do it again, God knows what would become of them."

"Okay, that's probably not a good idea. You're not that kind of person, Lin. Do you think it might be possible to learn to control the mayhem? Maybe there's a way that you could use just the right amount without blacking out?"

"That really seems impossible. Maybe I shouldn't say I have mayhem inside me. I should say there's mayhem inside, and it has *me*."

"Have you ever tried to control it?"

"No, I never have. I only try to stop it. It's scary. Controlling it seems impossible."

"Won't know until you try, right? You might not be aware of how, but you're limiting it and controlling it, even when you're justifiably mad at someone. You've never killed anyone with it, have you?"

"Not yet, Gabby. Not yet."

Chapter 21 – Grayson & Ronnie

Lin closed her new hotel room's door behind her, flipped on the lights, and scanned the layout. The sliding glass doors caught her eye, and the dark, flat blue shimmering to the horizon got a sigh from her before she dumped her bags on the bed.

She was alone, and she spent a long moment standing by the luggage, tapping her phone down on it, and staring out to sea.

With a scoff that nobody heard but her, she made the call.

"Hi, Dr. Grayson. It's Lin. Got a minute?"

"Lin, hi. Good to hear from you. Are you still in Georgia?"

"Yes, just a couple more days. I'm still planning to get back to the office on Monday. Does everyone miss me?"

"Of course, we do. You're part of the team—it just isn't the same without you. But we're managing to get by. What's going on? What's on your mind?"

"It's probably nothing, but I've been working at Sweet Pets for a long time now. I was wondering if you remember ever seeing me get . . . I don't know . . . light-headed or a little dizzy? The last couple of days, I've gotten like that a few times. Nothing serious, and I feel fine, really. But I also remember feeling like that many years ago too. I was just wondering if that's something you'd ever noticed. It's the kind of thing I might not remember."

"I don't remember you being sick much, Lin. There was that one time you had the flu, but that's about it."

"No, I don't mean sick. Just, I don't know, kind of light-headed. Like maybe if there was an argument or something stressful going on. This thing seems to get stirred up in uncomfortable, um, situations."

A moment passed before Dr. Grayson continued.

"Lin, there's only one thing I can think of. Do you remember Paul Sanders and his cat, Roxie?"

"Yeah, vaguely. That was quite a while ago. Whatever happened to them? They used to be regulars."

"You don't remember anything about the last time they were here?"

"I only remember that he wasn't happy. Something about us making Roxie scared. Or hurting her. Something like that. He wasn't pleased at all. I remember him complaining, and then he never came back. Why? What else is there?"

"It's probably nothing, but it might be something you're asking about. Roxie was in for her usual check-up and for whatever reason, it didn't go well. I don't think it was our fault. I remember that the cat was agitated and fidgeting around. It was hard to do anything with her. Sharp little claws, Lin! She was upset. Then, Sanders got upset.

"You were settling their bill at the counter, and Sanders was complaining to you. I was around the corner, filing something, and I could see you and hear the whole thing. You were wonderfully diplomatic and considerate, but Sanders wasn't having any of it. He started berating you, which was ridiculous because you weren't even the one that had taken care of his cat.

"While he was mouthing off, you stood there patiently, just listening to it, but it went on too long. I was about to come out and tell him to take his business elsewhere when something happened. I, uh, don't know what."

"Something with me, you mean?"

"I think so. I was watching you, and you didn't move, but your eyes started to close just a tad. Almost exactly at that time, Sanders stopped talking. I mean, he just stopped mid-sentence. I took a few steps closer to see, and it looked like he might be having a seizure because he got pale and started shaking some.

"Before I could intervene, you opened your eyes and walked into the back. Sanders took a deep breath, picked up his cat crate, and hurried out the door. I called to him, but he didn't even turn around.

He mailed in a check for his bill, and we never saw him or his fidgety cat again.

"I went in back to see how you were, and you were lying on the couch. You weren't really awake, but you weren't asleep either. I asked if you were okay, and you mumbled something that I couldn't understand. You looked fine, so I let you rest. Maybe ten minutes later, you were back to work like nothing had happened."

"I don't remember you ever saying anything about that. Did we talk about it after?"

"No . . . no, we never did."

"Why not?"

"I . . . I don't know for sure. I thought I shouldn't. I mean, it seemed best to just leave it alone."

Lin scoffed and said, "Mayhem."

"What, Lin?"

"Oh, um, nothing. It's just a word that, uh, it's about weird things happening."

"Well, Lin, I think that's about some kind of violence, isn't it? There was nothing violent with Sanders. Maybe that scratchy little cat of his, though."

"Oh, that's true. I mean, about the violence. Maybe if he hadn't left, though, then—"

Lin winced, unable to finish the thought.

"Lin? Are you alright?"

"Doctor, I think I got too much sun today. My mind is just all over the place."

"Uh, sure. I see."

"So, why do you suppose the topic never came up?"

"Well, Lin, it wasn't that odd. Just a tad odd. No real mayhem to speak of."

Lin scoffed loudly enough for Dr. Grayson to hear.

"Oh, excuse me. Just a little cough."

"Of course."

"Yes, that was probably best not to bother talking about it. It's a shame Sanders never brought Roxie back in, though. Sounds like it was all just a big misunderstanding. I don't even recall feeling faint that day. It was probably just exhaustion. I tend to try to do too much."

"Yeah, you're probably right. But you'll be back Monday, right? The place isn't the same without you."

"Yes. Yes, I will, Doctor. See you then."

*   *   *

Lin helped herself to a healthy swallow of Merlot and looked out over the sea. The clouds had cleared, and she could see nothing but blue sky. A glance to the right showed Jekyll Island, serene above the sound. But her gaze returned to the left, and she looked out over the deep sea.

"There's mayhem in that ocean, I'd bet. Lots of it. Way deep down."

She sighed, took another drink, and made another call, all while staring out at the darkening sea.

*   *   *

"Ronnie, it's Lin. Can you talk a minute?"

"Hi, Lin. I gotta say, this is a surprise. Are you alright?"

"Yes, I'm doing fine. How about you?"

"Doing okay. Landed a couple of decent parts. This is a tough career choice, but you know that. You're smart to have a real career to keep you going."

"And I love working with all those critters."

"Who wouldn't? But a steady paycheck—that's the beautiful thing."

"Ronnie, I really am doing fine, but I'm trying to figure out some things in my life, and maybe you can help."

"Sure. Anything. What can I do?"

"Lately, over the last couple of days, I've had this thing where I don't feel quite right. Like I get light-headed or something. It's not bad, but

113

it's noticeable. And when I think back, I can remember that it happened like that a few times when I was younger too. Not a big deal, but it's something I'm wondering about.

"What I want to know is, for that time we were seeing each other, do you remember any times when I seemed to get faint or a little dizzy? Maybe like if something unusual is going on? Because I'm finding that I don't always remember on my own."

Ronnie was silent for a few seconds before he spoke.

"There was one time, Lin. I didn't bring it up. It didn't seem like a good idea."

"What happened?"

"I'm not trying to make this awkward or anything. Really, I'm not. We were in bed this one time. You know you liked to play rough sometimes and yeah, I liked it too. But this one time, I got my hands around your throat. Not tight, I'd never want to hurt you, but just playing, you know? I didn't ask you if it was okay, and it's not like we planned it."

"Like the other stuff?"

He laughed and said, "Yeah. I just went ahead and tried it. You remember that time?"

"Yeah, I remember. It wasn't a big deal, but I don't remember what happened after that."

"I do. I'll never forget it. You seemed to be enjoying it, kind of playing the victim and all—like the damn good actor you are—and then, out of nowhere, you stopped moving. You were looking right at me, and your eyes were half-closed, and it creeped me out. A lot. Somehow, I froze inside, and I saw my hands pull away from you. I didn't want to, or try to, but somehow, I fell over onto the bed, like something knocked me over, and I couldn't move.

"And something so simple terrified me too. It was a windy day, and the curtains were blowing around. But while I lay there paralyzed, I could see the curtains were perfectly still. And one was frozen up in the air. Damn, it was just stuck there where it couldn't possibly be. I still don't know how the hell—"

"Ronnie. Finish the story, okay?"

"Sure. It was only a minute or two later that I could move again and when I could, the curtains began blowing again. I looked over and saw that you were asleep. So, maybe it was nothing. Maybe nothing really happened. Just my imagination, right? But I sure felt different after that."

"Different how?"

Ronnie hesitated.

"I was still extremely attracted to you."

"That's not a bad thing, is it?"

"By itself, no."

"Well, what else was it, then?"

Ronnie paused even longer.

"I was afraid of you too."

Lin slumped forward and let the phone drift down, then made an effort and brought it back to her ear.

"What do you mean, you were afraid of me?"

"I don't know, Lin, but I felt both: hot for you and terrified of you. That's why, when you said later we should go our separate ways, my fear let you go without any complaint. It was stronger than the attraction I felt for you."

"I don't really understand what you're saying or what happened, Ronnie, but okay. Thanks for remembering all that."

"You know, if you're—"

There was only silence.

"What?"

"This is so weird, Lin. I was going to suggest we get together sometime, but then I got this scared, creepy feeling, and I couldn't finish the sentence. Look, it's been nice talking to you again. You take care, alright?"

"You too," said Lin, but Ronnie had already hung up.

Chapter 22 – Arnie

Lin set her phone on the charger and poured another glass of wine. After downing half of it, she stripped everything off and wrapped herself in a towel. The lounge chair on the balcony lured her out with glass and bottle, and she stretched her legs one at a time before settling in.

Eyes on the sea, filled glass near her lips, Lin laughed and said, "Really, who lives a life like this?"

Giving up the sight of the waves far from shore and focusing instead on their incessant, gentle lapping on the sand, Lin finished drawing near the glass and tipped it back, chugging half of it.

Blindly setting it on the table beside her, the waves kept a steady beat that chased away any sounds of hotel neighbors, traffic, and even squeals and laughter from the few remaining children on the beach.

"Oh, I need that," she said, reaching for the glass. "Just the sound of the waves."

She finished it off, then laid it on its side as she let out a deep breath.

The orderly, soft pounding of the surf continued, then became, beat by beat, a driving drum strike from a band on the night club's stage, warming up for their set.

A thoughtful bass guitar joined in, rolling with it, the deep tones showing enough strength to shake the cold beer bottle Lin felt in her hand.

She heard herself say, "What? I can't hear you!" before opening her eyes.

"I asked when you started acting."

She saw the bottle first, then looked to her right. His eyes were dark, kind of mysterious, and she knew that kind of smile and what it meant even without looking directly at it.

A quick laugh, a clink of her beer bottle into his, and a shake of her head were the response, then she looked across the bar. In the mirror, she saw her twenty-something self, teased-up blond hair, and a pair of red lips. To her side sat a man about her age, and she remembered that he'd just sat beside her after she'd plopped down on her stool and received her first drink.

"Huh," she said. "Ask me if I ever stop."

"Do you ever stop?"

She turned toward him, grinned, and said, "No beginning, no end. How about you?"

"Me? I'm just trying to fight my way into this world. I just left an audition that I bombed. I mean, it really sucked. It'll take some work."

"Me too. I flew out from PA and thought I had more of a chance. To answer your question, I've been acting almost all of my life."

"Even as a kid, you mean?"

"Uh, early teens. Let's just say that my, um, life circumstances kind of forced me to do some serious acting."

"Sounds intense."

She scoffed, then hit the beer again.

"Missing out on a sweet role—that's intense."

"Poor baby. What kind of a role was it?"

"A detective. I even—"

"A sexy detective?"

Lin turned, gave each of his eyes a second of attention, then said, "Hmm, I'm detecting something right here."

He laughed, looked away, then said, "Yeah, me too."

Looking at Lin again, he said, "Sorry, I interrupted. You even . . . what?"

"I could tell you, but then I'd have to arrest you."

"I'm kind of, uh, captured already."

"Hey. Good ad-lib."

"Thanks."

"Alright, I'll tell you. And like a smart cop, I'm watching your eyes closely, looking for clues. You ready?"

He kept his dark eyes open and locked on Lin's as he nodded.

"I even . . . bought handcuffs. I like to get deep in my roles."

"Real ones? Or flimsy props that—"

"Hey."

He tipped his head, listening.

"You need to find out for yourself. You look damn guilty of something."

"What? No, I just—"

"Messing with you," Lin said with a laugh before becoming serious and adding, "Let's see your wrist."

"What, like this?"

He held his left hand out over the bar, and Lin quickly ratcheted it tight around his wrist.

"Hey, what the—"

"Told you I've been practicing."

"Okay, sure, but you need to—"

"Didn't think I'd be that fast, did you?"

"No, but I—"

While he stared at the shiny metal locked around his wrist, Lin clinked the other set to the polished brass pipe running along the edge of the bar.

"Hey! This isn't funny. Get this goddamn thing off of me."

Lin snickered and said, "Don't resist. I'll have to call for backup."

"Dammit, no! Come on. Unlock this fucking thing!"

He pulled at it, groaning and trying to not attract any attention. The drum and bass helped, and the few guests in the place weren't all that close and didn't care.

"Hey, it's just for fun. I just wanted to—"

"I'll kill you, goddamn it. Unlock this thing right now, bitch."

Lin caught a sharp breath and scooted back two stools, well out of his reach.

"What the hell's wrong with you? Calm down, okay?"

"You don't get it."

He covered the cuffs with his free hand when a couple walked past along the bar, oblivious to their drama.

His eyes bored into Lin's.

"I'm on the lam. This shit is freaking me out. Unlock it now, or I swear to God . . ."

"You're . . . what? You jumped bail? That's what you're saying?"

"None of your goddamn business. Get this shit off me."

"How much?"

"What?"

"The bounty. How much is it?"

"Look, you're hot and all, but if you don't—"

"If you hope to have any chance of me unlocking that, you'd better tell me."

"Fine. Goddammit. The bail is twenty grand."

Lin studied the cuffs for a few seconds, then looked up into his eyes. She scoffed softly and let a narrow grin appear.

"No. Don't even think of it."

"Huh. Even ten percent of that isn't all that bad. That would cover the cost of this failed audition trip."

"How the hell do you know so much about that?"

"I study for my roles, mister."

"I swear to God. If you—hey! Put away that goddamn phone!"

She laughed from two stools away, looking into his desperate eyes, which started to swell with the drum's pounding, keeping the beat.

And his hopeful smile from just moments earlier had flattened out into a tight, stressed line, a line that twitched like where sand met water, each wave shifting it, moving to the beat of the sea.

Lin's eyes popped open, and she flailed around until she'd found the wine glass. Laughing, she left it on its side, picked up the bottle, and tipped back what little remained.

Then, after letting the bottle roll away on the balcony floor, she laughed and squirmed around until comfortable, eyes closed, welcoming the steady beat of the surf.

*   *   *

Morning sunlight crept lazily up Lin's legs as she lay sprawled out on the balcony's only recliner, with the wine bottle on its side on the floor next to her. She awoke slowly as the sun's heat and the cool breezes off the ocean took turns caressing her, each in its own way. The towel had fallen open during the night, allowing a full dose of her skin to experience it.

With a groan, she sat straight up abruptly, pulling her towel around her and peering down over the balcony rail. Her heart rate climbed as she looked to the right and left, eyes darting around at the small areas of the hotel's parking lot flanking the building.

She rolled the tipped wine glass to the side and picked up her phone. A few taps woke that up, too, and she smiled when she read the message.

"Three hours, Jack? Oh, I'd better get moving."

A short, hot shower, followed by a glaze of cocoa butter sunblock all over, a quick blow dry, and she was ready to get dressed. She unpacked a simple sundress first, frowned at it, then tossed it onto the bed. She searched around and found instead a short white skirt, a light blue blouse, and matching heels.

With all of that on, and the blouse unbuttoned low, she topped it off with a white hat with a wide, floppy brim.

At the door, she looked back around her room, then let go of the knob. A quick race around got everything she'd brought packed and ready for a quick getaway.

Back at the door, with all of her stuff packed and slung over her shoulder, she gave the room another look.

Then, she stepped into the hall and pulled the door closed with a soft boom.

*　　*　　*

Barely thirty minutes after waking naked on her second-floor balcony, Lin was racing her rental car over the Causeway, leaving St. Simons. Even though the air conditioner was fighting the start of a steamy day, she left the windows down to catch some of the scents of the marshes.

The Causeway came to an end at Glynn Avenue, and she found what she sought after a short drive south. A modest motel merged with surrounding shadows on a side road near Glynn. The long strip building was separated from the road by a wide, concrete sidewalk.

Idling past, tinted windows up again, Lin noticed that around the motel there were retail stores, office buildings, and trees. She hit the brakes and gave extra study to an adjacent parking area that had a good view of the motel's doors.

Satisfied that she'd seen enough to work up a plan, she headed into the heart and simmering heat of Brunswick.

*　　*　　*

The stairs creaked even under Lin's light steps as she made her way to Arnie's second-floor office. A knock on the door generated a loud, "Come on in."

She pushed the door open and stepped inside, her sharp heels clacking solidly on the weathered wood floor. Across the room, Arnaldo Maldonado grinned like a school boy watching her walk in.

Arnie's office had a single window facing east, and the blinds were up, letting bright rays have a chance at cheering up the room. But the room resisted and remained murky and dim. Dusty file cabinets lined the wall to the left, and a couch past its prime sat off to the right. A slowly rotating ceiling fan trailed strands of spider webs that caught the sunlight on each trip around.

The ancient wooden desk faced the door, and sunlight bathed his balding head and sagging shoulders from behind as he looked up at Lin.

"Hi. Can I help you?"

"Yes, I called Tuesday about doing some work for you."

"Oh yeah, I remember. Jones's girl. Are you sure you want this? Not to sound sexist or anything, but you're not what I expected."

"Don't let the fashion show fool you, Arnie. I know what I'm doing. Been doing it for quite a while."

"You know, I got a local guy that could work with you. Nothing wrong with a team effort, right? I can call him if—"

"I work alone, Arnie. I'll be fine."

"Are you sure? He's a real professional."

"I'm sure."

Arnie's smile revealed several teeth missing.

"Alright, I'm sure you know what's best. That couch doesn't look like much, but it really is pretty comfortable. Why don't you have a seat, and you can fill out the forms."

"Great, let's do it."

Arnie handed her a few sheets of paper on a clipboard along with a well-chewed pencil.

"Hang on . . . that guy's info is here somewhere. There it is. Here, you'll need this too," he said and handed her a stained file folder.

Lin sat uneasily on the tattered upholstery, shifting herself into position carefully and managing mostly to get her skirt working its way up along her thighs. When Arnie shuffled over in worn loafers, she looked up only long enough to offer a distracted smile for his cell phone camera.

She'd just started writing when her phone chimed. She gave it a look and a quick smile, then she tapped it and looked toward Arnie.

"Arnie, I'm sorry, but this is urgent and kind of private. How about if I take these out to the car and fill them out? I'll bring them back up as soon as I can."

"Sure, why not. Take your time. I'm not going anywhere."

Lin pried herself up from the couch, gave the hem of her skirt a tug downward, and walked to the door, and Arnie stared, eyes cycling up and down at her every step of the way.

She closed the door behind her and risked the old stairs one more time. A short walk brought her to her rental parked in the road, and she started it up to cool it down.

"Jack, it's me. What's going on?"

"Hi, Lin. Everything is fine. It's just that my flight is delayed about two hours. Instead of 1:00, I probably won't get to my room until about 3:00. I thought you might want to know so you could plan the rest of your day. I could have texted, but it's an excuse to talk to you. This is good, though, right? More time to shop?"

"Well, there's not exactly much time for shopping right now . . ."

"Sorry, bad joke, I guess."

"It's fine, Jack. I do like to shop. Thanks for letting me know about your flight."

"Oh, hey, they've started to board, so I should probably go. See you later?"

"Wouldn't miss it, Jack."

"See you soon, Lin."

Lin sat behind the wheel, glancing enough at the fugitive's file to let a frown dominate her face. She tossed those notes aside, got busy with the forms, and occasionally glanced up at Arnie's office window.

Chapter 23 – Ivan & Doc

Arnie had held onto his desk as if trying to hold himself down until Lin had closed the door behind her. Its dull clunk was the starting gun for him to rise up, wince and hold his lower back, then turn enough to face the window. He got two fat fingers poking into the blinds, then spread them apart, giving him a view of the street and cars parked near his building.

He hummed, holding his back with his other hand, then saw Lin exit the building and walk toward her car. Her face was concealed under the wide hat brim, but most other parts of her were on full display: her bare legs and high heels, her short skirt, and the easy, teasing sway of her hips.

"Mm, mm, mm," he mumbled to himself, then followed that with a long, soft whistle.

He had to suck in another breath and launch a fresh whistle to last until she'd made it to her car and opened the door. And when she turned, leaned, and jutted out her hips to take a seat, Arnie choked on his own whistle and stared in silence.

Through the old glass, he heard her car door slam shut, so he ambled himself back around to frown down on the messy desk.

Only then did he notice the light traffic sounds working their way through gaps around the window behind him, but they weren't enough to block the sound of heavy footsteps on the stairs near his office door.

He waited for the knock. The sign on the door read, "Please Knock," but whoever was there didn't follow his instructions.

Keeping himself quiet, he sat and scooted his chair closer to the desk, eyes on the doorway.

As the door slowly opened inward, he gasped and reached for the desk's top right drawer. But the business end of a sawed-off shotgun quickly poked its way around the door and pointed directly at him. His hand froze midway to the drawer.

Everything about him froze, too, and he only stared at the black barrel with his trembling hand hovering above the desk.

The shotgun was followed by a clean-cut, well-dressed man with piercing eyes who didn't say a word. Arnie kept his eyes on the twin black circles at the end of the barrel, like two merciless eyes watching him back.

The shotgun man stepped into the dank office and moved to the side, letting Eugene "Doc" Lamont enter before closing the door behind him. Doc stood tall in a thin white sport coat, black t-shirt, and jeans. Despite his reputation for being ruthless and cruel, his features were delicate, almost fragile.

Arnie shook all over, including his outstretched hand, which he hadn't reeled back in. He scoffed when looking up at Doc, then gave a quick look at the other guy, whose muscular build gave him away as a veteran iron pumper from a prison yard.

Before Doc stepped any closer or even said a word, his partner smirked and slapped Arnie's hand away. He then grabbed Arnie's gun from his desk, made his way behind him, and let the blinds down all the way. A couple piles of papers and folders on the sill blocked it from bottoming out, so he brushed them to the floor.

"Thank you, Ivan. We need to keep this a private conversation. And it'll be more enjoyable if he doesn't have a gun."

Ivan only nodded as he scanned the entire room. He remained close behind Arnie.

"What do you want, Doc?"

After a long silence, Doc approached and looked down on him from across the desk.

"I have only two reasons for visiting you today, Arnaldo. One is easy and quick. The other . . . well, we'll get to that.

"As you know, I'm planning to do some traveling. Georgia isn't welcoming me like I'd prefer, so my friend and I will be leaving soon. We are in need of some walking around money. No doubt, you deal in cash, and somewhere in this smelly room,"—Doc looked around with a sneer—"you likely have cash. Pretend you're a smart man—tell Ivan where it is."

Arnie hesitated. When Doc gave him a quick glance, Ivan didn't. He brought the shotgun's stock down on the back of Arnie's head, which then tipped around in a few lazy circles. After wiping his wound, Arnie pointed with a bloody hand toward the file cabinet. Ivan retrieved the zipper bag full of bills, handed it to Doc, and moved back to his position behind Arnie.

"Well, that wasn't smart. Now, you're bleeding."

He unzipped the bag, looked in, and scoffed loudly before holding Arnie's gaze again.

"Quite the pathetic little operation you're running here."

"It's all I got. Leave me some for lunch, alright?"

"Gallows humor?"

"What? No, just that—"

"Hush, dear Arnaldo. I have a simple question for you. I'd like a simple answer from you. Who have you sent after me?"

Arnie turned enough to look back at Ivan, who smirked and gestured for him to pay attention only to Doc. Arnie groaned, rubbed at the blood dripping down his neck, and turned back around.

"No one, Doc. You just skipped a couple days ago. It's too soon. No one's after you yet."

Doc laughed and raised a hand.

"Oh my, that's bullshit, and all of us know it."

His raised hand sprung out a finger to point at Ivan. Another blow to the back of Arnie's skull made his eyes close and his head hang forward.

"Ivan, if you would, I'm tired of hearing lies on a sunny and otherwise pleasant day."

Ivan quickly wrapped the cord from the blinds around Arnie's throat and squeezed just enough to keep him quiet.

Arnie gagged and watched as Doc began looking through the files on his desk, taking his time. With each lack of a useful answer, he threw the files he'd examined onto the floor.

"Arnaldo, be a dear and hand your phone to Ivan, hmm?"

Ivan took the phone from Arnie's shaking hand and passed it to Doc, who wiped it all around on his jeans before checking it.

"Ah, this is interesting. You took this photo only minutes ago. Perhaps we even passed our pursuer on the way in. I'm a bit insulted, Arnaldo. What is she . . . a Vegas showgirl? You should be sending someone a little more imposing to get me."

Arnie tried to answer, but the string that Ivan kept tight around his throat wouldn't allow it.

Doc took his time and looked through every folder near the top of the piles on Arnie's desk. The final folder, another one with no useful info, got tossed over his shoulder.

The fugitive in the white jacket frowned for a moment at the emptied desktop, all of its gouges and stains visible, then looked again at the phone. He scoffed and give it a quick grin.

Doc gestured to Ivan to loosen the noose, and Arnie gasped and gulped in as much air as he could. But the cord still remained looped and ready to be tightened again.

"Now, Arnaldo, there's just one more thing I desperately need you to tell me. And when I say 'desperately,' I'm sure you understand that your cooperation is very important to both of us."

He let that sink in a while, as Arnie's gasping settled down.

"Who is this woman? Hmm?"

Ivan loosened the cord just enough for Arnie to offer a raspy answer.

"I swear, I don't know her name. We only got as far as the photo, and she had to leave. She said she'd come back another day to finish."

"Oh, it's not very smart to believe you can lie to me. Ivan?"

Arnie tried to get some fingers up between the cord and his neck, but Ivan grabbed his wrist and stretched his arm out to the side.

"I swear, I don't know her name."

Doc smiled and nodded his head, prompting Ivan to change his grip on Arnie's left hand, and he immediately bent his little finger back all the way with a solid snap.

Arnie started to scream, but Ivan quickly tightened the cord, and Arnie only gurgled and moaned.

Doc looked down at Arnie, not even fighting his amusement, and after a few seconds, shrugged his shoulders.

"It's an easy question, really. Who is she? You have nine more fingers, Arnaldo. Or seven more and two thumbs. Whatever. Ivan will happily ruin them all," he said and laughed.

Arnie groaned and tried to pull his hand away, but the grip was too strong. Ivan didn't hesitate a moment, and the sickening cracking sound was followed immediately by the noose choking off his scream.

Doc's sneer turned into a frown, and he leaned over the desk, both palms flat on the surface.

"I'll let you breathe a little bit, Arnaldo, and I promise no more of your fingers will be snapped. Doesn't that sound nice?"

Arnie nodded.

Ivan loosened the cord and a second later, Arnie vomited all over himself and the desk.

"You're a truly disgusting man."

Doc smiled up at Ivan when Arnie kept his head down and sobbed. Suddenly deadly serious, Doc said, "Now. The showgirl. Her name."

Arnie's voice still sounded pinched, even without the cord cutting in.

"God, don't you think I'd tell you by now? I really don't know! God, I wish I did . . ."

A look of satisfaction permeated Doc's soft features as he smiled at Arnie.

"Well, now *that* I believe. Which means you're of no further use to us."

He looked around the room quickly, then tipped his head to focus on the cord that was already partway dug into the skin of Arnie's neck.

"Ivan, I believe we're done here. Would you please, um,"—he looped his pointing finger in a few quick circles—"tie up some loose ends before we leave?"

Ivan didn't question the instructions and didn't hesitate, just quickly pulled the cord tight. There was only silence from Arnie and some weak flailing of his arms, with two fingers flopping loosely, before all of his motion stopped.

After Ivan had unwrapped the cord, a solid push to the back of Arnie's head left him leaning over the desk, dead in his own vomit.

"Ivan, I'd prefer we not leave any easy evidence of our conversation here. Could you please light a match? I believe our friend here fell asleep smoking. What a shame."

"Doc, I've already looked around. There are no ashtrays, no lighters or matches, nothing like that. He doesn't smoke."

"Oh, but soon he will," Doc said with a grin.

*　　*　　*

Lin glanced up from her paperwork and noticed that Arnie's blinds had been pulled all the way down. She made some adjustments to point the cool air from the vents more strategically, then got back to filling out the forms.

After she'd completed all of them, she took another look at the jumper's file. "Doc" he was called. The rap sheet was long and the crimes disgusting. She winced just from reading of his heinous antics.

Before opening her car door, she took another look up at Arnie's window. The blinds were still down, but something was wrong. The blinds seemed to be moving. No, they were burning, and she could see that the room was engulfed in flames.

"Oh, what the hell is this?"

She reached for the door handle, but she was stopped from even opening the door by the sight of Doc walking out onto the sidewalk. He stopped and stood outside the burning building and calmly studied a cell phone.

129

More people rushed out of the building, some brushing past Doc but not disturbing him at all. Sirens wailed and screamed, approaching, and she started her car and slowly idled past Doc. In her rearview mirror, she had a view of him still standing in front of the building, and he appeared to be whistling.

"This is the guy I'm going to capture? Wonderful."

Watching the road ahead only enough to avoid crashing, she kept a wary eye on Doc in the mirror. He still hadn't felt a need to flee the scene.

"Huh. Maybe I should use that partner. Like Arnie said."

She scoffed, aiming her car back toward St. Simons.

"Dead Arnie."

*   *   *

Lin raced along Demere, then whipped into the parking lot where she'd dropped John and Tommy. She managed a weak smile, anticipating that Gabby was waiting and would soon join her.

Under a sprawling live oak, she snapped the car into park and turned to her right.

"That fugitive that I'm after—I'm sure he just killed a guy named Arnie. And he set his building on fire."

"None of that is your fault, Lin. Are you still sure you want to go after that guy?"

"He just killed someone, Gabby! Someone needs to bring him in."

"Does it have to be you?"

"It's not like I want to for the fun of it. I need the money. You know why."

"Yes, I do."

The silence stretched out until Lin couldn't take it any longer.

"Go ahead and ask."

"Okay, why are we here?"

"To talk to John and Tommy."

"And they are?"

"They're the two guys from Pennsylvania—the two that were with the one that attacked me. The one that decided to gorge himself on gravel."

"And why are they on the Island?"

"Here's the weird thing, Gabby. They're infatuated with me. They don't know me aside from what they saw up in PA, but they found a way to follow me here. They quit their jobs. Tommy even left his family. They say they want to be with me. Help me with whatever I need. I can't seem to shake them."

"Do they like what happened to the other guy?"

"They don't seem to care. It doesn't upset them or scare them at all. But this whole thing is even weirder than that. Yesterday, I called my boss and asked him if he ever saw me acting strange, like getting dizzy. He said yes, once. And here's the thing: I think from that day forward, he's been kind of infatuated with me too."

"Could that all be some strange coincidence, Lin?"

"Sure, but there's more. I called Ronnie, Taylor's dad, who of course doesn't know Taylor exists, but that's another story. Anyway, I asked him the same thing. And he said yeah, once, and it affected him."

"Affected him how?"

"He said he was afraid of me but also still very attracted to me. Gabby, what the heck is going on? Is this all from the mayhem? How could it be?"

"Do you remember how we talked about the mayhem being a power? Is it possible that when you use the power, it affects people?"

"Well, sure. It tends to ruin them, mutilate them . . . stuff like that."

"But maybe it also causes people who witness it to be *impressed* by you? Maybe that's one way of looking at it?"

"I don't know, Gabby. It's a lot for me to get my head around."

"Good things aren't always easy things, Lin. And remember, this could be a good thing, don't you think? Have you ever hurt anyone for no reason at all, or did they all contribute to it?"

"I see your point. But damn, it's scary."

"Yeah, no doubt. I'd say you need to learn to control it."

"I don't think that's possible. I've tried. When I feel the mayhem start, it overwhelms me, and I black out."

"You said before that it's a lot for you to get your head around. Maybe understanding this, and hopefully controlling it, isn't about your mind so much. Maybe another part of you."

"You're losing me, Gabby. I know you're trying to help, but this is just too much."

Lin looked up to see John and Tommy wandering by the pool, looking in every direction.

"Hey, they're coming out. Over there, by the pool. Can you give us a minute? These guys are already jacked up. If I had to explain you to them, too, I just don't know. It'll only be a minute."

"Sure, I'll take off for a while. Talk to you soon."

*　*　*

Lin's guys had bought new clothes more suitable to the South Georgia heat and humidity. Both wore shorts and t-shirts, and Tommy even had a visor. Both sported sunglasses and looked completely natural there, like typical tourists.

With the window down, Lin called out, "Hey, guys, over here."

They practically ran over to the car and huddled close to the driver's door. Lin looked them up and down and shook her head.

"It's hot guys. Why don't you get in? The air helps."

They both climbed into the back seat, pushing each other and giggling.

"John, Tommy, have you guys gotten some rest? Are you eating?"

"Yes, Lin," said John. "This is a fantastic hotel. We're quite comfortable here, but we want to help. We want to be with you."

"And you will. Saturday. But for now, I need you to rest up and take care of yourselves. That means eating too. Did you get your clothes cleaned?"

"They're so clean, they're like new, Lin. New like us, since we came to stay with you in our new lives."

"Okay. That's just wonderful, Tommy," Lin said, rolling her eyes while looking in the mirror.

"Here's an address," Lin said and scribbled on a napkin before handing it to John.

"I need you guys there right at 5:00. Okay? Can you do that?"

"We'll be there right at five. Not a minute early or late. We'll show up. Showing up is ninety-percent of the thing, right? We'll show up and—"

"Tommy, what's this about showing up being such a big deal? We can do much better than that. Lin, we won't *just* show up—we'll do whatever you want us to do."

"And we'll try not to be dogs."

John said, "But you have to admit, we're kind of your posse, right?"

She looked in the mirror and caught Tommy's eyes.

Staring into the mirror and bouncing his eyebrows, he said, "Right?"

Lin let out a huge sigh as she stared straight ahead before turning to look directly at each of them.

"Right. Sure looks that way. And you'll wear your clean clothes too. Right?"

"Yes, we will."

*   *   *

The boys had their instructions and ambled back to their hotel, repeatedly turning back and waving. Once they were safely out of sight, Lin eased the car back onto Demere and aimed for the Village.

Grinning, in a pained way, she said to herself, "On my way, Jack. And I'll try to leave all this nonsense behind."

Chapter 24 – Together

Still warmed by the sun, Lin hiked the cool, deserted hallway toward Jack's hotel room. She held back her usual strutting, keeping her heels quieter than usual.

Standing at his door, she raised a hand to knock, then let it drop. After a look each way, then a deep sigh, she faced the barricade between them once again.

And she knocked.

The door swung in to reveal a dimly lit room, the blazing Georgia heat kept at bay by thick curtains and maxed-out air conditioning.

Slowly, as her eyes were still adjusting, Jack became visible. He wore only a damp white towel, and it was plainly obvious that he was quite happy to see her.

Without any talk, he moved toward her, reached around her with both of his strong arms, and pulled her into him. His calloused hands were rough against her back as he trapped her close, squeezing them together. Her aroma of coconuts blended with a rugged, natural scent as Lin lost herself in his arms.

He didn't kiss her right away and in the chilled air of his room, his heat easily got through her thin blouse, not just warming her but also giving her heart a not-so-subtle boost.

And then, he kissed her. A long, deep kiss that took her breath away.

Before she could speak or even catch her breath, he easily lifted her into his arms, kicked the door shut, and carried her to the bed.

Lin scoffed at seeing that the covers had already been turned down. She didn't have time for a snide comment as he almost dropped her down, letting her hit the soft mattress enough to bounce a few times.

Before she'd sunk completely into the cool sheets, Jack's lips were again on hers. He kissed with more urgency after the heartfelt kiss at the door was behind them. Like their animal needs could wait no more.

Lin lay back and accepted all of his kisses, each one hot and hungry. Without removing his lips from hers, he slowly unbuttoned her blouse and peeled it to each side. A soft moan escaped her lips as she arched her back, inviting him to take all that he wanted.

And he did take. And he gave. And Lin also took and gave. And despite the stress of Lin's life and the uncertainties in Jack's, then and there, in that cool hotel room, they came to the same powerful conclusion. Together.

*　　*　　*

Lin and Jack collapsed to their backs on the sheets they'd warmed. They lay there taking in deep breaths with the sweat hot on their skin before the room air began to cool them. At the same time, they pulled the sheets up to their chins and turned to look into each other's eyes. Still, not a word had been spoken.

"Oh, Cowboy . . ."

"My Cowgirl."

"I'm so glad you're here. It's so good to see you. That was amazing. Did I tell you I'm glad you're here?"

Lin rolled to her side and put her hand on his hot chest. They both laughed softly.

"I'm glad I'm here too. Wow, just when I think you can't possibly get any more attractive, you do."

"Oh, you're sweet. Same to you. You're looking damn good."

"Aw, thanks. I guess building houses can keep a—"

"Carpenter?" she said, giggling softly.

"Hmm. How about house builder? I don't want to get out of bed but if you want some whiskey to sip, I'll hit the mini bar."

She reached up for his cheek, turned him to face her, and gave him a long, wet kiss.

"That sounds wonderful. Just get back here quick, okay?"

In the dim light, she watched him make his way to the bar. His lean body showed the muscles that he'd earned from all of the hard work that his life required. He finished uncapping small bottles and filling two tumblers and when he turned to bring her the whiskey, she lowered her eyes and gazed with satisfaction at another part of him that could deliver some hard work.

Back in bed, they each held a tumbler of whiskey, sipping in between more kisses.

"I'm glad the room is so cool, because I want to stay right up against you. And in this Georgia heat, I'm afraid I'd smother you."

"Ha, that's not a bad way to go. Do your best, Cowgirl."

"Oh, Jack. It's good you're here. Do you have plans while you're here, or can I make plans for you?"

"Please, make plans. I'm all yours."

"My reunion is tomorrow night, remember? Would you consider being my date?"

"I can think of only one thing I'd rather do with you someday."

"Jack, don't you even—"

"Yes," he said, laughing, "of course."

Lin paused and looked into his eyes, and he smiled and quickly looked away.

"Thank you, Jack. Now it'll be a great time. I don't remember too many people from those days—just a few. And now, I'll have the best company of all. To us."

They toasted their plans for Saturday night, the soft clink almost lost in the humming from the air conditioner.

"Jack, I'm hungry."

Grinning, he said, "Oh, you want me to get up again to order something."

"I do."

"I like those two words."

"Hmm. How about room service for now?"

He laughed, looking away, then took her empty glass from her.

"How's your trip been so far?"

"Oh, just minor annoyances, that's all. Like any other trip. And all of those are out there somewhere, locked out of this dark oasis. I'm safe here."

"In my arms."

"Yeah, Jack. In your arms. But I'm still hungry."

"God, you're beautiful."

Holding her glass up and away, he leaned close enough for their lips to meet.

*   *   *

He'd just finished stacking the room service plates near the sink, then stood there, looking her over.

"I'm not leaving this room, Jack."

"Well, of course. Too damn hot out there."

"It's not the heat out there. It's the heat in here. Come back to bed."

"How could I say no to that?"

"You can't. Pussy Mayhem says get back in bed."

"Sure, anything for—"

"Be sure to say 'Mayhem,' too, Jack."

He hurried to join her under the cool sheets and thick blankets.

"Mm, that ceiling fan just makes it cooler."

"Want me to switch it off?"

"No, it's fine. As long as you keep me warm."

"You know I will. It's late. You ready for some sleep?"

She rolled away just enough to lie on her back and gaze up at the slowly spinning ceiling fan blades above them.

Her answer was to slowly and carefully peel the coverings down, just a little at a time, until she heard a scoff that evolved into a low, starving growl.

"You're still hungry, Jack. Ooh, and I need you to deliver some heat."

"I'm your guy. Then, we can sleep?"

137

"Hmm. We'll see."

Chapter 25 – Endless Depths

Lin's hammock rocked softly, nudged by tropical breezes lush with the scent of coconut. Nothing covered her naked body, which had been oiled and rubbed until she thought surely she'd melt. Lean young native men wearing only grass skirts tended to her comfort, slowly waving large palm fronds over her.

The bravest of her servants had been lightly sliding his fan across her breasts, just barely making contact. His smile showed his satisfaction with the obvious reaction. Lin struggled to keep pretending to sleep, not wanting to discourage his bold advances. The playful caressing and sounds of nearby crashing waves brought a peace she'd never known before.

Until the waves slowed and became strong, steady currents from deep within . . .

Her eyes remained closed as the dream slipped away, and she noticed the slow, deep breathing. She witnessed the breaths as if they weren't her own, each one flowing in and back out with a constant, unwavering force.

With each breath, the sheets covering her dragged a barely noticeable distance across her breasts. But she noticed. And it excited her.

Lin awoke completely but in a way she'd never been awake before. The breathing was purposeful and unrelenting, but she wasn't controlling it. Not interfering in any way. It had an intent of its own.

She became aware of every part of her body—every smallest feature, from the top of her head, to the tips of her fingers, and down to her toes. And especially her private places. She felt alive inside her Earthly vessel, the body she'd known all of her life and so often had taken for granted. She had never felt so completely alive.

Lin opened her eyes. She saw the ceiling fan spinning in the darkened room and felt the cool sheets against her skin. The air conditioner hummed softly, and the last trace of whiskey on her lips tasted sweet. She smelled the coconut on her own body.

And Jack's musky scent.

She rolled over toward him and gently laid her arm across his solid chest. He didn't wake, and she watched her arm as it rose and fell with his breathing. It entranced her to watch Jack moving a part of her up and down, strong and steady, over and over and—

How she needed him. She needed to *take* him.

Up on one elbow, Lin felt her way under the sheets and got busy waking Jack. Not all of Jack—not yet—just a part of him.

Soon, Jack was asleep and obscenely awake at the same time.

With the continuing attention, Jack awoke. He smiled and started to speak.

"Shh . . ." she said quickly, and Jack obeyed.

The breathing continued its slow, steady pace.

Lin rolled the sheets down off of them and felt the cool air rush against her bare skin. She rose to her knees and lifted her leg across, placing it tight against his side. With one knee on either side of him, she paused for a moment, relishing the anticipation. Showing only a trace of a smile, she effortlessly anchored herself just where she needed to be.

Jack remained silent, but he reached for her with both hands.

"No . . ." she said firmly and held his wrists to the sheets on either side of his head while leaning over him with her long hair spilling past her shoulders.

She began to rise and fall, her body moving in time with every breath. Jack watched silently, gazing up at her eyes.

Sweet pleasure hit her in waves, matching her rhythm and matching the breathing. She felt so alive, as if she had no limits. Her life seemed far too big to be contained by her body. All of her senses were hungry for the world, and she could perceive everything around her all at once.

Even though Lin moved slowly, matching the breathing, the pleasure increased rapidly.

She felt the torrent of ecstasy would soon crest and without knowing why or how, she took back control of the breathing. After a short lull, her breathing began at the same pace as before but now, her will commanded it.

As the pleasure continued to build, she purposely slowed her breaths and motions even more until they were barely perceptible. Still, the pleasure only increased.

Without understanding why, Lin took one last breath, slowly and deeply, and she held it.

She felt the immense power in that breath, a power that seemed to stop time itself. All of her senses were wide open, and she perceived the world stretching out to infinity in every direction.

Lin found herself at the center of the calm surface of a world built upon endless depths of magic. It was so plain to see—the entire world floated on a bottomless sea of magic, magic that twisted and churned in every direction.

The pause alone brought its own pleasure. From the breath she held inside, she felt the magic of the world pouring into her, flowing from that unimaginable expanse below to every cell in her body. She felt her life expanding from the magic, swelling her to the point of bursting from her flesh.

When the pressure had reached a sweetly unbearable level, she looked into Jack's eyes. With a feeling of falling through the sky, she moaned and set the breath free.

Her exhale was a boulder slammed onto the calm surface of the world. Instantly, a wave arose and rushed outward from her, as Lin's life burst through the bounds of her body in every direction.

The wave touched everything in its path. Lin rode that wave, because she was a part of it, in the direction that held her focus—toward Jack. The wave moved swiftly, but she was able to see that Jack's body lived in the surface, part of the world of reality. And his spirit lay just beneath it in the swirling magic.

She flowed with the wave as it washed through him. It carried her into the narrow space between Jack's spirit and his body—between the magic and the reality. From that gap, she could feel everything that Jack felt. It happened as she'd willed it. As she had intended.

Jack's eyes grew wide, but he didn't move. He *couldn't* move. His contorted face showed both pleasure and shock—the pleasure of Lin's touch and the shock of his soul being ripped from his body.

Lin knew that Jack was helpless, so she released his wrists and held the headboard. She was almost straight up, her tireless legs rhythmically flexing like coiled springs beneath her.

His helpless eyes gazed up at her as she raised and lowered herself slowly. And she'd invaded every part of him, including his eyes. She felt his pleasure mixed with terror as she looked up into her own eyes.

They were half-closed, staring down calmly, and burning with a green light of their own.

She swept her tongue lazily across the inside of her upper lip, teasing him and tormenting him while enjoying the sight of it through Jack's eyes.

Past her own blond mane, she saw the blades of the motionless ceiling fan framing her head like the rays of a dark, frozen sun in the absolute quiet of their chamber.

Lin knew that he felt the immense pleasure of them joining together.

But what she was doing with him also terrified him out of his mind.

Lin felt no terror at all. Only understanding. She saw clearly that this was how things had happened after she'd blacked out.

This was *mayhem* . . .

Lin could feel his abject fear and though the magic and pleasure nearly consumed her, she remembered that fear wasn't her intent for him. She'd wanted to bring him only pleasure.

So, from that narrow space, she directed the magic to what connected them—their union—and her focus raised his pleasure so high that she was sure his fear must have been forgotten. Lin was at the same time rising and falling with her breathing and driving her energy into the part of Jack that mattered the most to her at that moment.

On and on it continued, Lin aware of Jack balancing on the edge of insanity, and still, she wouldn't let it end. She felt lost in eternal ecstasy.

She used her own eyes again and looked down on him, knowing what he saw: a magical green glow. Her hair swayed on either side of her face as she moved gently. Silently.

Relentlessly . . .

After an eternity, Lin finally felt ready to let them both go. But at the last moment, she said, "Mm . . . ladies first, Jack."

She ignored that Jack was silently losing his mind while his bliss built to impossible levels. Helpless beneath her, he could only witness Lin release with all the power that she'd commanded as her own. It was as though the bed were tossed by a violent sea, and Jack's eyes grew even wider. But still, he couldn't move.

Lin shuddered like never before and felt all of the world's magic course through her. The measured rhythm of her flexing legs never slowed as she drove the ecstasy like beating on a drum.

When at last her own hunger had been sated, it was Jack's turn. As she continued her steady caressing of him, she applied her magic to him in just the right ways from that narrow space in between his magic and his reality until she felt that any more pleasure might kill him.

Just as Jack appeared to be losing consciousness from the raw rapture, Lin let the dam break, and the surge hammered him so hard that she could no longer feel his presence in that narrow space. She wondered where the wild flood had taken him.

Lin enjoyed a few stolen moments—for they truly were stolen—seeing and feeling the world through Jack's body. She'd felt his pleasure as she'd felt his fear, and she'd felt the power of each.

When she began to feel Jack's presence again, she returned completely to herself and looked down on him.

They were slick with sweat, and the cool of the room hadn't yet given them a chill. She placed her palms on his heaving chest and leaned close until their lips almost touched and her hair brushed his face on both sides.

She watched him closely and waited for his breathing to return to normal. Moving only his eyes, he looked to one side then the other, as if he dared not test his ability to move any other part of himself.

She kissed him quickly and pulled back.

"Jack, are you okay?"

"What was . . . what just happened? How did you—"

Jack was okay. A single fingertip on his lips silenced his voice.

But not his eyes. Lin clearly saw adoration in his eyes, much more than ever before.

And fear.

Now, there was also fear.

And the coldness Lin felt didn't come from the dark room's hold on them or the resumed spinning of the fan above them. It came from her calm realization that he wasn't the same Jack as before she'd taken him.

Jack had been touched by *mayhem*.

*   *   *

Lin rolled off of Jack and snuggled close under his arm. He shifted onto his side to hold her with both arms.

"Lin. Lin, I—"

She touched his lips softly.

"Shh, Jack. Just hold me."

Cool air from the fan prompted her to pull the sheets back up over them, and she wiggled herself in closer to him.

She'd kept herself apart just enough to watch his eyes batting slowly, then staying mostly closed, then completely closed.

Still holding Lin, he slept like a dead man. Or maybe like a man who'd had his life taken from him.

But only for a while.

She stayed awake in his arms, her head tipped enough to watch the fan blades cutting gently through the dark air of their room.

After tipping her eyes just once, convincing herself that Jack was too deep into sleep to hear anything, she stared up at the fan that she knew for sure she'd seen stopped.

Frozen above her as her eyes had burned a bright green.

"So . . . that's mayhem? Damn."

Chapter 26 – Crumbling Wall

"Gabby, we need to talk."

Lin had slipped out of Jack's bed early and traveled straight to her own hotel. He never woke, even though she'd dropped her brush on his chest as she stood and looked down on him before leaving.

It was a short hike back to her room, and she'd stayed vigilant, watching for any sign of Ben. She didn't see him or his truck anywhere.

"I understand the mayhem."

"What happened?"

"A couple of hours ago, I used it on Jack. Not to hurt him. No, it actually drove him crazy with pleasure. I drove him crazy. I was in control."

"You didn't black out this time?"

"No, not even close. And the usual confusion I feel—my senses all jumbled up—that never happened either. My mind was clear and calm the whole time. I had control. Maybe I shouldn't even call it mayhem after that, but I still like the name 'mayhem.'"

"You didn't hurt him, Lin? No one got hurt this time?"

Lin laughed.

"No, just the opposite. He enjoyed the hell out of it."

"What did it feel like to you?"

"Oh, Gabby, it was the most amazing thing. We had already made love a few hours before that, and we were sleeping. I woke up, and there was something different about my breathing. It was really slow and deep, and it was just flowing on its own.

"I felt a need to take Jack, so I started to. The breathing stayed slow and strong, and my body moved with it.

"Then, for some reason, I don't know why, I was back in control of my breathing. It was kind of like a dream to be breathing really deep, looking down on Jack, and feeling what was going on.

"I took a big breath and held it. I didn't know why, Gabby. I held that breath, and that alone felt amazing. Like magic somehow. But then it gets crazier.

"While holding that breath, the world seemed different to me. It seemed completely still. I felt I could perceive all of it at once. Like I could see infinity in every direction, all at the same time.

"After what felt like forever, I let the breath out. It seemed like something heavy crashed and created a wave. And I rode that wave straight to Jack."

"Why to Jack?"

"I think because I was so focused on him. I could sense everything around me, but I focused on him.

"But here's the really weird thing. As I got closer to Jack, I saw that there was a gap—some kind of a space—between his body and what I'd guess was his spirit. And somehow, I got into that space. He couldn't move after that—I had control of him."

Lin paused and looked down, staring and shaking her head.

"Gabby, I see now. That must be what happened those other times. I somehow took control of them. No wonder they were terrified."

"Terrified of you."

"Yeah, but those other two guys, John and Tommy, got infatuated with me, probably somehow from the mayhem, too, right? Why aren't they scared like the rest?"

"Did you do anything to them? Or were they just close?"

"I'll never figure this out."

"I'm sure you will. So, Jack never got terrified?"

"Oh, sure. He was afraid for a while. But I fixed that. I instinctively knew how to make him feel good, even better than from just what we were doing. He forgot about being afraid.

"And this went on for so long I think I lost track of time. Like there was no time. The pleasure kept building, and when I finally did climax, it was like all the power of the world crashed through me. I never felt such power, Gabby.

"Then, I let Jack have his turn. I could tell—no, I could *feel*—that it was off the charts for him too. It blew him away to somewhere else for a while. But he came back. And he didn't get hurt."

"That's quite an experience, Lin. You're sure no one got hurt?"

"I'm fine. No, better than fine. And Jack, well, he's not hurt."

"But he's okay, right?"

"It was more pleasure than he's ever felt before. But dammit, when it was done, I could see fear in his eyes. Fear of *me*. God, what have I done? What am I?"

"You're you, Lin. No matter what happened. As for Jack, maybe you can't help but to have people feel that way after they've known mayhem. Those other two—that guy in Erie and the one by the pond— weren't they afraid of you too?"

"God yeah, they were terrified. Ben too. But Jack isn't terrified anymore. He's just a little afraid. The fear's mixed in with how he felt about me before. I think his love for me is even stronger now. Gabby, he loves me and fears me at the same time."

"Where's Jack now?"

"He's asleep in his hotel room. I didn't think I could wake him up even if I'd tried. I had to get out of there. This is all new to me. But at the same time, I know it's part of me. Has been for years. Things are just starting to get clearer now."

"What do you think is going on with you, Lin?"

She started to speak but stopped herself and waited several seconds.

"I don't know, but I know it's powerful. And it feels right. This feels like me. This is an amazing power, and I need to have more control over it. Today was good, but I sense it's only the beginning."

"Only the beginning? What do you mean?"

"I mean, I think I can get more control over the mayhem. And I can use it. I can use it with some nasty problems I have ahead of me. Ben. And the fugitive in Brunswick. I'm not too worried about them anymore. They can't stand up to this. I don't think anyone can."

"So, it's a weapon?"

"Yeah, I guess. Or it can be."

"But all you did to Jack was increase his pleasure, right?"

"Yep, but that was because of how I feel about Jack. Gabby, from in that space in between, God knows what I could do to someone."

"Yes, God knows alright."

Lin shivered like a chill had run up her back.

"Is that what you want? You want to use mayhem to hurt them?"

"No. I want Ben to leave me alone. I want that fugitive to come along quietly. I don't *want* to hurt anybody. But I can. And I will if I have to."

"Do you feel you have that much control over it? Can you be sure you won't hurt someone by accident?"

"I felt so much in control with Jack that yeah, I think I do have that kind of control."

Lin snapped her hair back and broke into a self-satisfied smile.

"Why now? Why do you suppose this is happening with you now?"

"I can't imagine. Maybe I've just gotten to an age where things are happening. I don't know."

"Is there anything different about your life lately? Something that might have led to this?"

"Nothing significant. The only real change lately is that I started dressing better," Lin said as she attempted to pull her skirt down farther. She found that there wasn't enough material.

"I agree. Clothes probably aren't significant. But why did you change that?"

"That, I'm not sure. It just felt like the right time. Like I'd been hiding who I was, and it was time to take it straight on. It's not my fault I'm attractive, and I shouldn't have to downplay it."

"Lin, when you told me about the guy in Erie and that other guy, you said you felt kind of like you were holding back. Or that something was keeping you from hurting them worse."

"Yeah, it did feel that way. It was a vague feeling like I could have unleashed Hell on them. But I wouldn't let myself, for some reason."

"So, what was different with Jack? Were you holding back?"

"No, I didn't have that feeling. I rode that wave. I felt the power, and I used it."

Another big smile spread across Lin's face.

"Oh, Gabby, now I see. There *was* a difference. I felt so sexy when I woke up next to Jack. And I was completely proud of it. No, accepting of it is more like it. I felt empowered to be what I am."

"You didn't feel that with the other two?"

"No. I actually felt a little guilty, like maybe I shouldn't have overloaded them like that. But I can see now what led me to how I felt with Jack. It has something to do with changing how I dress now. That's when it started. I started accepting the real me. The power of my sexuality.

"Gabby, I feel another big piece of the puzzle falling into place. My sexuality is a big part of this. Even when I was much younger, I was kind of . . ."

Lin paused for a moment and looked around the room, and her smile dwindled, leaving nothing but a frown.

"Oh no, Gabby, this can't be true. I think I've been blaming myself for what Ray did to me so long ago. I've been carrying that with me all these years. I've felt attractive, and I've felt the power that comes with it. But I've also felt guilty about it, like I shouldn't just turn it loose.

"And lately, I *am* turning it loose. First the clothes, the sexy clothes, and then, finally, how I felt with Jack. I think I'm finally giving myself permission to be who I am."

"That sounds like a huge puzzle piece."

"But what is mayhem? What the hell is that?"

"There are countless mysteries in this world, Lin. Sometimes all we can do is accept that they exist. Maybe our only concern should be what choices we make."

"You mean, what I do with the mayhem?"

"Yes, exactly. You've seen that you can use it to bring pleasure. And you know you can use it to injure. Maybe even kill."

Lin scoffed and looked across the room.

"I'm not worried about it. I have control over it now. Before, I didn't. People got hurt when I didn't have control."

"Okay, but remember something. In the past, you had something holding you back. You felt guilt about your sexual power. What now? What choices will you make now that that wall is crumbling?"

"Oh, Gabby, you worry too much. I don't want to hurt anyone."

"I hope you always remember that."

"Of course, I'll always remember that."

Lin shook her head, scowling, then brushed her hair back and continued.

"It sure does help a lot talking to you. Things make so much more sense. God, what a good friend you are. How is it that you know so much?"

"I've been around a while, Lin. And God knows, the things I've seen . . ."

Chapter 27 – Center of Stillness

Lin's walk displayed a distinct strut on her way to Jack's door, which she'd keyed open, using the key she'd taken earlier, and closed the door quietly.

She didn't try to quench her smile when she got herself undressed, even making it a bit like a striptease for the sleeping man. The careless toss of her skirt toward the dresser shook around a lamp, and she rushed to steady it, snickering and seeing that Jack had barely stirred.

All stripped, she hesitated, let the room air chill her skin, then she slipped in beside him. He still hadn't moved, so she pulled the sheet and blankets up over them, watching his eyes, which still refused to open.

"Hmm."

She burrowed herself in closer, letting his heat elicit a soft moan from her.

Still, no Jack.

She leaned herself in close, let her warm breath wash over and into his ear, then moaned more loudly before backing away, waiting.

He began to lick his lips, smiling as the deep slumber began to pull back like a receding tide. But still, it wasn't until after a long yawn had run its course did he open his eyes.

He woke only halfway and smiled, his tired eyes drooping more closed than open. Then, he reached around her and pulled her closer for a kiss.

As he woke completely, he tipped his head back but didn't let her go.

"Lin. Good morning."

Lin bobbed her head around, trying to not make it obvious as she studied his eyes.

"Time to wake up, Jack. How do you feel?"

"Um, okay. Good."

"How did you feel before, when we, um, you know?"

She kept her eyes from squinting and waited with a quite calm appearance.

"Lin, I've never felt anything like that. It was ecstasy like I never dreamed possible. But . . ."

"But what?"

"Was the rest of that some kind of dream? Or nightmare?"

"I wouldn't call it either. Maybe we shouldn't dwell on it. Let's just say it was amazing . . . in a very good way."

"Yeah, okay, I'd like to . . . but Lin, I can't even describe what I felt. I'd feel crazy even trying to say it."

She let her eyes show the beginning of a squint.

"So don't even try, then. It was a weird night, okay? We have all day together. And tonight too."

"But—"

She silenced him with one manicured finger pressed to his lips and gave each of his eyes a share of her scrutiny as her smile grew.

And she didn't remove her finger from his lips. She slowly caressed first his top lip then his bottom, repeating that several times. And then, her finger slowly worked its way into his mouth. Just the fingertip at first, until she felt his tongue touching it. Then, it went in a little deeper. In and out, his wet lips holding it tight.

"Mm, just like that, Jack. Oh, maybe one more thing."

With her other hand, she reached down and got his full attention.

"That. Oh, somebody's waking up for me."

She slowly slid her finger from his lips, and they kissed long and deep. Jack rolled her to her back, and she welcomed him openly.

While he proved how awake she'd gotten him, giving the mattress beneath her a steady rhythm, Lin focused on her breathing.

She breathed in and out deliberately, consciously slowing her pace.

After a few moments, she flashed a quick scowl, then reached up and ran her fingers through his hair and returned his smile.

Again, she focused on her breathing, also staring into Jack's eyes and gasping with each of his powerful thrusts.

She gave it a minute, then scoffed and grasped his long, wavy brown hair in tight fists.

"Ooh," he said without smiling, just with uncertainty in his eyes. "Rough."

"Mm-hmm."

She released his hair and held him by his hips.

"You feel so good, Lin. Damn."

"Mm-hmm. You too, Jack."

Jack came to his usual, robust conclusion.

Lin faked hers, then tapped him and nudged him to roll over beside her.

"Jack, that was wonderful. See? Nothing weird. Nothing like a nightmare."

"Yeah, you're right. That was great, like always. I'm glad you came back."

"You knew I left? I thought you were out cold."

"One eye opened. Just a little. Only for a second when the door closed behind you. Then, yeah, I was out cold again."

"Hmm. I need to try harder next time, then."

"No, you don't!"

"You're funny, Jack."

"Can you stay awhile, or do you need to get ready for the reunion?"

"Trying to chase me out?"

"No, never. Just, um, trying to be considerate."

"Well, that's sweet. I have some time. Why don't we just relax awhile. It's so good being close to you."

"Yeah."

She saw his eyes, then looked away.

"Close is good," he added, then tipped his head, trying to catch her gaze.

Still looking around, not at his eyes, she said, "Just hold me, Jack. It sure is chilly in here."

Lin spun herself around, and Jack held her close while she stared across the room until they both fell asleep.

*　　*　　*

"Jack. Jack, wake up."

"Uh, I'm up. Not like before."

"You could be,"—she bounced her eyebrows at him—"but I think I'd better get going. It'll take me a while to get ready. I have the rental car, so I can pick you up. Say, 4:45? How does that sound?"

"That sounds good. I'll be ready. I'm thrilled to be going with you, Lin."

"And I'm thrilled that you're here to go with me. We'll have a great time."

She jumped up out of bed, got dressed quickly, and waved a quick goodbye.

"See you in a bit."

"Okay, Lin. We'll have such a good time."

She nodded and slipped out into the hall, pulled the door shut, then leaned her forehead into it.

"Sure. But will you ever call me Cowgirl again?"

*　　*　　*

Lin hiked the short distance back to her own hotel room, with not nearly as much strutting as when she'd gone to see Jack, opened the door with a hard shove, then closed it with more resolve than necessary.

"Gabby, I have problems. Sorry I was impatient with you before. I guess maybe it was too much excitement for me. This is almost too much to comprehend."

"You never have to be sorry, Lin. What you're going through, I think, is bigger than even you can imagine."

"I don't know. My imagination's pretty good."

"Not good enough. What happened?"

"I had it. Late last night, the mayhem was mine. I was in complete control with Jack. It was like nothing could get in my way. Not even slow me down.

"I was just with Jack, and I got him worked up again, and I thought I'd kick in a little bit of mayhem. Not enough to scare him. Just enough for me to feel it."

"For fun?"

"Uh, more like practice? Okay, kind of for fun too."

"Not surprising."

"But it didn't work. Not even a little. I tried the breathing. I felt sexy as hell, and that seemed right. Not a trace of guilt. And still, not a bit of mayhem."

"Is there something you're missing, Lin?"

"I don't think so. That wall, where I wasn't accepting my sexuality— I think that's gone. Just now with Jack, my sexuality was a power I had over him. And that didn't bother me a bit. I enjoyed it. I found it exhilarating."

"Okay, and what else were you feeling? Think hard. This might be important."

"I hate to admit it, but I was still kind of frustrated or maybe even angry with you. I felt like you were trying to hold me back, and that bothered me. It was still bothering me at Jack's."

"What did you tell me, from the night with Jack, about the world? How did the world seem to you?"

"Oh, Gabby, it was amazing. I could see, or feel, the world spreading to infinity in every direction."

"Seeing infinity is good. The world is definitely an incredible place. But there was something else about the world . . ."

"Let's see. I was breathing right, I think. I felt sexy. No guilt. Everything was—"

Her eyes snapped open, and she shook her head before speaking.

"There's something else. When I saw the world, the real world, it was still. It was a calm surface. I didn't see that just now with Jack."

"It was calm? Nothing about it was moving?"

"No, it looked completely still."

"And when it worked, were you also part of that stillness?"

Lin tried to open her eyes even wider, which made her laugh once.

"Yes! Yes, I was part of that stillness. I was still too. My God, Gabby. I saw all that magic below, and I—"

"Magic, Lin? That's what you're calling it?"

She squinted, saying, "Well, I guess. I don't know what else to call it, that's for sure. So, I was breathing it all in, and I was at the center of the stillness. What does that mean?"

"Lin, is it possible you have to feel that stillness in yourself first before you can feel the stillness of the world?"

Lin stared at Gabby without blinking. Her mouth hung open.

"So, I was kind of mad at you, so I wasn't at all—"

"Still."

"Inside, Gabby. Still inside."

"Yes."

"Gabby, this is incredible. I see what you're saying. I was calm, still, that night with Jack. And then, I was at the center of all the other stillness out there. Is that how it works? I have to be completely still inside?"

"You won't know that until you try."

"But I don't even know where to begin! How could anyone cause that to happen? We all have so many feelings running through us all the time. What kind of person could turn all of that off?"

"Nothing anywhere is completely free, Lin. Some gifts ask that you do something in return. This gift—this power—*demands* what you must *be*."

Chapter 28 – Witnessing Infinity

Lin stood over the clothes she'd laid out for the reunion, all neatly arranged on the hotel bed. She picked up the blouse, never really looked at it, and dropped it back onto the bed. Leaving her hand out, she watched it sometimes steady, sometimes shaking.

She snapped it back and held it close.

"I'm not running back to PA. Mayhem will just have to help if that damn Ben shows up."

Her wardrobe waited patiently, but she only stared down at everything she planned to wear to the reunion. The silky top was more revealing than usual and tighter too. The skirt was short, also quite snug, and the heels were higher than she'd ever worn. She grinned at that, touching gently one of the sharp heels.

"Uh-huh. Yep."

Postponing dressing for a time, she sat at the foot of the bed and gazed into the dresser mirror. She saw a beautiful woman looking back. Maybe not a Greek goddess, although she'd been cast as one more than once. Her wavy blond hair draped down below her shoulders, framing a model's face with green eyes. And it might have been from the overhead lighting in the room, but the green had a subtle shine to it.

She lay back on the smooth blanket, smashing down her party attire, and opened the towel. The ceiling fan's breeze cooled her skin, and she took a deep breath. She lay there looking at the lazy rotation of the fan hanging onto the ceiling.

She stared up, controlling her breathing for only a few moments, then she snarled and rubbed her face with both hands.

With a loud exhale, she stuck her arms straight down along her sides, blinked slowly, gently, and let her breaths find their own pace.

Moments later, the softness of the bed cradling her, the breeze from the fan above, even its low humming, conspired to convince her eyelids to begin to close.

The fan kept humming, spinning tirelessly, and sleep began to take her. She shifted herself around gently, then let everything almost melt into the warming blanket and clothing beneath her.

She noticed that the fan's low sounds were somewhat like a flowing stream. It was steady. Continuous. Never speeding up. Never slowing. Just lazing its way through the surrounding land.

In the twilight region poised between being awake and sleeping, she had the distinct feeling that she lay on her back in a tiny boat, floating down the stream.

But she was also awake, with her unfocused, barely-open eyes watching the fan's motion.

Her eyes finally closed completely, and the room and its fan faded away as she shifted to being entirely drifting down the stream.

The fan's sounds hadn't changed but for Lin, they were nothing but the gurgling water lapping against her boat.

"No," she said without thinking about it. "Not confusion. Not that."

She looked up at the calm rotation above her, her eyes open only as narrow slits but focused on fans, not water.

The room around Lin became more real. The floating boat feeling began to fade but not totally, and she found herself back to being mostly on the bed and barely in the boat.

She sighed and let her eyes close, and the fan became water and again drifted her along in her tiny, private boat.

Back and forth, bed to boat to bed, Lin traveled many times.

And as she started to slip again into the confusion of floating in a boat, she said, barely even a whisper, "No. Stop thinking."

She breathed strong and easy several times.

"Remember. Remember how it felt with Jack."

As her thinking slowed and memories of the bizarre night with Jack took hold, it was no longer her breathing. It sank, gained strength, and became slower and deeper. A force of its own.

She smiled with her eyes half-closed as the breathing slowed even more.

With each inhale, she felt the pleasure of that magical encounter with Jack.

With each exhale, she felt the pleasure that he'd felt.

With every complete breath, she was feeling both of their pleasure and not thinking about it at all.

Then, like a theater curtain being drawn to the sides, all of her senses opened wide, and she saw the world around her become still. She saw infinity in every direction, and there was endless magic below.

It was as it had been before but this time, she had no goals for it. She only witnessed it.

Infinity wherever she looked. Crazy, unimaginable magic below.

Lin took control of her breathing. She took a last deep breath and held it. She felt the power flowing into her and filling her. She was at the center of all that she could perceive, a coiled spring of power. She lingered there, savoring it. Making it a memory.

Remembering the feeling.

Then, she very slowly exhaled that power-filled breath, so slowly that she created no wave. All remained calm, and she felt infinity gradually recede, rolling back toward her and giving the world its limits.

Her breathing returned to normal, and she was again lying on the bed, quite comfortable under the fan's breeze. The fan's humming was again only that—a sound.

*   *   *

Lin awoke with a shiver from the fan's breeze and stretched her limbs across the cool blanket, folding and crumpling her clothes.

"That place," she mumbled, still half asleep. "That feeling."

She stretched again, then laughed.

"Remember it, dammit."
She spun off of the bed and let the towel slip to the floor.

Chapter 29 – Party by the Sea

A stained and shredded sheet of cardboard only partly covered him as he lay on his back, in the weeds beneath an overpass. Under that crude covering, he held close to his gut the weapon that had taken almost all of his coffee can cash to purchase.

He tipped his head, snarling in the oblivion of his late afternoon nap, and swatted at his face. Like being hounded by a swarm of spiteful mosquitoes, Ben palmed the pistol with one hand and nearly beat himself with the other, twitching and slapping and almost awake enough to do some real cussing.

A spasm sat him up, instantly and angrily awakened to a constant drip from the bridge's steel girder splatting on his face.

"Dammit. That's why I was dreaming it was raining. Goddamn filthy shit."

And it wasn't clean rainwater like in a pleasant dream. A crew had been hosing the roadway above, and the water had picked up a collection of dirt, dead insects, and rusty metal flakes by the time it struck him.

Looking up while shifting to one side, he mumbled, "Bastards" at hearing the road crew talking and laughing while they sprayed cold water all around after whatever construction work had been going on.

Still looking up, he made sure that the barrel of his gun was scoping out those who had dared to wake him with their nonsense.

"Boom," he said, then laughed and stuck the barrel behind him, down behind his belt.

But he didn't let it go. He kept a hand on it, feeling the hard, reliably dangerous advantage that he'd need later.

To battle the witch.

Because it was salvation day.

*　　*　　*

While hiking away from the artificial, grimy rain of his outdoor hotel, Ben slipped out of his pocket a folded, somewhat wet piece of paper.

"Goddamn reunion."

He glared at the party center's address for a few seconds, then crumpled it and left it in the weeds.

"See you there, witch. Good luck against a gun."

*　　*　　*

Lin snatched up the bath towel and held it in front of her as she stood at the foot of the bed, looking down at the clothes she'd selected for the evening.

She pointed at each item, saying, "Skirt's short. Blouse is a size too small."

Leaning some to see the shoes on the floor, she scoffed and said, "Highest heels I have too."

Dropping the towel, leaving her naked, invited the ceiling fan to give her a quick chill. She looked up at its relentless blade spinning and scoffed again.

"You. Like to pretend you're water, huh?"

The fan ignored her honest question and kept busy spinning, so she looked again at a steady, outstretched hand.

"Huh. Can I do it when it matters? If Ben crashes the party?"

She scoffed again and got dressed, stretching tight material over every curve, and sat on the bed's edge to get the ankle straps secured.

At the mirror, she rolled on some lipstick while studying her eyes, then dropped that to pick up a hat. With that in place, she eased her mane back over her shoulders on both sides, then walked to the door, where she paused to look around the room.

While walking out into the hallway, she smiled and shrugged and said, "Broken hearts or broken bones."

*   *   *

Ben continued the march to where he'd left his truck, a few blocks over at an all-night shopping center in Brunswick. Halfway across the parking lot, a beverage shop caught his eye, so he aimed his stomping hike in the that direction, checking that his t-shirt covered the pistol at the small of his back along the way.

He dropped the six-pack on the counter and glared at the clerk.

"Hey," he said to the lanky young man minding the register. "Run a sale. Free six-packs."

"Sir, I can't do that. Come on."

"Bet I could convince you."

The clerk swallowed hard as he looked up at Ben's scowling face.

"Just kidding. Here."

He tossed some bills on the counter, grabbed the beer, and punched the door open.

As he drove through the city with a cigarette clenched between his lips and a cold beer in his hand, he squealed his brakes to stop at a red light.

To his left, the Causeway to the Island waited, the path to the reunion party clear of traffic and inviting him to turn and do some driving that way.

To his right was any one of countless other paths that could lead him back to his life on Shotgun Road, and the shack he called home, and the woman he often beat.

He reached around to the small of his back and felt the pistol's steel warmed up from his skin and the Georgia heat. He slipped it up and out and laid it on the littered seat beside him.

He looked to his right, toward home, then scowled and looked to his left, toward the witch.

"No. Dammit, it ends right here."

164

With a strong drag on the cigarette and a quick downing of the entire can, he ignored the red light and squealed the tires, aiming his truck and himself and his gun to crash the gate and party with Lin.

*　　*　　*

Lin pulled up a few minutes early in front of Jack's hotel, parked in the street, and shut down the engine. After a quick glance at a pair of green eyes in the mirror, she got out and stood next to the driver's door, then took a few steps to the front end and gave all of her attention to scanning the traffic in both directions.

She barely noticed the warm ocean breezes washing over her and toying with her hair in the hot Georgia sunlight. A stronger gust threatened to donate her hat to any of the locals or tourists that could catch it, so she held that in place with one hand and left the other against her hip.

At the sound of footsteps behind her, she turned enough to see that Jack had stepped out of his hotel and was walking toward her. Still a few steps away, he called to her.

"Wow, Lin. You're absolutely stunning."

Before answering, she tried for a better look at his eyes, but they were greedy and still focused on her legs.

"Aw. Thanks, Jack. You too. Are you ready for the big party?"

He walked the final steps to the passenger door with a lot less swagger, Lin saw. He finally held her gaze, smiling, but the sight of his eyes prompted Lin to look away.

"Yes, of course. Thanks for picking me up."

"Of course, Jack."

He kept smiling and after a short, awkward silence, he continued.

"You really do look wonderful, Lin. Are you anxious to see anyone from school? Were there people you've missed or people you'd hate to see?"

She snapped her head to look one way, then the other before facing him again with a deliberate smile.

165

"Oh, um, I didn't have too many friends in school, and I didn't make an effort to keep up with anyone after my family moved back home. And wow, it's been more than a few years. I doubt we'll recognize each other."

"If anything, you're more beautiful now. They can all eat their hearts out."

"Oh, Jack. You're sweet. I think we'll have a great time tonight. And it's at such a cool place just up the road. If we drink too much, we can walk, or stagger, back to our room."

As she brushed her hair back over her shoulder, she laughed at Jack saying, "I already know I'll drink too much, then."

"Jack, you're silly."

He shrugged, and he didn't let his eyes focus on hers for too long.

"I guess we'll have to play it by ear," he said. "It sure is perfect weather. Is it being held inside? It'd be a shame to waste all this sunshine."

"No, I believe it's out on the lawn. We'll have ocean views, ocean breezes, and oceans of . . ."

She bounced her eyebrows and waited.

"Uh, booze?"

She laughed and said, "Why not? Come on. Let's get going."

After the short drive, Lin parked the car, and they sat a moment before getting out.

"Hey," he said, "classy place."

"Oh, yeah. Really nice. As long as it's not too classy for some mayhem."

"Huh?"

"Nothing, Jack. Let's do this."

*　*　*

Jack sometimes scraped his western boots while walking toward the entrance, then he stopped to glance back at Lin. She'd stopped at the front of the car and was stretching her arms to her sides. Her eyes were

166

locked on the ocean over the low fence and beyond the grassy party grounds, and light winds coasting in were giving her hair a subtle bounce.

She turned to him with a smile and said, "What?"

"Uh, you're just incredible."

"Not too incredible for a carpenter, though?"

He looked down, smiling, and said, "I hope not."

"Jack, you're being silly again. We'd better get inside, okay?"

As they drew near the entrance, they looked ahead and saw two men standing outside the doorway. Both stared only at Lin, and one of them waved, then the other joined him. Both had huge grins and eyes as wide as they could go.

Lin laughed once at seeing that they'd gotten their clothes laundered, and there was no trace of gravel dust anywhere on them.

"Who are those clowns?"

"Oh, I forgot to mention them. That's John and Tommy. They're from high school, but I didn't really know them too well. John called me yesterday and asked if I could help get them into the reunion. They were in a different grade, but they'd like to go too. I told them I'd help if I could. They're goofy but harmless."

"They went to school with you? No offense, but they look too young."

"They seem to have aged well, that's for sure. They won't be sitting with us, though. Once we all get in, they'll go off on their own."

"And just how are you supposed to cheat those guys into the party?"

"I wouldn't call it cheating, Jack. Just influence. I don't think I ever told you, but I was a cheerleader all through high school."

"That's going to do it?"

"Well, we shall see."

As Lin and Jack got nearer, the smiles grew and Tommy's waving picked up speed.

"Hi John. Hi Tommy. Glad you guys could make it. This is Jack."

"Hi, Lin," John said, his eyes locked on Lin.

"Hi, Lin," said Tommy, not once looking in Jack's direction.

"Shall we?" said Lin, and they all walked to the entrance.

"Hello. I'm Lin Finnerty, and this is my date, Jack."

"Very good, you're on the list plus one," said the former class president checking in guests.

"Oh, I know they didn't make it to the list, but this is John, and this is Tommy. I was hoping they could join us as well. It's kind of a last-minute thing. Would that be okay?"

"Well, I don't know. It's supposed to be classmates plus one, you know?"

"Yeah, I know, but I was a cheerleader all four years of school. You probably don't remember me . . ."

"Oh, Lin. Yeah, now I remember," he said after he'd gotten a good look at her. Or at least as much as he dared with Jack glaring at him.

"I guess there's no real harm. Y'all have a good time tonight, alright?"

*   *   *

Ben jerked his truck to a stop in the street with a sharp squeal just before turning into the party place parking lot. Staring toward the entrance, he rummaged around and found three empty beer cans and gave them a toss out the window.

He popped the top on the fourth. With half of that one down, he lit a cigarette and laughed before sucking in a deep drag.

It was time.

He began cruising around the lot.

Chapter 30 – Stolen Breath

With John and Tommy snickering and in the lead, they all walked through the main entrance and toward a metal detector. Lin let out a loud sigh.

"Oh, Jack . . ." she said with a big smile.

"What?"

"Nothing. I just think it'll be a wonderful evening. Let's get a drink," she said and squeezed his hand tight and touched the security feature with her other hand on the way through.

They were right on time, but most of the guests hadn't yet arrived. They passed through an ornamental arch and took a few steps past empty tables draped in white cloths before stopping to look out at the ocean.

"Hell of a view."

"Mm-hmm. Oh yeah, Jack."

After several seconds, Lin sighed again and leaned over to kiss him. He spun her toward him and wrapped his arms around her waist, and they shared another kiss.

"Where do you want to sit, Jack? Do you mind if we sit more out of the way? We'll still be able to see the ocean."

"Anywhere you want, dear girl. This is your party. I'm just the luckiest guy here."

"Oh, Jack. You're too good to me."

She steered them to a table that could be seen by John and Tommy and was also close to an exit.

"Jack, maybe this isn't the time or place, but can we agree that sometime, we'll talk about stuff? All kinds of things?"

"Yeah, of course. You probably won't believe this, but talking with you is at least as good as anything else we do. I truly enjoy your company. Maybe later? After the party?"

"Yeah, that might be good. Let's see how the night goes."

"Alright. How does it feel to be back in St. Simons? Does it feel like home even a little bit?"

"Yeah, it really does. But Pennsylvania is still more of a home to me. I only lived here for a while. There were good times here. And some not-so-good times."

Jack looked down and didn't ask. After a few seconds of silence, he looked up.

"Well, let's hope tonight, it's nothing but good times."

"Yeah, Jack. Tonight—"

She looked past him at the sound of a vehicle backfiring somewhere in the parking lot, then back at him.

"—I'm hoping for nothing but good things."

* * *

Ben's truck rolled into a parking spot with two more empty beer cans thrown out along the way. He jammed it into park and sat there a moment, not really thinking—just sucking in smoke and staring toward the entrance.

After a deep pull on the cigarette, he flicked it out through the open window, where it gave a dying burst of sparks as it struck the neighboring car.

"Luanne was right. That day changed me."

He dragged a rag from the seat beside him all around on his bald head, blotting off some of the sweat.

"And right now, Lin, you goddamn witch—you're paying for that."

He sucked on the cigarette and looked out every truck window at the shiny, expensive vehicles all around him.

"In front of all your goddamn fancy friends."

*   *   *

"Lin? Did you hear me?"

"What? Oh, sorry, Jack. I guess I'm a little distracted. Seeing some of these faces brings back memories, some not so good. What were you saying?"

"I just asked what you wanted from the bar?"

"Oh, that. Um, I think I'll keep it simple tonight. How about bourbon on ice?"

"That sounds perfect. Me too. Be right back."

She watched him making his way to the bar for only a moment, then her eyes snapped back to the entrance.

She looked down and saw her hands shaking, so she jabbed them on her lap and let the tablecloth hide them. But the crisp white fabric shook lightly, betraying her actual state as she kept her gaze toward the door as calm as possible.

Finding that she'd been holding her breath, she snorted it out quickly, then tried to impose a deep, steady pace. But after a short try, she groaned and rushed out another breath.

Jack set her drink in front of her and took his seat, looking at her with adoring eyes. She leaned to study his eyes better before speaking.

"Thanks," she said, smiling at him. "Cowboy."

"Anytime."

Lin slumped more in her seat and looked away.

"Another drink anytime I need one, Cowboy?"

She turned her eyes enough to see that Jack was mostly staring down at his drink as he swirled it around.

He looked up briefly, then back down. The swirling continued.

"Yeah. Just let me know."

*   *   *

Ben checked that his pistol was secure and stepped onto the pavement. He swallowed the last of can six and tossed it back inside the truck. With a burning cigarette hanging from his lips, he began his trek to the door.

His low growl with every exhale kept pace with his steps as he dropped one heavy boot in front of the other. The South Georgia sun forced his face into a squinting, angry scowl as he stared straight ahead. When he neared the door, he grunted at the sight: a metal detector on the way in.

He kept walking without any hesitation, never showing that the security setup was of any interest to him. He steered off to the side and continued past as if he wanted only to look around the place first, and that's what he did. He became a sightseer, enjoying a look at the ocean for a while, then he walked a direct path back to the truck.

After grinding his cigarette out beneath his boot, he got back in the pickup.

"She's just a woman. And no bullshit witchcraft is going to help her this time."

He reached around, retrieved the gun, and held it on his lap a moment. He stared down at it, caressing its hard edges and testing the weight of it.

"Dammit."

Grunting, he wrapped the gun in a rag and stuffed it under the seat.

He lit another cigarette and jabbed it between his lips, and he again walked toward the door.

*   *   *

"Jack, do you remember our first date?"

"Of course. It was the best first date ever. You impressed the heck out of me. I'd never seen anyone I wanted so much."

"Same here. And the things you said really hooked me. Do you remember the chocolate?"

"Yeah, of course. I put four pieces on the table, and you probably thought we'd split them. But then, I pushed three over in front of you and said something about you getting at least three before I get even one."

"Yeah, that's right. And I've learned that that's how you are, Jack. You're so giving and unselfish. And the poems you write to me. I feel lucky to know you."

"I feel lucky for every moment that I can spend with you."

"I hope you always feel that way, Jack. There are things I need to tell you. Things that I haven't told anyone, and . . ."

Lin hesitated.

"And I hope you always feel that way about me. No matter what happens. Even if bad things come our way."

"I can't imagine anything changing my mind about you."

*　　*　　*

"Hey, Ben Johnson. Here for the reunion."

"Hello, Mr. Johnson. Um, I don't see your name on the guest list. Did you RSVP?"

"No, I didn't. I didn't know if I'd be able to make it, but here I am."

"I'm sorry, Mr. Johnson, but we have a strict policy on that."

The check-in crew got good looks at Ben's tattered jeans and stained t-shirt, and the smell of alcohol was drifting around with the light ocean breezes.

"You can shove that policy up your ass. Get the hell out of my way."

Ben pushed the man aside and stomped his way toward the party. The man took a step back with his mouth hanging open, then he glanced behind him at the office, then he watched Ben walking away. In those few seconds, Ben had made it almost to the main party area.

He dug his boots into the manicured turf, sometimes bumping into chairs and elbowing people aside.

He turned the corner and stopped to look over the crowd. It took a moment for him to spot Lin and when he had, a loud, slow groan carried all of his breath out of his lungs.

173

The winds off of the ocean were flirting with wisps of her hair, sometimes letting strands cross, then uncover, the generous portion of her blouse that she'd left unbuttoned.

And her green eyes were staring directly into his.

"Damn."

And he hesitated there, gazing at the beautiful witch that had ruined him when they were both just kids.

*   *   *

"Never say never, Jack. You just don't know—"

Lin stopped abruptly and looked past Jack and over his shoulder toward the entrance.

"Oh, God," she said, too softly for Jack to hear.

Ben stood near the door, dressed shabbily and swiveling his bald head to look all around at the guests populating most tables and standing with drinks in hand.

With the next head rotation, Ben's eyes focused on her. But he didn't immediately rush over to their table. He stood there with an odd look on his face. His rage was obvious, but there was more written there.

"Lin, you okay?"

Still looking past Jack, she said softly, "Turn around and leave. Dammit, just go."

"Lin?"

Ben began his march toward her.

Chapter 31 – Seaside Showdown

"Lin," said Jack, "what are—"

He spun around at seeing Lin staring past him, checked her eyes again, then stood when he saw the large, filthy man approaching their table. It was more than just his grimy clothes that set him apart from all of the fashionable guests. They all wore smiles as they talked and laughed and shook hands, while Ben displayed a frown and wild eyes. His cigarette hung at the corner of his mouth, and he puffed out smoke like a train about to derail.

Ben bumped into people and chairs as he plowed through the crowd while staring directly at Lin. If someone remained in his path, they were shoved aside.

The man stood at least six inches taller than Jack, and his fists were clenched.

"Goddamn witch," he mumbled. "No good, lousy, evil . . ."

His bald head glistened in the hot sunlight.

Jack looked back at Lin, saw her staring and shaking he head, then took a few cautious steps to block Ben's path. As he got nearer to their table, Ben's eyes were still focused only on Lin as he flicked his cigarette onto the closest table, where it ignited a napkin.

"Hey!" said a woman as her date brushed the fire to the grass and stepped on it.

"Shut the hell up."

Jack stood his ground but before he could speak, Ben punched him hard in the gut. He dropped down to one knee and fought to take another breath. The next punch was to his chin, and he collapsed and took a chair and sliding tablecloth down with him.

Ben turned to glare at Lin.

She had risen from her seat and hid her pepper spray in her hand by her side. But she was controlling her breaths, pulling in way more than needed then letting it rush out in chops as her body shook from the effort.

She ignored his squinting eyes to study his hands, which were by his sides, fists clenching. But neither one held a gun.

Still, he hesitated, his head leaning as he scowled at her. But Jack was trying to get himself back in the fight, and it took only Ben stepping into him, on his way to confront Lin, to send him back to the ground.

He approached her slowly, staring at her and snarling. He grabbed her by the shoulders, much like when they were fifteen.

The screaming all around them began to fade, and Lin stared up into the eyes of the monster that she, and the mayhem, had created.

"You goddamn witch. You ruined my life. And now, I'm ruining—"

Lin aimed and fired directly into his eyes. He never finished.

"Goddammit!"

He backed away quickly, holding his face.

"You goddamn witch!"

John and Tommy appeared from the crowd. They'd been trying to come to Lin's aid and had just then arrived. They both pounced on Ben, fearless in her defense.

Against the unreal silence, Lin heard John screaming.

"Go! Get out of here! We got this! Please, just go now!"

Even nearly blind, Ben became a storm of violence. He easily shook the two off of him and landed a couple of hard punches in the process. John and Tommy were more suited to giggling than fighting, and what little strength they had was gone. But still, they attacked.

Lin helped Jack to his feet, and she hesitated, watching the boys take her beating. She saw them get slammed to the ground, and they stayed there, both writhing and holding parts that Ben had struck.

Her plan had worked but not for long, and it was time to run.

Before Lin hurried a stumbling Jack around the corner and to her car, she looked back to see security swarming around Ben.

"Good," she said. "Lock him up."

Jack held his chin and his gut, leaning over, as Lin led him toward the car. She got a better hold on him, trying to keep him on his feet, as she reached for the passenger door handle.

"Just where the hell was the mayhem . . ."

"What?" said Jack.

"Nothing, Jack. Just get in. We have to leave."

She slumped him into the passenger seat and to the sound of approaching sirens, they fled the scene.

*   *   *

Two guards kept a solid hold on Ben as they helped him up from the grass, leaving his arms free enough only to wipe at his eyes. One of them let go to wave to the small group near the entrance.

"Hey, call the locals!"

He tried to regain a hold on Ben, but he'd begun swinging that freed arm blindly, a tight fist at the end of it. The guard wasn't quick enough in leaning away, and the backhand snapped his head, sending him unconscious into the grass.

Ben laughed and said, "Got you, fucker!"

Tommy was near, so he hugged one of Ben's legs."

"Why, you little shit."

He immediately went for a quick, jerky ride that ended with him rolling loose, then taking most of Ben's weight when he stepped on his back.

"Got you too. Who's next?"

He shook loose from the other guard, fumbled around to find him, then slung him to the side, crashing him onto a table and wrapping him in the tablecloth.

Free for a moment, Ben rubbed at his watering eyes and looked around him, seeing only John untouched enough to mount any further attack.

"You."

"No! We're done!"

John let his head drop and rest in the grass. Snarling and spinning, with his vision clearing, Ben took a bead on the exit.

There were bodies between him and his escape but not for too long. Most of them self-moved at the sight of him approaching them like a charging rhino, and the rest—male, female, it didn't matter—got lifted, shoved, or swatted out of his path.

In seconds, they were all down, and Ben was free and running outside.

But not to his truck. Sirens were wailing north and south on Ocean Boulevard, and the truck would have to wait.

Chapter 32 – Old Style Magic

Lin kept an arm around Jack as she swiped the hotel room key, then bumped the door open with her hip. Jack largely held himself upright, but he'd staggered a few times walking the hallway.

Still guiding him, she let the door swing shut on its own, flipped the light switch, and started nudging him toward the bed.

"Jack, how do you feel? Are you going to be okay?"

She set him on the bed's edge, then leaned to see him better as she tugged at her skirt.

"Oh . . . yeah . . . I think so. Damn, that dude can hit."

The tugging did little, so she smoothed it down all around, then sat beside him.

"Thanks for being my knight in shining armor, Jack. You fought for me, and I can't thank you enough."

"Huh. I never got the chance to fight. What was that all about? Who was that guy?"

Lin pulled back her arm from around him and crossed them both in front of her. The deep breath that she'd dragged in and used to puff up her cheeks trickled out as she looked ahead at her eyes in the mirror.

"Jack, that's one of the things I wanted to talk to you about. His name's Ben. I went to school with him here in St. Simons."

"That guy? He went to school here? He looks more like he escaped from a chain gang somewhere."

"I know. His life, well, it took a different path. And I'm to blame. At least partly."

"How? How could you have possibly caused that?"

She bit her lip and sighed, watching it in her reflection.

"Jack, my life here on the Island started out rough, but that's another story. I just mention that because I think those experiences led me to acting in a way that I'm not proud of, and it affected Ben."

"Was he your boyfriend or something?"

"No, no. Nothing like that. We were only friends, but I think he did have a crush on me.

"At that time in my life, I was more ornery. I didn't want to take crap from anyone. I had a mean streak, which I think was there because of some problems I had. It was at a very tough time in my life and one day, I turned it on Ben. I didn't mean to. I was just having fun, but it didn't end up fun at all."

She hesitated, her arms still crossed, and said, "Jack, I don't know. Maybe I—"

"No. Keep going, Lin. I really want to know."

"Alright. Um, he and I and some other kids sort of broke into this construction company's place. We were drinking beer and just being stupid and when I saw the keys in their dump truck, I couldn't help myself. I had to take it for a ride.

"It was a blast cruising around in that big truck. But at some point, I decided it would be fun to put pressure on Ben and try to make him take a turn driving it around. You see, Ben was basically a good kid back then. I think he had a bad home life, and he seemed to never want to take chances. It was just too easy to back him into a corner.

"So, that's what I did. I challenged him, and he wouldn't drive it. Of course, kids are cruel, right? The rest started teasing him and after a short while, he kind of snapped. He attacked me, Jack. I didn't know if he was going to hurt me or not, but he was big, even back then, and no one there could have stopped him.

"Oh, by the way, on that day I got the name Pussy Mayhem. When I was driving the truck, they started calling me Ms. Mayhem. But when Ben was panicking about driving the truck, they started calling him a pussy. One thing led to another, and that's where that name came from."

"You didn't just make that up for online dating?"

"No, I didn't, but it's a pretty good name, don't you think? Worked with you."

"Oh, did it ever."

"So, Jack, do you remember really early this morning that, um, weird experience?"

"Oh yeah, I sure do. What was that?"

"I don't know how to explain that to you, Jack. It's just something that happens. Well, something similar happened that day to Ben but not in a sexual way. Not sexual at all. But it hurt him. Kind of messed with his mind too.

"He was totally humiliated in front of all of us. He couldn't understand what had happened to him. His life took a nosedive after that, and you see how he ended up. Jack, he didn't have to turn out that way. Somehow, I did that to him."

She watched as his eyes changed. When he looked away, it was as if a door had begun to swing closed. She wiped at a tear beginning to roll down her cheek.

"Come on. Some fresh air could only help."

"Sure. Okay."

She took his hand and led him out on the balcony where they sat facing the sea.

"That same kind of thing happened between you and Ben?"

"No, not the same, Jack, but it was something weird, that's for sure."

"Is this something you do all the time? I've never seen it before this morning."

"It's rare, and I can't control when it happens. With you, that was the first time I've ever not blacked out from it, and didn't I treat you well? Didn't you enjoy it?"

"I enjoyed it like you can't imagine. But it was scary as hell too."

"Oh, I can imagine. It was incredibly good for me too. I really can't explain what it is, Jack. One day, I hope that I can. I only brought up all of this to explain who that guy was and why he was after me like that. He blames me for his entire life."

Jack looked away from her and stared silently at the endless blue. After a moment, Lin looked away, too, and sighed, but she didn't let go of his hand.

They sat quietly, her hand above his, as they gazed at the sea.

*   *   *

"Lin, you said your life here was rough sometimes. Is that something you can tell me about?"

Her sigh could have been a scoff, and she lifted her hand up off of his. But she left it close, patted his a few times, then let it cover it again.

"Alright, here goes. Jack, I was sexually abused when I was a kid."

"Oh, Lin. I had no idea. I'm sorry. That must have been horrible."

"And it wasn't just once. It started when I was twelve, and the last time was when I was fifteen."

"God, that's even worse. How did that happen? Who did it?"

"It was an uncle, my dad's brother, who came to live with us when I was twelve. Mom and Dad couldn't find decent work, and we were about to be out on the streets. That's when Ray moved in. He had money, and he helped pay the bills. He used that against me. He said if I told anyone, he'd stop paying, and the family would be ruined. And it would be my fault.

"So, I kept it all to myself. But Jack, as traumatic as that was, I never looked away from it. I didn't bury the feelings. I think I must have somehow gotten stronger all that time. I wanted nothing more than to make him stop. I wanted to make him *want* to stop.

"And one day, I guess I was strong enough because I did make him want to stop."

"How the heck can a fifteen-year-old do that?"

"The same way I messed with Ben. Yeah, that happened to Ray too. I was mostly blacked out, and I don't have any clear memories of what happened. But his abuse stopped that day."

"Whatever happened to your uncle?"

Lin froze with the horrible truth straining to spill out and send him screaming from the room.

"He, um, he changed from the experience—let's put it that way. He was never the same after that."

"Did you ever see him again? Did you ever tell anyone?"

"No, I never saw him again. And no, I've never told anyone. You're the first."

She kept looking into his eyes, waiting to see what effect her revelations would have on him. She held her breath until she was sure that he wouldn't turn his eyes from her.

"I know it's none of my business but just recently, you started dressing differently. I have no complaints, believe me. You're looking so damn good lately. Is that related to your past in any way?"

"Yeah, it is, and I'm only just now figuring out what's been making me tick. Jack, I never knew that I partially blamed myself for what my uncle did. I went through so much of my life not understanding that. So, I guess that's why I dressed more frumpy for so long—up until a couple months ago. Something changed in me. It felt like I had to stop hiding from who I am."

"I'm glad you stopped and not just because you look so damn good. You should always feel comfortable being who you are.

"And Lin, you must know that my feelings for you aren't just because of how you look. You do know that, right?"

"I hope so, Jack. Yeah, I guess I know that."

She gave him a small smile, the first since they'd returned to his room.

He smiled back, and she waited while postponing her next breath.

"Of course, you *are* the hottest Cowgirl the world has ever seen."

"Oh, Jack, I'm still your Cowgirl?"

"Always, Lin. You shouldn't even have to ask."

They leaned toward each other for a quick kiss. The quick kiss led to a much longer one, and their lips finally parted as they rose from their chairs. Without a word, they walked hand-in-hand to the bed.

No mayhem joined them, but magic still filled the room like they'd always shared in the past. A calm, powerful magic beneath cool sheets in their safe hideaway as the sunlight faded and their hungry souls danced to the rhythm of crashing waves.

Chapter 33 – In the Park

Lin leaned back against the picnic table and let the warming air touch all of her exposed skin. Even the trees were silent, as if the birds had already begun to hide from the Georgia heat that would soon take hold. Weak air currents, not yet teaming to form even a breeze, occasionally rattled the drooping leaves.

She looked in every direction but saw no one else.

"Gabby, I feel like my life is crashing in on me. It's just too much to juggle. Things with Jack, with the mayhem, with Ben . . . all of it. Maybe especially the criminal I'm going after later today. It's just too many things, and—"

"Lin, why don't we just slow down. Don't problems always seem overwhelming if we try to take them on all at once? Why don't we pick one to talk about?"

"But they're all twisted together. There's no clear line anymore between anything. It's all just a huge pile that's about to land square on my head."

"Let's start with what you call mayhem. The last I heard was that you controlled it. You used it and not to hurt anyone. Isn't that right?"

"Yeah, but since then, it's all fallen apart. I thought I had it figured out. When I woke up next to Jack early Saturday, it felt like I had so much control. I guess I didn't because I really needed it yesterday, and it was nowhere.

"And it's more confusing than that. This is so mixed up. After I talked to you, remember that I went back to see Jack. I thought it would be fun to use a little mayhem. Sort of test it out again. Nothing happened.

"But later on, after that, I was alone in my room, and I did get the mayhem going again. I found a way to get the breathing like it had been earlier. I took it pretty far, but I didn't do anything with it. But still, after that, I felt sure I knew what to do.

"Then, last night at the reunion, I needed to use it so bad. That guy that attacked me Thursday showed up and who knows, maybe he wanted to kill me. I tried, but I couldn't get a trace of mayhem.

"Now, I'm facing this violent criminal in a couple hours, and I know I can't rely on any mayhem to be there. This is bad . . ."

She pulled her hair down with both hands and looked into the trees.

"You know, it sounds like you do know what to do but only when you're perfectly calm. You can learn to use it anytime, I believe, if you can calm yourself when you need to."

"Like when someone's trying to kill me? How is that even possible?"

"No one can answer that for you, Lin. But I'm telling you, it can be done."

"I hope you're right. I really do, but there's no way I can learn something like that soon enough.

"And Jack. I've changed him, Gabby. He adores me—I have no doubt of it—but he's afraid of me too. What a ridiculous relationship. I think he loves me more than ever."

"He probably always did love you, and the mayhem shouldn't scare him away. Maybe what you see as fear is more like respect? Or wonder? It's good to be a mystery, you know."

"Yeah, maybe. But I also told him about my past. About what happened with Ben. And Ray. Not every little detail about Ray but enough. He got pretty quiet, and I'm not sure what he thinks of me now."

"It's good you're being more open with him. That's the right thing to do. Things will work out."

The breeze had picked up, and the brim of Lin's hat began waving in her face. So, she held it on her lap and continued.

"But there's something else. After I used the mayhem on him, I saw that he'd changed, whether it's fear or respect or wonder. But I felt kind of indifferent about it. Like it didn't matter. The mayhem mattered more to me than Jack. Right now, that doesn't make sense to me, but that's what I felt then."

"That gift, or power, changes you too, Lin. There's no escaping that."

"But what if I don't want to change like that? Most of the time, I wish I could have my old life back.

"And then, other times, that power draws me in and attracts me like nothing else."

"I'm not sure you can turn your back on it now. It's part of you. You didn't know it at the time, but you were paying your dues to get that power when you didn't buckle under Ray's abuse. You asked for it, you worked for it, and you have it."

"But it's not any good, Gabby, unless I have complete control of it. Today, I'm going after that fugitive, and this guy's really bad news. The report said he's suspected of molesting and killing a child, but they don't have enough evidence yet. And remember, he just killed a guy Friday and burned his building down. This could get bad today, and I wouldn't be concerned if I could control mayhem."

"You have other skills, Lin. You're a good bounty hunter. Just plan to handle things like you usually do, and be careful. I'm sure you'll be fine."

"Oh, yeah. That's another problem. The guy Doc just killed was supposed to register me so I could legally hunt in Georgia. Now, I have to make other arrangements."

"You're still going after him? Is it really just about the money, Lin?"

Lin bit her lip and exhaled heavily. She drew in a deep breath and held it a moment before continuing.

"No. Listen to me, Gabby. He's a really bad guy. He's a child molester. How do you think I should feel about that?"

"I hope you're not going after him for revenge. Ray is already gone, Lin. But I can tell you're determined to go, and I just want you to be careful. And don't worry. Sometimes things work out way better than you can imagine. Don't be surprised if it all goes well today."

"Right. Things will work out," Lin said and shook her head.

"What about Ben? Is he still a concern?"

"Oh yeah, he's a concern but maybe not for a while. After he attacked me at the reunion, security grabbed him, and I imagine he's in lockup right now. There were lots of eyewitnesses to him assaulting me and Jack and John and Tommy too. I'm hoping he won't get turned loose anytime soon. By the time he gets out, I'll be back home, and he doesn't know where that is.

"All of this would be so much easier if I had control. Except for Jack. I'm not sure anything will help with that now."

She wiped her cheeks lightly just below her eyes.

"This is all stuff no one can help you with, but I do have some advice. When you didn't accept your sexuality, that was a wall built up inside you. You knocked that wall down, no one helped, and that led to you getting some control over the mayhem, at least that one time.

"Is it possible you're not completely accepting that mayhem is now a part of you? Is that another wall? What will happen if you knock down that wall too?"

"I feel like I'm accepting it, Gabby. I want to understand it and control it, but that doesn't mean I'm rejecting it or anything."

"No, you're not really rejecting it, but—"

"How much more can I accept it? I really don't understand what you're saying."

"Perhaps in time, you will, Lin."

Lin began forming a response but stopped and said nothing. After a few seconds, she shrugged and continued.

"Gabby, I'm going to do something I haven't done in decades. I'm going to church. We used to go as a family when I was a kid. I remember the pastor being a kind man, and I wished then that I could tell him about Ray. Of course, I couldn't. I couldn't tell anyone. I wonder if he's still there."

"That's a great idea, Lin. I'm sure he'd be very happy to see you again after so long. And keep an open mind—you never know who might help you put all the puzzle pieces together."

Chapter 34 – God's House

Lin kept her speed down as she cruised her rental car into the church parking lot. All around her, trees that had grown to be giants since she'd left the Island provided a leafy shield against the increasing sunlight, but she easily found her way through the twists and turns since they'd never redesigned the parking areas.

She set the car in park and let it idle, keeping the air on high. She'd just picked up the notes on her quarry, but the file got tossed aside when she saw the pastor propping open the door in anticipation of the congregation that would soon appear. She knew him at once, even though his kindly features were now framed by gray and badly cut hair.

She hurried to the entrance with her heels clicking on the concrete. Before she'd finished climbing the stairs, the man looked down on her with a puzzled expression.

Lin smiled up at him and said, "Good morning, Father."

After several seconds of staring blankly at her, a smile appeared.

"Lin? Is that really you?"

"Yes, Father, it really is. It's been a long time."

She finished the climb up the stairs, and they embraced. Lin gave him a final squeeze after a few seconds, and they separated, with his hands remaining on her shoulders for a few moments longer.

"Oh, my. Thank Heaven. It's wonderful to see you again. What brought you back to us? I haven't seen you in what . . . thirty years?"

"Yeah, it's been about that long. I was in town for a high school reunion, and I'm heading back to Pennsylvania later today. I was hoping I'd get to see you, but I didn't know if you were still here."

"Yes, still here. This is my home. I hope everything is going well. How are your folks?"

"Oh, I guess you wouldn't know. They passed away several years ago. They always spoke highly of you. You were a good influence in their lives."

"I'm sorry to hear about your parents. And your life? Did I do any good for you back then?"

"Well, those times sure had their difficult moments. You helped our family so much, Father. You remember that we went through some tough times and shortly after high school, we went back to Pennsylvania."

"But you're here today at Mass, and that's a good thing. Do you plan to continue attending, in Pennsylvania, though?"

"I don't know. I really don't know. Life is becoming more mysterious to me than I ever could have imagined. It's changing me. I'm changing, Father. Things from my past seem to be catching up with me. Things I couldn't figure out then, and I'm still having a hard time now."

"I'd like to help if I can, Lin. What's catching up with you? What are you trying to figure out?"

From Lin's view, standing in the bright Georgia sunlight, the church interior seemed as if it existed in perpetual night. She couldn't see that the organist had crept down the stairs from the balcony, and he lurked just inside the main doors. He held sheet music in front of him, but his eyes looked off into the darkness as he listened to their conversation.

"Father, I feel like I'm becoming something else. Like I have some kind of ability that no one should have. Maybe it's a power of some kind."

The organist's eyes opened wide at the mention of a "power."

"I want to be good, but it's so confusing. I don't know where I might end up."

"None of us are able to be good all of the time, Lin. Do you have something you want to confess? There's time—we can do that now, if you'd like."

"No, not really. I admit, I was just hoping that I'd find an easy answer here. I'm not possessed. At least, I don't think I am. But something takes over, and I see the world in a different way. I can't explain it, and I know it sounds crazy, but I can see that the world is magic."

The organist couldn't continue to fake that he was looking at his music. He froze on the spot, with one hand covering his mouth, at hearing the word "magic."

"Well, of course it is, Lin. All of God's creation is something we can't comprehend. Isn't it good that you can see that?"

"It's not like that. It's magic that's full of power, and I can use it. At least, one time it felt like I was using it."

"You might just be feeling God working through you. Trust Him, and let Him use you. There's no harm in that. God's will is always a good thing."

"But Father, it's hard to trust Him if I think I might do something bad with it, you know? How can I possibly let go, let things happen, then just accept whatever happens?"

"Lin, God is mysterious, and He works in mysterious ways. It's not easy to trust, for any of us, but we need to trust. It's called faith. You have a good heart, Lin, I know you do. Have faith in God too."

The bells in the steeple began eight rings, and many people had already filed through. Both Lin and the pastor had paused their discussion while parishioners passed them.

"Thanks, Father, but I should probably go. Mass is about to start. I feel like a lunatic trying to describe this. Maybe I'm just exhausted and overstressed. It's probably nothing."

"Won't you attend Mass, Lin?"

"Not this time, Father. Speaking with you is what I needed most."

Once again, he held Lin by her shoulders.

"Well, take good care of yourself. Get more rest, and try to find some peace in your heart. And have faith, Lin. Usually what we're looking for has been inside us all the time."

"It was very good to see you again, Father. I hope it's not another thirty years before we cross paths again."

With a sincere smile, he let her go.

Eyes in the shadows kept a close watch on her as she strode across the parking lot, back to her car. She climbed in, started it, and got the air blasting in defiance of the growing heat and humidity.

"Inside us all the time? That's your advice, Father?"

She put the car in gear and got it rolling toward the exit.

"Mayhem. That's what's inside me."

Chapter 35 – Easy Split

It was mid-morning on a day that was promising to deliver an abundance of South Georgia heat. Without the constant cool air hitting her, her tight skirt and blouse would have caused more squirming in her seat. Her hat lay beside her on the passenger seat, and its wide, floppy brim remained still since every fan vent pointed only at Lin.

She drove east after leaving the church and then north on Glynn. Traffic was light, and the few pedestrians moving about were dressed for the warmth and looked to have a sense of purpose. Children, holding hands of the adults leading them, seemed to dance as they jumped about in the sunlight.

A dog barked from the left, and Lin turned to look. And when she resumed watching the road, she slammed the brakes and squealed the car to a stop. Traffic in front of her had locked up and far ahead, ten or more cars away, she saw a procession of ducks and ducklings waddling across the street.

"Oh, wonderful."

She looked at her watch, then back at the road, which still had her trapped in place. With a quick spin to look behind her to the left, she saw the road clear.

"Ben would just make a U-turn."

She scoffed and tapped on the steering wheel, and the air kept lifting her hair.

"Maybe God is telling me to forget this guy."

The brake lights ahead winked off like a timed light show, and the line of cars began moving, so Lin gave her car some gas and followed, ignoring another dog barking somewhere nearby.

"Nope. Sorry, God. This is for Taylor."

She drove for another thirty seconds, then said, "I'd ask for help, but even Gabby said I had to figure it out on my own."

*　　*　　*

Just a short distance before the Causeway, she reached her destination. Pausing at a stop sign, she gave it another quick study and saw nothing different from the many times she'd driven past it in the last couple of days.

The narrow building looked deserted, and the sidewalk in front held only one rusty bench and some trash scattered around between all of the doors to the rooms. On each side of the building and across the street, there were stores and other businesses, many with parking lots and a fair amount of activity.

She parked the car at a small shopping center behind the motel and checked her looks in the mirror, lingering on the green eyes looking back at her.

"You ready?"

The mirror Lin didn't answer, so the Lin with a mission scoffed and exited the rental car.

Her heels clicked sharply on the hot pavement as she walked in the direction of the motel. On the way, near the building, she kept an eye on the broken asphalt, dodging deep cracks with her heels, then stopped and took out her phone.

But she stashed the phone when movement near the motel caught her attention. A large four-door car, rather old and with out-of-state plates, cruised slowly in front of the building, coming from the other direction. She watched with a sideways glance as the car crept to a stop a couple of car lengths from the motel's office.

"Just wonderful. Probably one of your buddies, huh, Doc?"

She took out her phone and tapped a few times, then scowled and put it back away.

"Hell. Could be anybody, right?"

She tugged down at her skirt, not moving it much, then fluffed back her hair.

And she began a relaxed strut toward the car.

* * *

The car's windows were heavily tinted, but both of them in front were down. Lin strutted along the motel and toward the car, swaying her hips and sometimes brushing back her hair She approached the car from its front, and she'd seen the driver look up briefly, noticing her.

She'd passed the office entrance and was nearing the front bumper. When she was next to the open passenger side window, she leaned over and flashed a bright smile.

"Well, hello there! I hate to bother you, but I seem to have misplaced my car. Too much partying last night! The cops don't go crazy towing cars around here, do they?"

Lin was leaning on the car and giving the driver a good view while she looked directly at him. He focused an intense stare her way.

"I know why you're here, lady. Beat it. This is my territory."

His voice was deep and relaxed, like he was used to being in charge.

"Why, whatever are you talking about? I'm just looking—"

"Save it. I can spot a bounty hunter anywhere. Now, get those sexy high heels walking back down the street. You don't want any part of this guy. Trust me."

The driver again looked toward the motel, and Lin gave him an overall study. He was a little rough looking but not like a criminal. His clothes were tasteful, and his hair short and neat. There was no sign of tattoos.

His story was believable. He might even be the bounty hunter Arnie had tried pushing on her.

If she partnered with the guy, that would solve the issue of her not being registered. They could team up and split the reward. Easy.

Plans had changed. She walked around to the driver's side.

"If he's that bad, let's team up and split it."

195

"I work alone. Get lost."

"It'll go better with me."

She leaned down on the window frame, her buttons popped low and giving a nice view level with his eyes and close enough to touch.

"Come on, you have to admit I can be a good distraction. He won't have a chance."

He looked to his left, at what Lin was showing him, and blew a kiss there before looking up into her eyes.

"Hmm. My kind of distraction. That's how you work?"

"All the time," she said, giving him a good smile. "Even when I'm not working."

"Hmm."

He turned to look back at the motel entrance and stared in that direction for a moment.

"If we're going to do this, you'll need to—"

He snapped his head around to look at Lin.

"He's coming out of his room. Get in the back, quick. Get down on the floor. If he walks this way, he won't see you anyway. Move it. Get in right now!"

Without arguing or even questioning, Lin got in. The back door was unlocked, and she almost dove into the large back seat and found herself on the floor. Her knees ground into the carpet behind the driver's seat, her bent legs keeping her sharp heels pointed up, and her head was near the rear passenger door. Her hat had fallen off onto the seat, and her hair hung down on both sides of her face.

Realizing her unladylike position, she reached back and tried to force her skirt down farther along her thighs. But there was just no way to do it. Anyone that might happen past and looked in wouldn't have to wonder if she was the kind of woman that wore anything under her skirt.

"Maybe teaming up was a good idea after all because—"

"Quiet. He's coming this way."

Lin's breaths were raspy, and she didn't conceal them too well. She heard footsteps on concrete in the distance.

"I hear him. He's—"

"You really need to stay quiet. Stay down. He won't see you."

"He'd have a hell of a view if he was on the other—"

"Shh. Seriously."

Lin held herself still, looking at and smelling musty old floor mats, as the sound of footsteps got louder.

Chapter 36 – Cold Steel

Lin held her breath as the footsteps sounded like the man would be passing the car any second.

Then, she heard the passenger door open.

Almost instantly, the driver pressed the icy barrel of a pistol against her exposed lower back. She heard the man behind the wheel scoff just once.

The front passenger seat sagged with the squealing of old springs, and the door slammed shut.

The three of them remained silent for a moment, and Lin lost control of her breathing. Air was getting sucked in at whatever speed it wanted, and it rushed out like small, scared explosions.

"You probably guessed by now . . . I ain't no bounty hunter," said the driver without a trace of emotion.

"Let me go right now. This doesn't have to get any worse than it already is. Let's just forget it happened. Just get your pistol off of me and let me up."

He laughed and said, "Right. No, that's not going to happen. You see, my buddy here is wanted on some serious shit. So am I. Lucky you, you caught us on a day when we got nothing to lose."

His slow laughter sent a shiver up Lin's spine, and she squirmed to try to get away from the cold steel pressed against it.

"But don't worry. We'll take good care of you. At least until we've had enough. 'Cause I really like what I'm seeing here, even more than the photo on Arnie's phone."

He poked around with the gun barrel, taking turns moving her blouse around, dragging the barrel over the smooth skin of her back. Then, Lin felt him prying her skirt up even farther.

He whistled softly, then said, "Damn. My kind of Sunday morning."

And the steel of his gun felt so much colder than against her back.

"Hmm. Maybe we just take her back in that shitty motel, huh, Doc?"

"There's no time."

The high-pitched voice had come from the passenger side.

Lin scoffed and hung her head.

"Alright, fine. Funny thing about phones, huh, lady? I knew you as soon as I saw you."

"Dammit."

"Thanks for that little tease job, though. Leaning, forgetting how to button up that pretty blouse."

"Let me go. You'd better—"

"No. No way. We're going to have some serious fun with—"

"You know that's not my type, Ivan."

"Oh, yeah. You and your particular interests. Okay, more for me, then."

"Did Arnie tip you off to me?"

"Well," said Doc, "he didn't want to, but we convinced him. Poor Arnaldo—he didn't survive the questioning."

"Will I?"

There was a pause, then Ivan said, "I got not questions for her. You, Doc?"

"Not a single one. I don't even like being this close to her."

"Yeah, I get that."

"Floozy showgirl."

"Yeah, she kinda is. So, Doc, how you wanna play this?"

There was a long pause. Lin dug her fingernails into the carpet as the two men sat in relaxed silence.

"Drive. Try south."

"Got it.

"You just stay right where you are, lady. Do as you're told, and you might get through this. Pick your head up, or scream, or any other stupid shit, and I'll put a hole in you right here."

He tapped on her spine with the barrel.

"It'd be a downright shame to mess up such a nice body."

Lin stayed quiet, contorted in the backseat of that old car as it headed south, unable to get up or even properly cover herself.

If the men in front heard her labored attempts at controlling her breathing, they didn't say anything. And it didn't matter to them anyway.

No mayhem seemed to be along for that ride.

*　　*　　*

About ten minutes of driving had passed with no one saying anything else. Lin knew the area well and by her guess of the speed they'd been traveling, she figured they'd blended into Route 17 from Glynn. With the windows down, she listened for the roar of 95.

Less than thirty seconds later, the traffic on 95 barreled through the open windows and seconds later, they were past it.

*　　*　　*

Doc said, "Take the next right."

"Oh, okay. You wanna play it kinda like last time?"

"Yes, like last time. I like being close to the water. Water hides things so well."

The car rumbled on, carrying two criminals and a partially undressed bounty hunter that couldn't find a speck of mayhem to a park not much farther north on the road.

"Fox Trot, this time?"

"Yes, Ivan. Exactly. I've already placed some heavy bricks in the trunk."

"Got it. They never found him. That's a good plan."

"I do tend to think about these things a lot, dear Ivan. Maybe fantasize is more correct."

"Whatever. Let's get this done."

Lin's heartbeat echoed through her.

* * *

The car slowed as they approached the park entrance, but it didn't stop.

"What the . . ."

"Don't stop, Ivan. Just keep driving."

"Of all the times for there to be an accident right there. Damn, what happened? It looks like a camper wiped out a bunch of bicycles. I hate bikes. We can't sneak past the cops either, Doc. This car might have been reported stolen by now."

"Yes, perhaps. Another spot, then."

"Huh. Probably without water. Some other plan, then?"

"Yes," he said, chuckling. "I'm fantasizing about it right now."

"What exactly are you—"

"Shh," Doc said, grinning. "Don't interrupt."

In silence, they continued north.

Lin was practically in shock from the unexpected turn of events. She'd been prepared for the fugitive to resist, and even fight with her, but not this. Being abducted by two desperate, hardened criminals hadn't even been in the cards.

There was no mayhem to be found, and she fought to not fall into despair, a feeling that she'd always managed to keep at bay. But this was simply too much for her. They had every advantage. She began resigning herself to her fate.

"Take the next left," said Doc.

"Sure."

Lin felt the car turn several seconds later and resume cruising speed. She hadn't given up yet, though, and she still tried to plot their course. They'd passed the park entrance almost a minute before, so a left turn could probably be Blythe Island Drive. If that were the case, very soon, she should again hear the roar of 95.

A minute or two later, she did hear the traffic. And after that rumble had faded behind them, another minute or two passed before anyone spoke again.

"There. Quick. Take that left."

"Over there through the trees?"

"Yes, that's secluded enough. We can't drive around with her forever."

After their turn, the car slowed and bumped up and down and when Lin twisted her head to the right, she could see tree branches passing close by.

"Yeah, secluded is right," said Ivan.

Lin saw that she'd lived an interesting life. She'd loved and been loved, and she'd even witnessed miracles. She corrected that thought, almost laughing out loud. No, she'd *performed* miracles. How else could mayhem be explained? What an unbelievable gift she'd been given, even if only for a while. She felt deep gratitude that mayhem had been part of her life.

Lying on the musty carpet of a car driven by her captors, she had another realization: she'd felt guilty about mayhem ever since Ray and Ben. She knew that it had saved her from Ray, but it was out of control when it struck Ben. And Ben had paid a horrible price.

After Ben, she'd made a conscious effort to hold herself tight inside, not even knowing what that meant. It was a feeling, a sense that she was holding something in—something terrible and dangerous. She'd forced mayhem into the box where she'd refused to hide herself. She'd lived her life as well as she could, but she'd never let down her guard. It could never escape again.

She saw then that mayhem didn't have to be something terrible and dangerous. She'd controlled it, sort of, with Jack. There was probably a way to learn how to use it safely, but it was too late, and that was okay too.

Lin felt all of the anger, frustration, and rage at those two men breaking apart and melting away. She was left feeling only thankful for every moment of her life, especially mayhem. She'd miss Taylor and everyone else that had shared time with her in such a magical world. And she'd miss not gaining a deeper understanding of the powers within her.

But she vowed that she wouldn't give up without a fight. Her decision to fight wasn't based on panic or fear or anger. It was the principle, and it no longer mattered what the outcome would be. She realized that she couldn't control the situation or its ending, but she could choose the focus of her intent. Her intent was all she had.

She saw clearly that her intent was everything.

The car came to a stop and again, the two in front just sat a moment. Lin felt the cold gun barrel removed from her back, and both front doors opened. She didn't dare try anything from her facedown position on the car's floor.

Quickly, they opened both rear doors. Doc grabbed her hair on his side, and Ivan leaned in from his side to place the gun at her back again.

"Hey," said Lin, "I'm not even fighting."

"Good. Slowly," said Ivan. "Helluva view, you should know."

Lin rose up and began crawling toward the open rear passenger door, and Ivan followed her, keeping the gun touching her back. Doc had let go of her hair, though, and wiped his hand across his pants.

She could stand again, and she laughed once at the sight of Doc so repulsed by the touch of her. She straightened her clothes, pulled her skirt back down, and smoothed her hair back over her shoulders.

All around them, there were thick trees and brush in every direction. An opening directly above them, about as big as the car, showed the sky's deep blue. Not a cloud to be seen.

"Ivan, we have a schedule. You can have fun some other time. Finish it."

"This won't take long. We have time."

Ivan stood behind her with the gun in his right hand and the barrel pressed into her ribs. His left hand had begun its investigations by getting a good feel of her backside, through the thin skirt and sometimes under it. Then, he worked his way around to the front, where he had free rein over everything he could reach. He'd just started unbuttoning the next button down, then Lin spoke.

"You're a loser. This is the only way you could ever get a woman."

"Bitch!"

He spun her around and backhanded her with the gun still pressed into her abdomen. Her hips were jammed against the rear fender, and she had no escape route.

"Ivan, we don't have time."

"Cool it, Doc. We got time."

Lin thought she must really be going into shock because she simply didn't care anymore. She knew that the men were evil. She was helpless, and it had no chance of ending well. So, she might as well ruin it for them.

"You're a piece of shit, Ivan," she said as she stared straight into his eyes. "You know that if I saw you on the street, I wouldn't give you a second glance. You could never have a woman like me . . . not voluntarily."

"Well, too fuckin' bad because I just decided I'm having you now anyway. I bet this is your kind of foreplay too."

With his left hand, Ivan touched everything, and an evil smile spread across his face. Lin said no more and only stared at him coldly.

"I already know you got nothing under that skirt. Always ready for anyone, I bet. Tramp."

"Well, Ivan, she's a showgirl," Doc said, snickering. "What would you expect? But we don't have—"

"Just cool it, Doc."

He reached down to undo his belt, and that was a good enough opportunity for Lin, who quickly knocked the gun out of his hand. She followed with a sharp punch that almost caught him in the throat, but he was ready and blocked it. He quickly wrapped both of his hands around her neck. His body pressed her tightly against the car. She couldn't kick, and she couldn't even swing a good punch.

It felt like a death grip to her. She knew that she couldn't trick her way out of it. She couldn't fight her way out of it. And she couldn't find a trace of mayhem. She observed all of that, completely honest with herself, because she had no choice.

It was over.

As she felt the air in her lungs consumed by her pounding heart, Lin lost her fight and dropped her arms to her sides.

Chapter 37 – Lonely Road

The branches all around danced on the light breezes, with an occasional rattle and scrape as they collided and slid against each other. The late morning sun beamed through the opening above, bathing them in heat and light. Birds flitted from limb to limb, chirping and going about their business as if nothing on that deserted road were amiss.

To Lin, it felt like it could be home. All was right with the world.

Except that her last breath was trapped by two strong hands wrapped around her throat.

She observed with some indifference that that was the last breath she'd ever take. But it was a good breath, full of the rich air from that quiet place in the world. She was grateful for it.

"Now, that's good, Ivan. Even her voice annoys me."

Her breath felt heavenly inside her. Science could never explain it to her completely, but she knew that it couldn't be just oxygen. It was a sustaining force, like every breath she'd ever taken in her life. From the moment of her birth, her breaths had connected her to the world, rolling in and out like endless waves on a beach. Each and every one had given her the power to continue to live.

She saw then that every breath during her life could have been her last. Each was special and such a gift. That breath, her last, was the most precious of all.

"You brought this on yourself, bitch," said Ivan.

She didn't hear either of them.

Lin's last breath brought life deep within her, even during those final, hopeless moments. It gave her the strength to survive a few seconds longer and for those seconds, she looked inside. She studied her breath from every direction. From every possible angle. With every sense she had. Until she knew it intimately. Its shape and its color. Its flavor and its scent.

Its calm silence.

Its stillness.

Yet it was only an ordinary breath. So commonplace. Just one of many.

Her last.

She felt a cold smile coming up from behind. Death's eager arms began Lin's final embrace.

And at the very end of her very last breath . . . as death's hold tightened . . . Lin saw it.

Lin saw the *magic* in her breath.

Just a pinpoint at first, but there it was—like a single star in a night sky. Lin watched it and studied it, remaining calm and quiet.

It widened and began to open like a door, and all of her senses felt a gust, each in its own way, and she could see beyond the door endless, swirling magic . . . every color and shape and flavor and scent and taste . . . every substance and every possible creation all mixed together, twisting and spinning . . . a scattering of thoughts and memories and feelings and dreams, all exploding and being reborn and flying in every direction.

Amid the roar, a silence thundering through eternity.

And a stillness that shook the Earth.

But nothing in all that magic made sense . . . nothing that could be known . . . nothing that—

Lin broke her gaze of the magic, sensing that she'd be lost. Her mind survived but couldn't keep the memory of it, and some other part of her, something deep inside, connected her to the magic.

She'd witnessed it just long enough to know that it was her intent that linked her to the endless magic.

From seeing that, from understanding that, she got an unbreakable hold on her intent.

And she would never again have the slightest doubt of it.

So simple, she saw . . . like a switch on a wall. It was nothing more than being what she had to be. What mayhem demanded her to be. Her intent to raise mayhem was all that she needed.

It was all intent.

The switch had been there all along since the day she'd destroyed Ray. She'd created it, nurtured it, and strengthened it—piece by piece, day after day—every time she'd withstood his abuse.

She wondered how she'd never seen it before. But she knew she'd never lose sight of it again.

Lin looked back out at the world, knowing where to find the switch. How to be what mayhem required.

Her eyes began to close as she intended mayhem, and every tiniest bit of her life poured into her intent as it focused sharply on the magic inside her. Her intent opened the door. All of her senses opened wide. She felt the magic flowing into her, and she saw infinity sprawling out in every direction.

She held the view of both men, and she smiled.

A soft green glow lit her eyes.

"Ivan? Ivan!"

"Doc! What the hell is—"

Time stopped.

Small birds in the trees close by fell silent and remained motionless. Some were perched on branches. Some not.

The world around her had become a calm surface, balanced atop towering mountains of magic that extended downward beyond any possible comprehension. Just as Lin felt she was about to burst from the magic flowing into her, she felt herself falling from an impossible height. A powerful wave rose up and rushed out from her in all directions, washing through the two men and everything else nearby.

Ivan's hands loosened, and his arms dropped to his sides. Doc froze where he stood.

Lin had invaded both men and held each of them upright.

Death whispered in Lin's ear and backed away, laughing.

Mayhem was finally hers.

She stayed leaning against the car with half-closed glowing eyes and a faint smile on her lips. There was no longer any need to escape. There was no need to hurry. It was time to make them pay.

Doc would be first. Doc, the child molester and probably child murderer too. Doc's practice had to end. Doc had to end.

In the space between his spirit and his body, Lin took her time and caused pain in every way she could imagine. She heard the silent shrieking from him, much like what she'd heard from Ray. Doc's shrieking didn't cause her any anguish or even slow her down. She knew that he deserved worse.

Lin could sense that at that moment, Doc was sorry for all that he'd done. He admitted it all, trying to save himself.

Her mayhem had humbled the monster.

It satisfied her to hear his confession. He silently screamed about all of his evil work, including how he'd earned the nickname "Doc." She understood just how horrible he had allowed himself to become, and she decided that it was simply too late for him. She learned that he had in fact killed that child, plus much more.

Maybe his confessing will help him after she's through, she thought, but she wouldn't be the one to decide that.

She gripped his heart, that cold, twisted heart that would allow him to harm children, and she squeezed. Just a little at first so that he'd be aware of it happening. Then, harder and harder until the shrieking dwindled to a murmur.

Finally, the pressure had become too great. Doc's weak sobbing had stopped, and the heart could beat no more. Lin felt that he'd died appropriately—the monster had died with a whimper.

Lin was holding a dead body above the ground.

It was no longer worth the effort, so she let the corpse crumple to the dirt.

She turned her focus to Ivan. She didn't know Ivan's past and though she knew that he was bad, she didn't know if he deserved to die. But he'd witnessed all of it. Something had to be done. There couldn't be an eyewitness to what had happened there.

That's the answer, she thought.

From that narrow space, she used the magic on parts of his eyes— not to destroy them completely, just enough to make them useless for a while. Long enough for her to be safely back home. His vision would never again be as good as it had been. Even though he wouldn't be blind, he would never be able to identify her.

Ivan's silent shrieking was tolerable, and Lin found that she wasn't upset by it at all. It was easy to complete her work. She didn't even mind that he hadn't had time to confess to anything.

She let the nearly blind man slump to the ground and retreated back to her own body.

The birds snapped their heads around to look at the source of the wave. They'd seen three people standing near a car, and then two were on the ground. The wave had passed, so they went back to their lives.

Lin reached out to Ivan, who trembled and tried to back away. But she got a hold on his arm and left him sitting up against a tree. All of his fight had left him. Another humbled monster, she thought. She picked up the pistol with a leaf, wiped the barrel where it had touched her, and quietly set it on the ground several feet from him.

Doc lay contorted in a grotesque pose where she'd dropped him. She reached inside his jacket and retrieved Arnie's phone.

Back at the car, she found a blood-stained shotgun. She carefully placed that near Ivan too. She paused to look at both of them.

"Well, gentlemen, that was mayhem. My mayhem. Broken hearts or broken bones."

After closing the other three doors, she got in and backed out to the main road. Before driving any farther, she put the car in park and stretched over the seat to reclaim her hat. She spent several seconds attempting to pull her skirt back down, then she sped away.

On the drive back to Doc's motel in Brunswick, Lin looked into the rearview mirror only to check her eyes, never to see what might be following.

She smiled as she said aloud, "Broken hearts or broken bones. Easier than ever."

She parked the car in a secluded area a block from the motel. It took only minutes to wipe down every surface that might have her prints. She also noticed a single long, blond hair on the carpet where she'd been held captive. She laughed and shook her head, and she removed the evidence.

The late morning sunshine was hot and invigorating as she walked the short distance to her rental car.

During the ride back to her own hotel, Lin looked for the mayhem switch, and she found it there in her breath. Just by finding the switch, just by having the intent, she began to see infinity all around and felt magic billowing up from the depths. She'd never lose it again.

She considered anonymously reporting the incident, but she realized that the police would eventually find them anyway. And all that they'd find are two criminals—one with bad eyesight and one dead from a heart attack.

Doc was dead, and Arnie was dead too. There remained only one living person that knew of her involvement.

Ivan's pistol would probably match more than one crime—maybe even a murder. The blood on the shotgun would also incriminate him, so he would surely end up in prison.

Lin calculated that the only surviving witness would likely live out his days in a cage, telling tall tales of a murderous witch on a lonely Georgia road.

Chapter 38 – Infinite Future

"You did good, Tommy. You didn't tell them Lin's name. I thought you might, but you didn't."

"I'd never betray Lin, no matter what. We were just helping some lady in trouble. Some big creep was trying to hurt her. We had to help. That was the plan. Lin told us to be ready, and we were ready. We were."

After being questioned and released, John and Tommy had nowhere to go, so they started walking north. It was just a block or two before they found a small park, and they sat on a picnic table until darkness fell. It wasn't easy to find two small places to hide out for the night, but they did. When the sun came up, they'd claimed their table and sat with nothing else to do.

"We have to find Lin, John. I don't know where she is. Do you? Do you know? Is she still in St. Simons?"

"I don't know. I really don't know. All I know is that we saved her. You and me. Just like we said we would. We'll find her and man, she's going to be happy to see us!"

"Yeah, that's right. Real happy. Let's start walking, John. Maybe we'll find her. Let's go back the way we came."

"That makes sense. She's got to be here somewhere."

"I'll know her when I see her, John. Those eyes. She had magic eyes. They were magic, right?"

"For sure, Tommy, and I think she had blond hair, didn't she?"

"I think so. I'm not sure. Yeah, it was blond. Probably blond. I'll recognize those eyes, though."

"Right, we'll know her eyes, but shouldn't we know what kind of hair she has? It doesn't make sense that we wouldn't know that."

"You know what else doesn't make sense, John? I'm having a hard time remembering why I liked Lin so much. I mean, I still like her, but not like the last five days. I was crazy about her and now, I like her, but I'm not crazy about her."

"Damn, I didn't want to mention it but me too. I can't remember what it was about her that made me want to be with her so much. She's wonderful, of course. Amazing, even. But damn, Tommy, I quit my job to come down here."

"That sucks for sure, but I left my family. And for what? I feel like I've been crazy, and I'm just now getting my mind back again."

"What are we doing here, Tommy?"

*　　*　　*

Fresh from spending the night hidden near the marshes, Ben had emerged, clothes streaked with dried mud and skin marred by scratches, bruises, and dried blood. He'd snarled at every passing car, and his outstretched thumb didn't convince anyone to stop for him.

Only one car had slowed enough to yell to him, and they never came close enough for Ben to grab ahold of a door handle.

"Mister, you alright?"

"Hell, yeah. Gimme a ride?"

"Not with you all bloody and dirty like that. I'll call an ambulance, though. Would you like that?"

"Get the hell out of here, then."

"You ungrateful son of a bitch. Howsabout I call the cops, then, huh? How about that?"

Ben had lunged at the car, and the laughing driver rolled away quickly, one middle finger held high out of the window.

Cursing to himself, he took a look and examined his arms, then his legs, and confirmed all of the cop caller's accusations.

Laughing, he said, "Shit, I'd call the cops too."

Not waiting for sirens to surround him, he'd hiked in the growing heat through yards and between houses to shorten the trip back to the Village.

The unremarkable house on his left contained a barking dog, but the one on the right was silent. And a window was open.

He peeked in, didn't see anyone, and climbed in to find himself in a bedroom.

A quick look through the dresser drawers produced jeans and a polo shirt, in a size adequate for him, and he swapped his wardrobe quickly.

After tossing his dirty clothes in their laundry basket, and laughing about it, he checked the fridge, found a six-pack, and popped the first one before leaving the house.

A short walk got him out from between all of the houses, and he continued on toward the party center lot, eyeing his truck from a distance and scanning around for any kind of a stakeout.

It looked clear, and he tossed empty cans two and three in with the thin plants keeping a small tree company in front of a shop, then crossed the street.

No one accosted him as he climbed into his truck, and he quickly got his pistol out and ready. With his other hand, he scrounged out the paper that he'd taken from Lin's hotel room, the menu for a restaurant in Pennsylvania.

"This isn't over, witch."

His truck cooperated and started right up, and he cruised slowly out of the parking lot, not attracting any attention. It was an easy ride back to his home on Shotgun Road and as usual, he left a trail of beer cans to mark his travels.

*   *   *

Jack picked his phone up from the table beside him for the fifteenth time.

"Huh," he said as he laid it down gently.

Seated out on the balcony, watching the light waves dancing in the sunlight, was all that had occupied him since he'd dragged himself out of bed only to find Lin already gone.

Without even a goodbye or a note about where she went.

The phone rang and vibrated around, getting a gleeful laugh out of him as he scooped it up, tapped it, then lost his smile.

"Oh, it's you. What?"

"Shit, Mr. Sunshine. Nothing big, Jack. I just won't have that flooring to you until Tuesday. I thought you might—"

"Hey, I'm on vacation, alright?"

"Sure, Jack. Sorry to bother—"

"No, it's alright. Look, I'm just at a sort of low point here. Nothing big, though. Things are mostly fine. I just thought the call was somebody else."

"Yeah. I can guess who."

"Yeah. You know who. She—"

"Well, get your ass off the phone, man! She's probably going to call any second!"

Jack laughed and said, "Sure. Yeah, I bet. Okay, just deliver all that whenever."

"Alright. Be cool!"

Jack tapped the phone and put it back where it had sat for a couple of hours.

He scoffed and said, "In this heat? Right."

*　*　*

Lin swiped her key, turned around, and bumped her hotel room door open. With it latched behind her, she paused there to look around before walking over to turn up the air conditioning. She kicked off her heels, slipped off the rest of it, and lay on the bed below the ceiling fan.

Looking up, watching the leisurely rotation, her breaths seemed to naturally flow easy and strong, never slowing, never hurrying.

"Mm, Jack would like this next step," she said with a soft giggle.

215

She drew in a deep breath, expanding her chest, and held it.

But only for a few seconds.

She let the air rush back out with her laughter.

"Forget him," she said to herself. "Just for now."

She drew in another breath and locked it inside, then let it flow out like a calm riptide. To her, the air conditioner had frozen solid and the ceiling fan had died.

And her eyes had flashed a green light of their own, though she hadn't seen that.

She let her breaths resume a natural pace, and her eyes, bright with green light, faded to their natural shade.

"Wait a second," she said and got up on her elbows. "With Jack. My eyes were—"

She glanced down at how she'd positioned herself.

"Hmm. He'd like this too. I'll check with him later."

She curled up enough to swing her legs over the edge, then stood and walked toward the dresser.

Facing the mirror, she brushed her hair back on both sides, then looked at her hands, rotating them. She flexed both fists, then held both palms up toward the mirror

"Still no blood, Mr. Detective."

Her breathing fell into a strong and steady pace immediately. Just that alone brought a smile, then a shake of her head too.

"You'll like this, Jack. And you'll probably be afraid of it too."

Her smile faded, but her breathing never changed. She pulled in a full measure of the air salty from the ocean so close, expanding her chest and drawing her eyes to the sight.

Serious again, she looked into her normal eyes and let the tide of ocean air flow out, smooth and controlled and filled with power.

And she saw her own eyes become two points of bright green light. Even when smiling again at the sight of her mayhem shown in her eyes, the light never faded.

Behind her, the mirror showed her that the ceiling fan had again cooperated and locked itself in place.

She raised one hand, leaving the other on her hip, and pointed at herself.

"You can see infinity. Infinity everywhere and in everything."

She let her pointing finger sag, but the smile remained.

"So, who are you?"

Two blazing green eyes stared back, unchanged by the smiling lips below them.

"Come on. Say it. You know who you are."

Without planning it, she drew in another, unnecessary breath and held it, creating a much more compelling image.

She scanned all of it, nodded gently, and returned her gaze to the blinding green mayhem eyes.

"I'm Lin Finity."

Chapter 39 – Innocent Touch

Lin Finity had swept out of her hotel dressed in her usual short skirt and heels with a thin yellow sweater and a blue floppy hat. Her arms and legs boasted a subtle tan from the South Georgia sun, and her bouncing hair had some distinct lighter tints. She'd seen in the mirror that her green eyes still shone brightly, but she felt a new coolness inside.

Again, she hesitated at Jack's door. With a hand raised to knock, she winced and looked each way along the empty hallway before sighing and facing his door again.

While shaking her head, she knocked.

Jack opened the door wearing only short pants and a ball cap tight over his long brown hair, and a big smile lit up his face. She waited in the hall outside of his reach, glancing down once at his hands, which weren't reaching for her.

"Lin, glad you're here. Come on in."

He turned and led the way into the room, and Lin followed, letting the door swing shut behind her.

"How are you, Jack?"

He turned, still out of reach but still showing a smile.

"No complaints. It's been quite a weekend. You'll be leaving soon?"

Lin gave his non-reaching hands another quick look.

"Yep. I'm heading back down to Jacksonville in a couple hours. Then, it's back to wonderful, freezing Pennsylvania. God, I'm going to miss this weather."

She walked past him, toward the balcony.

"How about you?" she said after she'd gotten a grip on the railing with both hands.

"Yeah, of course, I'll miss it. I do a lot of work outside, remember?"

She laughed at the ocean and said, "Oh, I remember. Yep."

"So, I have a flight out later this evening. I can't say I'll be happy to be back home, though, except for the fact that you'll be there. I've really enjoyed your company."

"We've had some incredible times, that's for sure."

She kept looking out over Jack's balcony rail at the ocean.

Jack paused to look up and down her figure barely concealed in the tight clothes. He took his time and viewed from her heels, up the backs of her legs, across all of the curves not disguised by the thin cloth, all the way up to her wavy hair lifted by the incoming breeze.

He looked down, took a deep breath, and walked up behind her, where he wrapped his arms around her waist. Lin sighed and reached back to place both of her hands on his hips and tilted her head back to rest on his shoulder. He reached up and gently moved her hair to one side and began kissing her neck and brushing lightly against her ear.

"Jack, we probably don't have time, do we?"

"We have time. I'll always have time for you. You must know that I adore you, right?"

Lin smiled but continued a cold stare out over the waves.

"You feel so good up against me, Jack."

He spun her around and with both hands, he held her with palms tight against her skirt. He kissed her several times, saying in between, "You're an angel, Lin."

She looked past him, over his shoulder, then up at the ceiling. A moment later, she sighed and turned enough to kiss him.

"Oh, I'm no angel, but we do have time, Cowboy."

*　*　*

219

Lin lay in bed, staring at the ceiling and taking slow, comfortable breaths. Jack wasn't beside her, but she still wore an easy smile from what they'd just shared.

The running shower added some tones to the steady buzz of the air conditioner. She squinted up at the lazy fan blades, then pointed at them.

"Wait. What happened to John and Tommy . . ."

She tipped her eyes toward the bathroom, then gave the fan her attention again.

"Could it?"

She had a silly grin while considering the playful, innocent plan until her breathing, all on its own, slipped out of her control, slowing and deepening at once. She rolled herself over, slid a sheet to partly cover her, and didn't interfere with the breathing in any way.

She allowed her breaths to continue slowing while she became overly aware of her life force. It filled her body to its ends as if it abhorred her boundaries. She felt the world around her stretching out to infinity, with her at the center. It was such a calm, continuous surface, and it was supported by unfathomable magic.

A barely noticeable smile appeared as she gazed into it.

Lin hungered to know that magic. To touch it. But not then. There would be time.

She heard the shower stop and knew that Jack would dry himself off for a minute or two. She waited a minute, then took control of her breathing, and it remained slow and very strong. She drew in a deep breath and held it. She forced herself to stop smiling.

Her life became flooded with the magic in that breath. Her spirit longed to break free and join the vast magic of the world. She held that breath until she heard the doorknob turn . . .

. . . and she let it out sharply, felt she was falling from the sky, and felt the wave rise up and spread out from her in every direction. But she didn't ride the wave. She had no intention of stealing Jack's life, even for a moment.

She watched as the wave rushed through Jack—through that space in between. Jack was again touched by her mayhem but this time, she'd held herself back. She was an observer. She remained only the source.

Her breathing quickly returned to normal, and she stayed as she had been: naked on the bed except for a teasing layer of thin sheet material.

*   *   *

Lin remained still, her head turned away, and heard the door open all the way but no sound of footsteps. Jack stood, wrapped in a towel and staring at Lin, who lay naked and hardly covered by a sheet. After a long moment, he approached, his footsteps giving him away, and the bed sagged under his weight.

Hey laid himself beside her but not tight up against her. Several minutes passed, then he began gently caressing her hair and brushing it back softly as if to avoid waking her. He did nothing but that—just stayed near and touched her hair.

Lin still lay still like she was asleep, and her eyes, looking away, watered up from Jack's innocent touch. She gave the impression of waking up, rolled over slightly to reward him with another memorable view, and looked into his eyes.

"Oh, Jack! Nice eyes!"

"Huh? What about them?"

"Nothing. I just like the way they look!"

"Lin, you're being silly. They always look like this."

"Mm-hmm. I hope they always will."

She yawned while stretching, tipping her head to his eyes from different angles.

"Jack, maybe we—"

"Shh . . . go back to sleep. We don't have to rush."

He wrapped his arms around her like he'd never let her go again. They lay there long enough for the shadows to inch across the wall, and then he began softly touching her again. Just a chaste caress. Just the contact was enough.

Lin chased away her smile and feigned sleep in his arms.

But only for a few minutes.

"Jack, we really should get moving, don't you think?"

"Did you say drink? Great idea. I'll be right back."

Jack kissed her, got out of bed, and returned quickly with a glass of whiskey. They held each other and sipped the strong drink, both quiet and sometimes smiling at each other.

She nudged the glass closer to his lips, raising her eyebrows, and he laughed and finished what was left.

"Jack, I really need to get some clothes on and get going. Thanks for a wonderful afternoon."

"Yeah, I know. It's getting late. I've had a wonderful afternoon too. I'm going to get dressed and give you some privacy."

As he retreated back into the bathroom, Lin switched on the news and began getting dressed. She'd gotten as far as her skirt and heels when a news report came on about a fight the night before. She watched as a police lieutenant gave a statement about the incident, the description of the suspect, and a warning for area residents to watch for him because he was dangerous and probably armed too.

Lin had a view of both the TV and herself in the dresser mirror. In the mirror stood an attractive woman wearing only a skirt and heels, and an artist's sketch of the suspect filled the TV screen. Lin and Ben— two drastically different lives.

"I have mayhem. You got ruined by it."

She watched for a few more seconds, then said to the sketch, "You don't have a chance anymore."

After switching off the TV, she finished getting dressed and brushed her hair lightly, leaving it looking wild.

Jack returned and backed her into the dresser. He hugged her tight and smiled at the view of her in the mirror.

"Mm, you look so good from any angle."

"Hey, you're peeking at me."

"Mm-hmm. Every chance I get."

He leaned back, and they shared one long kiss.

"See you in Pennsylvania, Jack. It's going to be so cold."
"I'm afraid so."
"But you're not afraid of me, are you?"
He squinted at her, then said, "Why would I be? Lin, you're silly."
He gave her a quick kiss, said, "I'd better go."
"Okay."
She watched him walk out and close the door, then she pumped a fist quietly and let her smile loose.

Chapter 40 – Airport Justice

After a quick checkout, Lin piloted her rental car up King's Way, weaving around the traffic, then over the Causeway with the windows down for better sights and scents of the marshes.

Ahead was a quick loop down and around on Glynn, then the open ribbons of 95 would take her to her flight out of Jacksonville.

"You seem to have a lot on your mind."

"I do, Gabby. My life has changed so much this week that I don't feel like the same person. So many things are different."

"Different bad? Or different good?"

"Both. I won't have nightmares again. I control my mayhem, and I don't black out anymore. I control what happens now."

"What has happened?"

"Well, let's just say it's been mostly good. It's saved my life, and that's good."

"Of course, that's good. What did you mean, 'mostly?'"

"It's probably best if we don't go into details. Things happened, that's all."

"You can tell me anything, Lin. You have for a very long time."

"Yeah, I know. Okay, here it is. I went after the fugitive in Brunswick, and it was my own stupid mistake, but I got abducted by him and one of his buddies. Those were bad guys."

"Were?"

"I'll get to that. They were going to kill me. They took me to this deserted road and all the way there, one was talking about what he was going to do to me. And the other, Doc was his name, he basically admitted that he'd molested and killed a child not long ago. Bad men, Gabby.

"The driver, who was Doc's friend, well, we struggled, and he—"

"You started a fight with him?"

"It was either that or just let him have sex with me."

"Oh."

"Yeah. So, he got a grip on my throat. I was dying, and I'll never forget the feeling. I accepted that I'd had a good life, and if it had to end right there, so be it. Even while being choked, I saw the beauty of the world and was thankful for that last breath inside me.

"Then, I saw it. Well, I didn't really see anything, but I found it. It's like a switch that I can find in my breath. It's really just knowing what I need to be for mayhem. I flip that switch, and mayhem rises up.

"And boy, did it rise up. I killed Doc—crushed his heart—and I nearly blinded the other guy."

She'd merged into light traffic on 95 and quickly got up to her cruising speed for the drive south.

"You killed a man."

"A bad man."

"Have you ever heard, 'thou shall not kill?'"

"Gabby, you know the true words are really, 'thou shall not murder.' And I didn't murder. I killed a murderer to save my own life, and that monster will never murder again."

"What happened to the other guy?"

"I messed with his eyes. He's not blind, but he'll never be able to identify me."

"The perfect crime?"

"It wasn't a crime, Gabby! They were going to kill me. My mayhem changed everything. I don't regret any of it. In fact, it was satisfying to kill that lowlife criminal. It felt right. It was justice."

"So, you pass judgment now?"

"Yes. When I have to."

*　　*　　*

With an hour left before boarding for the flight back to Pittsburgh, Lin took a turn into a restaurant for lunch. Very few diners were seated, and she sat at a table near the entrance.

The server, a man in his early twenties, took the order and tried unsuccessfully to keep his eyes off of Lin. She'd crossed her legs, and the skirt left little for his imagination. She noted his wandering eyes with satisfaction and sat back to sip her water and watch the travelers milling about.

Minutes later, a couple came in, walked past, and took seats behind Lin two tables back. They both looked to be in their late thirties, and they seemed weary of each other. There was a distinct tension between them—a lack of closeness, as if they'd rather sit at separate tables.

The man dressed well, but he appeared impatient or angry about something. The woman made a striking impression in a subtle way. Tight faded denim stretched over her thighs showed that she'd paid her dues at the gym. Her long black hair hung straight down, and the heels of her black snakeskin boots punctuated each solid, confident step.

Lin noticed most the look of determination in her eyes as she passed. She'd never looked directly in her direction, but Lin could see a strength there, like the woman had faced demons and conquered them.

The food arrived, and Lin started eating and paid no more attention to the couple two tables behind her. She made short work of her cheeseburger, and she was swabbing around the last of the fries in streaks of ketchup.

The last two fries were pinched, coated, and about to meet the same fate as all the rest, then Lin looked up.

"Gabby, I feel like I'm disappointing you. My world has changed in such a big way, and I'm still sorting it out. I don't know how I fit into my life anymore. I never asked for any of this. I never asked for Ray."

She stuffed in the last of her lunch and listened.

"No, you sure didn't ask for Ray, but it seems you were born with a strength, or maybe you picked it up along the way. And when Ray happened, you had the strength to not be a victim of it. You couldn't stop him, but you were never a victim. Your strength took it head on."

There was a clatter behind Lin, and the man said, "You think you're so tough. You wanna try living without me helping you out?"

The woman only looked coldly at him and continued eating. After a long pause, she said, "You know I'm tough. Leave if you want."

Lin turned back to her empty plate and picked up her drink.

"So, Gabby, are you saying whatever strength I had led to my mayhem?"

"I'm saying that your strength carries you along through your life and whatever happens, you meet it with that strength."

"I met Ray's abuse with that strength, and it turned into my mayhem?"

"How else would you explain it, Lin?"

A hand slammed a tabletop behind Lin.

"I'm just about done with you. I don't think you appreciate how much I do for you. You want this to be over? Is that what you want?"

Lin looked over her shoulder again. The man's face was contorted, and his jaw stayed mostly clenched as he spoke. His hands remained at each side of his plate, but they were balled up in shaking fists.

The woman still sat without any reaction and gazed at him while she continued to chew. The man didn't notice, but Lin saw the woman slowly place her hand over the steak knife next to her plate.

The woman said, "Do what you want. Right now, I want to eat."

Lin turned back around with a smile.

"That amuses you, Lin?"

"Yeah, it does. That guy looks like he could go off at any time. She looks like she's taking it, but she's preparing for whatever he might do. I have no doubt she can handle the situation."

She took a big sip of water and set down the glass.

"I can't explain my mayhem, Gabby, but I'll never again not know how to use it. I think I'm just beginning to learn all that it can do."

"Remember that it's always your choice what you do with it. You can choose to use it for good or bad."

"Who's to say what's good and what's bad? Isn't it more important to know whether what I do is just?"

"Lin, I believe—"

"Like Doc, up in Brunswick. That guy was such a dirtbag. He was evil, Gabby, and—"

A whining squeal from a chair being forced across the floor caused Lin to look back over her shoulder.

The woman had pushed her chair back and stood up. Her hand still covered the knife.

The man remained seated and stared at her with squinting eyes as he shook his head slowly.

"You sit your ass back down, Lee. If you don't, I'm leaving for good, and your little family can go to Hell for all I care, and it'll all be your fault."

The woman sat, but the knife remained ready.

Lin groaned while turning back around and put a hand over her gut.

"He just said it would be her fault."

"Lin, I don't think—"

Lin's anguish had passed, and she was completely calm.

"Ray said that. That bastard said that. To me."

"Lin—"

"Not now, Gabby."

Lin focused on her breath deep inside, and she intended her mayhem as her eyes began to close. She felt the magic rushing into her and filling every part of her. Her eyes began to glow, and the world became a calm surface above boundless layers of magic. She felt the sweet pressure of the magic inside as she sent the wave out toward the man and woman, but she focused only on the man.

She took complete control. She felt the man's terror, and she liked it. Time seemed to stand still as she kept the man sitting at the table. For a moment, it seemed like terrifying him would be enough.

It wasn't.

She found the man's heart and this time, she didn't squeeze it like with Doc. She focused her energy on it and increased the rate. Then a little more. More. The man's heart raced, and Lin found profound satisfaction in his excruciating level of fear. He tried to instill fear in others, and that's what he deserved.

She observed without emotion that the man had no idea what caused his agony, and that's probably why she could hear no pleading. Only silent screaming.

When she felt that he'd about reached his limit, she let him go. He collapsed to the floor unconscious.

She heard his body slump out of the chair and back completely in her own body, she turned to see. The man's bladder had let go, and he lay there twitching with his mouth hanging open.

Lin nodded, smirking, then glanced over at woman.

She stared directly at Lin, and her hand was no longer near the knife.

Her eyes were calm. She looked curious, even understanding, and without a trace of fear. Or adoration. And no smile. She'd never looked down at the man.

Lin spun back around and said, "Something isn't right, Gabby. She was close—why isn't she acting like John and Tommy?"

"Lin, it might just be—"

"Gabby, we have to go."

She grabbed her carry-on bag and stopped just short of the door to take one last look back. The woman still stared directly at her, and she'd begun to rise up from her seat.

*　*　*

After hurrying through the concourse, Lin boarded her plane and settled in. She hadn't said a word since the scene at the restaurant except what was necessary for passing checkpoints.

"What was that, Lin?"

"You know what that was. That man was abusing her."

"She seemed to be handling it. Why did you do what you did?"

"Because she deserved better than that. And he might have gotten violent with her. I was happy to stop it."

"Did that help her life?"

"Damn right, it did. He'll carry that fear with him for quite a while, I'd bet. And he'll be happy to have her around instead of taking her for granted."

"Maybe. Or did it help you more?"

"Oh, you think I did that for selfish reasons?"

"Did you?"

"Well, maybe a little. I did get some satisfaction out of it, but why shouldn't I?"

"Just be careful how you travel down this path. Don't lose sight of what's right and wrong. Always try to see what's necessary and what should be left alone."

"I've never hurt anyone that didn't deserve it. Like that fugitive in Erie.

"Yes, he did attack you."

"Yeah, and that punk in the gravel."

"He wasn't very nice to you."

"No. And Doc and Ivan, they—"

"The one you killed and the—"

"One I blinded. Yeah. They all deserved what they got. So what if I enjoy it too?"

"Maybe it isn't that easy, Lin. Maybe the choices you make change you too. Be careful that you don't lose yourself to your mayhem."

"You're wise beyond your years, Gabby," Lin said with a smirk.

After a pause, Gabby replied, "No, that's not really accurate."

"Okay, but I'm always thankful for your advice. I think I'll be okay."

Lin allowed her weary eyes to close.

Chapter 41 – Comfortable Space

Ben had maintained the posted speed limits all the way from the party center parking lot back to his shack on Shotgun Road. He'd glared many times at the silent, beaten radio, coming close many more times to punching it again.

Beside him lay beer cans, some full and some emptied. And a gun, still wrapped in a rag.

Whipping onto the gravel drive sent stones flying and dug in more deep ruts. Amid the cloud he'd kicked up, he sat and stared at a house almost as broken up as his truck radio while he finished the open can.

He downed it, tossed it to the floor, and cracked open his door.

He slammed the truck door, rattling the loose exhaust pipe near the passenger side, and it continued to rattle as he walked up the path. It wasn't so much a path by design as just a length of ground kicked clean of clutter and snaking to the front door.

Halfway to the house, he paused to light a cigarette. A scrawny cat saw that as an invitation and circled his legs, rubbing against the clean denim of his stolen jeans. He exhaled a cloud of smoke and looked down.

He brought one boot back, ready to kick, then set it back down gently. Not smiling, he leaned over and stroked the cat's back but only twice.

"Stupid cat," he said aloud as he took another drag and walked to the front door.

The door never quite latched all the way, as if it were hoping to make its opening easier and avoid being hit again. He pushed the door open and walked in.

He stared around the room without any surprise at the sight. It was as he'd left it. It was a mess. The night under the highway overpass no longer seemed so bad.

The house was quiet except for TV sounds drifting in from the bedroom. Luanne had long ago given up trying to make the shack any kind of home. It was a place to keep the rain off their heads, nothing more. And even that probably wouldn't last much longer.

He paused again and slowly drew his breath through the cigarette while looking toward where he'd soon find Luanne.

"Dammit, Lin."

He ground out his cigarette on the first bare spot of floor he found.

*   *   *

Back in her Temt8tion, Lin sank into the snug curves of the car's supple leather seat and roared down an on-ramp and onto the freeway. Both hands on the wheel, she stared straight ahead.

"I hope I'm leaving all that chaos behind me in Georgia. All the loose ends seem to be tied up, though. Things will be even more normal with Jack, that is, if I still want that."

"Why wouldn't you want Jack?"

"I'm just wondering if maybe too much has happened. I haven't told you, but I used my mayhem on him again. Just a little. Just enough to make him adore me. I think it worked—the fear seems to be gone. I have no idea how that works, Gabby, but it did that to John and Tommy too."

"Because of those two, and how they ended up, you decided to try it with Jack?"

"Yes. Wild, huh? It worked, but I have absolutely no idea how. Sure didn't work on the abused woman at the airport, though."

"That sounds like another mystery. I'm sure you'll understand it eventually."

"I wonder, too, if that weird effect has a shelf life. Does it wear off? I kind of doubt it—I think those two got changed forever."

"Another thing you'll understand someday."

"Maybe. Oh, what I said before: I was wrong before about loose ends. Ben is roaming around out there again. He got loose. The cops never took him in."

"Is it possible he'll leave you alone even if he does know where to find you?"

"That man hates me. I have no doubt of it. But I can handle him, and I will."

"He doesn't deserve to die, Lin."

"No, maybe he doesn't. And neither do I. I'll do what I need to do."

$$*\quad*\quad*$$

Luanne looked up from the dusty TV on the cardboard box to see Ben standing in the doorway with a rare confused look on his face.

She laughed and said, "New clothes? That a new look for—"

"Never mind the goddamn clothes. I'm throwing these out anyway."

"Uh, okay. What's wrong, Binge?"

"Nothing."

"Have a nice trip?"

"Um . . . yeah. It was okay. I'm just here to get some more cash. I'm heading back out."

"You didn't do anything crazy, did you? Did you find Lin?"

"Yeah, I found her. And no, I didn't kill her. But this ain't done."

"Just stay, Ben. Let it go. Lin isn't important."

"Says you."

"Look, you can't go on hating her for the rest of your life."

He dragged the back of his hand across his eyes and forced them to stay open.

"You don't know nothin' about it, Luanne. There has to be a reckoning. Go get that money you've been squirreling away for Christmas. And don't tell me you haven't. You don't want to be a problem to me right now."

Luanne opened her mouth, but she quickly closed it at the look on his face. She got a good wince going before pushing it.

"God, what are you gonna do this time, Binge?"

"I don't know. I just don't know."

While he had the stolen polo shirt pulled up, blocking his sight of Luanne, she sneaked out of the room, saying, after she was out, "I'll get you some of your usual things to wear."

He scoffed and said, "Because you just did laundry?"

He waited, shirt almost off, then grinned at receiving no answer.

*　　*　　*

Lin piloted the sleek black car out of the airport parking and turned it onto I-76 east.

"It'll be a relief to be home. Just six hours or so, and I'll be walking through the door."

"If Nomad lets you."

"Right. I'll have to deal with him too. He sure is a challenge."

"You've certainly had quite a week. You've done a lot and learned a lot."

"Gabby, so many things in my life have come into focus. I won't be having blackouts anymore or the dizzy confusion before them. And no more nightmares. They're just memories now."

Lin's high heel shoe pressed down on the accelerator, and the car reached cruising speed. Lin's cruising speed. No one would be passing her.

"Are you that confident now?"

"Yes, I am. My mayhem is part of me, and I know where to find it. The only thing is that I can't have my feelings running wild, or it doesn't work. I need to stay pretty even."

"That can't be easy."

"It's not as hard as it sounds. I know it's not how I've been, but I think my mayhem is kind of channeling me in that direction. I'm growing into it. Adapting."

"Maybe you won't have to try so hard after you're more used to your mayhem. How about the whole good versus evil thing?"

"I'm good, Gabby. You know that."

Lin clenched her jaw and stared ahead.

"If your new power is luring you in its own direction, will you always be so sure?"

Lin sped the car up a notch.

"I'll make an effort to only use it if someone's threatening me in some way. How's that?"

"So, that guy just a little while ago at the airport . . . that won't happen again?"

"Gabby, that was different. He was about to hurt that woman. How could I just let that go?"

"You can't save the world, Lin. That's not your job."

"Of course not, but I can help."

*　　*　　*

Ben lit a cigarette and climbed into his truck, then rattled the exhaust pipes with the slamming door. The dusty windshield kept the view of his house out of focus, but he saw enough to remind him that it was about all that he'd accomplished over the last thirty-plus years. That and long stretches of jail time, pissing off friends and family, and doing his part to keep the liquor industry afloat.

He looked down at his right hand, already clenched tight and ready for its next target. He slowly relaxed the fist and rotated his hand so that he could see it from every angle. He saw a strong hand, capable of more than just punching. Maybe even something useful and positive.

He scoffed, stabbed a cigarette between his lips with his left hand, and turned the key with his right. The truck roared to life, and he backed it to the road, chasing chickens and cats to either side.

It was time to drink.

*　　*　　*

"Whiskey, Duke."

"You got it, Binge."

Ben planted himself on his usual barstool and downed the first shot. He scowled as he took a good look at Duke as he walked over to pour his second. Holding that one, he looked around the bar at the junk hanging on the walls, the cracked paneling from that fight he'd started last summer, the pool table's torn cloth . . . he took it all in. Even the faint lipstick stain on his poorly washed shot glass.

After downing shot number two, he held it on the bar and held up the other hand, flexing and relaxing his fist.

"Uh, easy with that, Binge."

"It ain't for you. Not this time."

He slid the shot glass down the bar to get the third one on its way. Duke was still nearby, caught the speeding glass, and turned to fill it.

"Who's it for, then?"

"That witch."

"Oh. Yeah, you were talking about some witch."

"Not just some witch."

Duke held the bottle up and away, not pouring. He swiveled his head just enough to see Ben's eyes, but Ben was looking ahead, into the mirror.

"A . . . beautiful witch."

"Oh. Uh, maybe you shouldn't be beating on her, then, huh?"

"Just get that goddamn whiskey moving. Dammit, Duke, you don't know shit about witches."

Duke delivered more whiskey, and Ben shot it down, then set the glass on the bar gently.

"That did it," said Duke. "You always talk about that comfortable place. Three shots, right?"

Ben finally looked at the spindly owner of the bar.

"Yeah. Comfortable. Not enough, though."

"Sure thing, Binge."

Duke slowly and carefully took the glass from Ben's hand, then retreated to refill it.

"You got a little thing for this particular witch?"

Duke's smile wilted quickly at Ben's eyes boring into his.

"Could be your last day, you stupid man."

He tipped his eyes to the empty glass in Duke's shaking hand.

"Do your goddamn job."

"Uh, sure, Binge. Right away."

The bottle clinked around on the shot glass as Duke poured it, then he nudged it along the wet bar surface until it was close enough for Ben to grab, lift, pour, and swallow.

He dried his fingers from the cold wetness of his fourth shot glass and took out the paper with the restaurant address in Allentown.

"More than that, Duke."

"Huh?"

Ben only glared at him.

"Oh, okay. I get it. More than just a little thing. So, you're not going to beat her?"

"We'll see."

*   *   *

Lin drove in silence on the final legs of the trip back from the airport in Pittsburgh. She hadn't spoken a word with Gabby all the way up Route 33 and before heading for home on Route 248, they parted company. It would only be minutes until she finally made it home as she purred her powerful car into the neighborhood.

The lawns all around her house could have been on the cover of a magazine, even in November. All of Lin's neighbors were fanatics about keeping up with the leaves, trimming, and everything else.

She turned into her driveway and clicked the garage door open. After pulling in, she killed the engine, clicked the door shut, and sat there for a few moments. She let out a deep breath and felt a soft smile turn into a laugh.

It was time to see Nomad.

Chapter 42 – Nomad

Lin gave her car door an impatient shove open and stepped onto the garage floor. With a coffee cup in one hand and her purse in the other, she kicked the door shut as loudly as she could. After setting her things on the hood, she straightened her short skirt and walked back to slam closed the trunk that she'd popped.

Laughing, she said, "He'll just chew up my travel stuff anyway."

A few quick steps brought her to the house door.

"Okay, big boy. I know you know I'm home."

She didn't reach for the knob but instead held her ear close to the door and listened. No sound betrayed the presence of the animal waiting inside.

Several long minutes crawled by as Lin struggled to contain her laughter. Still, there wasn't a sound.

She reached for the door but pulled her hand back before a single manicured finger touched it.

"Come on, boy," she said softly to herself. "You know I'm home."

Another long, silent minute passed.

Finally, after she'd shrugged and sighed and began reaching for the knob, she heard a single, deep, "Woof!"

"I win again."

She gathered her hair back over her shoulders and braced herself as she turned the knob. She'd opened the door only a few inches when a gigantic red snout pushed its way into the opening and forced the door all the way open. With a burst of thick red fur, her two-hundred-pound Tibetan Mastiff stood in the open doorway reaching for her shoulders, then settling in to rest all of his bulk on her.

"Nomad! Nomad! I've missed you so much!"

It was all she could get out before Nomad's huge tongue began washing her face clean of every trace of makeup. He leaned heavily on her, straining her legs, and she could feel his massive back paws alternating in attempts to climb up into her arms.

"Oh, Nomad, you're so heavy! You want my legs to stay in good shape, don't you?"

Her leg muscles burned, and all the affection made her laugh and brought tears at the same time.

"Okay, my big boy. Let me in. You must be hungry."

Nomad dropped with a heavy thump on the wood floor and padded off to his gigantic silver bowl. Lin laughed at his thick, swishing tail as she followed him and grabbed the heavy bag from the pantry on the way. She filled the bowl, scribbled the weight on a napkin, then kicked off her heels. She sat next to him while he devoured most of it, hugging him and playing with his ears.

He'd been put up for adoption at Sweet Pets, and it soon became apparent to Lin that he'd be hard to place. Anyone that looked up his breed got scared away by how big he'd become. And besides his size, the dog was known for being very headstrong. He'd need a firm leadership presence.

Lin had loved him from the start, and she'd been secretly relieved that no one had come forward to adopt him. She'd given it a week, and she figured that should have been enough time. She wasn't concerned about his size. There would just be more for her to hug and squeeze. And he could be as stubborn as he wanted—she had no doubt that she'd always be the alpha.

She didn't like to dwell on it, but something about having control over such a large, male animal appealed to her too. She knew that a small dog just wouldn't bring the same satisfaction.

As the sound of Nomad crunching his dinner rang through the house, Lin got up and read the note on the refrigerator from her dog-sitter.

"Nomad is wonderful! Can I keep him?"

Listening to Nomad nose his emptying bowl across the floor, she stared at the note for a few moments, lost in thought.

"Maybe," she whispered to herself. "Like, if I'm gone?"

Nomad had rammed his bowl into the wall, spilling chunks all around.

"All filled up? Let's go, Nomad. Couch time."

She plopped down on the couch where she had a view of the neighborhood, and Nomad draped himself across her and pushed her deep into the cushions. She tried to hug him but could barely get her arms around his neck for the bushy mane. She spoke to him while rubbing his ears and scratching the top of his head, and he answered with low, thoughtful sounds from deep in his throat.

"Oh, Nomad, why can't all of life be this peaceful? We don't need that world out there, do we, boy?"

Still fussing with him, she glanced again out through the wide window at dark yards lit dimly by the streetlights.

"You still love me, don't you, boy?"

His answer was to lick her face.

"I haven't changed too much for you?"

He barked softly at the ceiling.

"Thanks, Nomad. I want you to always love me. Even if I had to leave because I'm, uh, different now, I'd always miss you."

He tipped his head, and he rarely blinked as he gazed into her eyes.

"I would, Nomad. I really would miss you."

He leaned closer and licked her cheek.

"You just said you'd miss me too? Hmm, maybe not as long as someone kept feeding you."

Nomad whined and burrowed his wet snout under her chin.

"I knew you'd miss me. Okay, boy. I need to change."

She wiggled her way out from under him, and he expressed his displeasure with deep grumbling and tried to hold her down.

As she changed into sweatpants, a t-shirt, and slippers, she shivered from the coolness of the house.

"Goodbye, South Georgia . . ."

Back on the couch with Nomad, Lin looked through the mail that her dog-sitter had brought in. She found nothing of consequence and turned on the TV. Twenty channels later, nothing there had caught her interest.

So, she tossed down the remote and rubbed Nomad's big ears with both hands as he lay with his head on her lap.

"I like that I can tell you anything, my big boy. Nomad . . . I'm obsessed with my mayhem."

She looked down on Nomad's big head with sleepy eyes that were beginning to droop closed, and said, "Hmm, I sure do wonder."

Nomad kept his head down but turned his eyes up to hers.

"Whatcha think, Nomad? Worth a try, boy? A little bit of my mayhem?"

She no longer needed to focus on anything as if she were following a set of instructions. She needed only to have the intention of mayhem and it began.

Instantly, she found herself at the center of the calm surface of a world hovering over bottomless layers of magic. That vast expanse of magic was mind boggling. But she suspected that that wasn't a place for her mind. That was a place of sensing. A place of action.

She felt the power from the breath expanding her life from the inside, and her life energy grew too large to be contained by her body. It was such pleasure to perceive all of the magic, to see it stretching to infinity, to feel the anticipation of—

A low growl interrupted her musings. She still held her breath as she looked down and met Nomad's eyes looking directly into hers. His growling could barely be heard, but she could feel the vibration from it on her thighs.

She let her breath out in small amounts, slowly and randomly, not wanting to risk making the wave, until the magic was no longer visible.

His growling stopped, but his eyes were still fixed on hers.

"Oh, Nomad. It can't be that bad."

She continued stroking the top of his head, playing with his ears and softly saying, "Nomad, Nomad . . ."

It took ten minutes for him to again close his eyes.

"Maybe it was just too sudden. Could that be? I'll ease into it this time."

She focused on staying completely calm, not changing how she petted him, and keeping her body totally relaxed. She intended her mayhem, and infinity rolled out in every direction. She kept her breathing slow and even so as to not alarm the big dog. She felt the pleasure begin, and—

More growling. Before looking down, Lin released her breath as before. Nomad's eyes were open wide and locked on hers.

"Don't be a baby, Nomad. You're big. You can take it."

Again, she allowed time for him to relax and close his eyes. He seemed reluctant to take his eyes off of her, but he was too tired to keep them open. When his big, heavy eyes had been closed again for several minutes, she intended her mayhem again.

With the intent came her mayhem and a focus on the breath inside her, filling her with magic. While basking in infinity and glancing at Nomad, she intended the wave of mayhem. It wasn't forceful. Just a gentle ripple. The growling had started, but she didn't change the plan.

The ripple trickled outward from her and she along with it. She looked for the gap between the growling dog and his spirit, but she couldn't find it. After several seconds, she caught a glimpse of what appeared to be an opening, but it was so narrow, almost just a line, that she didn't see a way in. And she needed to get in there.

Nomad could still move, and he did. His teeth were bared as his growling got louder, and he jumped to the floor. He was facing her, lying flat on the carpet, looking up at her and snarling.

Lin pushed harder to get into the narrow space. Nomad bared his teeth even farther as he crawled backwards on his belly away from her, and he didn't stop until he hit the corner of the room. From there, he sat up and leaned into the corner. He held his shaking paws out straight, and he looked at Lin between them. He never broke his stare, and his growling continued.

She pushed harder, committed to the experiment, and Nomad's growling got louder. She looked around Nomad's spirit and found a spot that appeared wide enough for her to squeeze in. She pushed hard to get in that gap, and he let out a shriek that all the neighbors must have heard. Through his outstretched, shaking paws, Lin could see that his eyes were red and watering, but he wouldn't stop staring at her.

Lin's heart jerked inside her, and she faced the fear that her mayhem was causing. No experiment was worth scaring her Nomad!

"Oh my God, what am I doing?"

She quickly ended her mayhem and watched him as his eyes closed and he slumped down into the corner. The growling had stopped, and no fangs could be seen.

Lin leaned each way, saw that he was breathing easily, and stayed safe on the couch.

After several minutes, his eyes opened, and he fell forward to lie there on his belly. His breathing had slowed, and he stared at her with red eyes.

"Nomad?"

He had no reaction.

She started to get up, and he bared his teeth with a low growl that continued until she sat back down and said, "Okay."

She settled back into the couch and continued to hold the dog's gaze. After several more minutes, she looked away and flipped TV channels for a few minutes. When she looked back, Nomad still stared at her.

"Oh," she whispered to herself, "what the hell was I thinking?"

She forced herself to ignore the giant, staring animal and keep her eyes on the TV. After a long while, she turned only her eyes toward him and saw that he was sleeping but still backed into the corner.

Again, she started to rise from the couch and instantly, his eyes snapped open to stare into hers, and he bared his teeth with a growl.

She shivered as she sat back down, staring at a formidable beast that could likely snap her neck with one violent shake.

She whistled softly and said, "And obviously, my mayhem won't help."

Lin snuggled under a thick blanket, parked on the couch for the night. And the last she saw before falling asleep was the very large, very dangerous animal keeping a close watch on her.

Chapter 43 – Striking Evil

Dr. Craig Grayson loved animals, and they loved him. He knew from an early age that being a veterinarian was the only life for him. The debts that he'd racked up for vet school were staggering, but he took a chance after graduation by leasing a storefront in downtown Allentown. Dr. Grayson's Sweet Pets then opened its doors to all animals large and small.

He credited much of his success to having chosen quality associates for his team. He had a sense about people—whether they truly loved animals, or if they were just looking for a job. His screening process filtered out a lot of applicants long before they could expect an interview. His interviews were rigorous but light-hearted. Knowledge of pet care was essential, but enjoying life and having a true love for the patients was at least as important.

Lin Finnerty's application had met all of the criteria: solid education, a history of volunteering, and a cover letter that convinced Dr. Grayson to schedule an interview. She'd nailed the interview with intelligence and charm, and she quickly became a model employee.

And he needed that valuable employee back from vacation already. She'd been gone a week, and it was difficult to keep up with the steady procession of cats, dogs, hamsters, and the occasional goat.

He couldn't hide his wide grin.

"Lin, good morning. It's good to have you back."

"It's good to be back. Did I miss anything?"

"Yes, you missed a lot of very fine critters that wanted to see you."

His smile was so big that Lin broke down and let go a little smile of her own.

"Well, I'd bet you all handled it very well, and there will always be many more fine critters, I'm sure."

She kept up her smile, but the memories of leaving her home to get to work were threatening to wipe it away.

It had been an ordeal even to get out of the house that morning. Nomad watched her every move. She learned quickly that if she needed something in his direction, it was best that she not face him and just move to the side and try to work her way around him. If he sensed that she was moving directly toward him, she got nothing but growling and fangs.

"Was it a good vacation? You went to Georgia, didn't you?"

"Oh, it was an interesting vacation, that's for sure. Very busy too. There was a high school reunion, and I got to catch up with some people from my past."

His eyes dipped down briefly to where Ben had struck her.

"I see you've noticed the bruise on my cheek. Too many margaritas can cause you to walk into a door," she said.

"Well, you deserve to have a good time. Watch out for those doors, though, huh? You must be tired from all that. I bet it's good to settle back in at home. How's Nomad? Did he miss you?"

"It sure is good to be home, and yeah, Nomad missed me. He's, uh, not really taking his eyes off me."

"He's a sweet boy. A big boy, though. I'm still glad you took him in. That's an amazing breed. So loyal but kind of wild, too, I suppose. Best not to get on his bad side, huh?"

"Oh yeah, that would be kind of scary."

"So, don't make him angry, ever!"

"I really shouldn't, that's true."

He looked toward the exam rooms, then focused on her again, letting his eyes drift lower.

"Doctor."

"Yes, Lin?"

He looked her in the eye again.

"I'm ready to get to work. What do we have going on?"

She held his gaze, forcing him to lock on her eyes too.
"We have a line of patients for routine shots and check-ups in Exam Room 1. You feel like jumping into that?"
"Sure, I'll just wash up and get started."
She brushed her hair back and headed for the sink.
"Fantastic. Good to have you back."

*   *   *

Lin immersed herself in a stream of needy patients and thirty minutes later, Dr. Grayson called the office manager into his room.
"Gina, come on in. Close the door, please."
"What's up?"
"It's great to have Lin back, but I don't know, she seems kind of down. Maybe she's just tired. Vacations can do that to you. Maybe I'm wrong, but she seems kind of out of it, like something is bothering her. Have you noticed that?"
"Yeah, now that you mention it. I thought she was just tired, but the more I think of it, she doesn't seem tired—she's just saying that she is. You think she's depressed?"
"Maybe. Or maybe it's just from having to come back to work."
They both laughed.
"That could be, Doctor, but maybe things didn't go well at the reunion. You never know what kind of bad things from the past can get dredged up."
"I think you're right. I was wondering . . . tell me what you think. How about if we have a work get-together tonight? We'll all have a few drinks, a good meal, and hopefully, a ton of laughter. I mean, that could only help, right?"
"That's a great idea. Where were you thinking?"
"My favorite place, of course—that place on Broadway. What do you think?"
"Sounds perfect. I'll make sure everyone's invited."

*　　*　　*

Mondays were short days at Sweet Pets and after some quick goodbyes and a fast drive, Lin arrived home for a couple of hours before heading back down to Allentown. She sat in her car in the garage before climbing out.

"Well, here we go, I suppose."

The usual contest at the door didn't happen. She'd waited quite a while, but Nomad hadn't come to greet her. She'd only sighed, opened the door noisily and waited, then, still not being mauled by her lovable beast, she'd closed the door quietly and tiptoed through the house.

She made it to her bedroom without seeing him and without considering it first, she closed the door.

"Huh. First time for that."

After changing into sweats, she headed back to the kitchen, where she noticed that Nomad's bowl was empty.

She shook the bag of food over his bowl, and the sound rang through the house. She paused, looking and listening, and within seconds, his big eyes scanned the kitchen from around the corner. Lin was about to write down the weight for her records, but she quickly pushed the tablet aside.

She started to step away from the bowl but stopped herself. Instead, she stooped down right there, forcing the confrontation.

His eyes looked up into hers, then back down to the bowl several times. He cautiously approached and ignored her while crunching.

She held her breath and stroked his thick fur while he ate, not hearing any growling and not seeing any bared teeth.

When he'd had enough, he turned to face her, and he paused for a long moment. He looked directly into her eyes with their noses almost touching. Her hands froze on either side of his mane as she held her breath and gave him no sign that she might wish to run for her life.

After his examination of her was complete, he moved closer and began licking her face.

Giggling, she said, "Nomad, you forgive me?"

He barked once very softly and kept his calm gaze locked on her.

She wrapped her arms around his thick neck and buried her face in his fur.

"I'm sorry, Nomad. I'll never do that to you again."

He seemed to accept her apology and allowed the hug to continue.

"Never again, big boy. I don't know what I was thinking."

She sighed, gave him a final squeeze, and got up to get ready for the evening. She saw that there was time enough, so she picked up her phone.

"Gabby, do you have time to talk?"

"Of course, Lin. How are you? How's your dog?"

"I'm fine, and how did you know?"

"I've known you a long time. It just makes sense that you'd try it. How did it go? Is Nomad alright?"

"I never should have tried it. God, what was I thinking? He seems okay now, but for a while there . . ."

"You weren't thinking, Lin. Your mayhem will push you if you're not vigilant."

"It didn't feel like anything pushed me, Gabby. I chose to do that because I need to learn, but I shouldn't have done anything at Nomad's expense."

"At least, he didn't attack you. He really does love you."

"He must! But it didn't work. My mayhem didn't work on him. It just made him kind of crazy. It took a long time before he'd trust me again."

"What was different about using it on the dog and every other time you've used it?"

"I couldn't get in. There wasn't enough room. The harder I tried, the more it aggravated him. I don't get it."

"Are you saying that there wasn't much space between his spirit and body? They were so close that you couldn't squeeze in between?"

"That's exactly right. God, you're amazing, Gabby. I don't know how you understand so many things."

"I've seen so much over the years, that's all. Remember that, as it's been said, there's nothing new under the sun."

"What? You've seen mayhem before? When?"

"Oh, it was a long time ago. What's most important, still, are the choices you make."

"Really, you've seen it before?"

"It's not important now, Lin. Good or bad—that's what's important."

"I'm still making good choices. I didn't want to hurt Nomad, and I didn't. I don't want to hurt anyone at all, but I want to learn what the heck this is."

"You're learning, even now, but you'll never understand it completely. The layers of magic, as you call it, are boundless. Incomprehensible. I can't stress this enough: what you do with it is the most important thing. You're capable of great good and great evil. Which will you choose?"

"I can tell you're trying to keep me good, Gabby. Thanks for that."

"I'd rather you choose good, but it has to be your choice. I can't make that decision for you."

"But there seems to be a fine line, like if Ben attacks me again. Why shouldn't I strike back? Wouldn't I just be correcting some bit of evil in the world?"

"Perhaps. But you must be absolutely sure of your decision. Be sure that you're truly in danger. Otherwise, you risk becoming just another 'bit of evil in the world.'"

"Gabby, I've never used my mayhem for anything but good. So far, everyone has deserved what they got, including Ray. Especially Ray.

"Be very careful with your choices, Lin. What you choose to do with your mayhem can have profound effects not just on the subject of your mayhem but on you as well."

"I get it. But if Ben shows up and tries to kill me, here where I live, he'll deserve whatever he gets."

Chapter 44 – Barely Breathing

Jack almost sleepwalked around in the Pennsylvania house he was rebuilding. The coffee pot in the kitchen bubbled and gurgled in the cold unheated kitchen, and he poured himself a hot cup before it had finished brewing, then leaned against the cabinets that had been waiting a while for a countertop.

He'd fled Georgia quickly, almost in a trance, after Lin had left him there. The flight black was a blur, the night an incessant rehash of his times with her there, both unbelievably good and just plain unbelievable.

Not so much waking as just getting his day started, he'd sat on the edge of his bed, head in hands, staring at a small box on his dresser.

But there was no time for that, and he'd gotten dressed and sped his pickup over to the project house, not exactly eager to get started.

Spreading that load of gravel across the driveway would have to wait. Only lighter work could be faced in his mood, so he got busy nailing trim around a doorway. He was old school, a man who still used a hammer, and his distraction led to a solid strike against his thumb.

"Dammit."

It hurt, but he allowed no reaction other than that. Injuries were often just part of the job. Resting the thumb wouldn't help the throbbing, but he decided to rest all the same. The hammer dropped to the floor, and he found the one chair in the house.

Coffee in one hand, smashed thumb on the other getting studied, he mumbled, "I should have just told her."

As the throbbing began to fade, he finished his drink and tossed the cup across the floor.

"Dammit, I'm just going to tell her."

He got out his phone, tapped a few numbers, then abandoned the call and stuck the phone back in his pocket.

"No. A poem. She likes poems."

*　*　*

Several hours later, after Jack had sat at his makeshift workbench covered in scribbled notes on paper, broken pencil in hand and crumpled sheets scattered all over the floor, he laid the pencil down.

He closed his eyes and sighed.

"It's not coming. I can't find the words."

The sheets and dull pencils remaining on the bench got swept to the floor, and he took a small box out of his coat pocket. He set it directly in front of him but didn't open it.

He only stared at it until he began to nod, then a smile sprang up too.

"Hell. I'll just ask her. What's the worst that can happen?"

*　*　*

Lin remained standing next to her bed, staring down at the silent phone that she'd tossed there.

"I meant it, Gabby," she said, shaking her head. "If Ben—"

The phone rang out, she picked it up, and she saw that it was Jack calling. She hesitated, wincing at the phone, then shook her head and tapped it, then held it to her ear.

"Hello, Jack."

"Hi, Lin. How was your trip back?"

"Oh, it was fine. Nothing too out of the ordinary. How about yours? Are you back in PA?"

"My flight was fine, and I'm at the house, trying to get some work done. But I'm really mostly just thinking of you. Would you like to have dinner later? I have something important I—"

"Oh, Jack, I can't. It was my first day back at work and for some reason, they all want to go out tonight. I feel like I have to go. How about a rain check?"

There was a long pause.

"Sure. Another time, then. Where are you all going?"

"A place in Allentown up on Broadway. Really nice place. You and I have been there, and maybe we should try it again."

"Sure, that sounds great. Is everything going okay? You sound a little tired. I guess that was quite a trip, huh?"

"Yeah, I think I'm just a little run down. It's good to be home, though. Look, I don't mean to cut you off, but I need to leave soon, and I'm still in sweats. Talk to you later?"

"For sure. Have a great time, alright?"

"I will. Bye, Jack."

"Bye."

Lin dropped the phone onto the bed and lay down, not in any rush.

*   *   *

Jack put the phone back in his pocket and picked up his hammer. He almost immediately put it back down.

"Shit," he said while looking at his watch.

He flipped a few switches, unplugged a few tools, and ran to the back door, where he'd parked his truck. Holding the knob, he gave that last switch a hit, then immediately tipped it back up.

A quick run, laughing, got him to the workbench where he scooped up the small box. He stuffed that in a pocket, made a hasty exit, and roared his truck to life.

"Tonight. It'll be tonight."

*   *   *

Eleven hours on the road, in a truck about to rattle itself to pieces, had left Ben numb. And those eleven hours of driving were after a restless four hours cramped up on the front seat trying to sleep, which were after six hours of driving the day before, which were after a fifth shot for the road.

Ben had rumbled his old truck through the streets of Allentown, leaving trails of black smoke choked out of the exhaust pipes pointing up behind the cab. He'd been dazed by what looked like a foreign country: no gravel roads, no shacks surrounded by junk, and no roadside dives with trucks and motorcycles swarmed all around it.

But still, there were bars, and he wheeled into the nearest one, shut down the engine, kicked the driver's door after slamming it, then hiked inside, scowling at the non-country music.

"What'll you have, mister?"

The neatly groomed man behind the bar smiled and refused to look at any other part of Ben but his eyes.

"Directions."

He held out the menu from Lin's hotel room in St. Simons Island.

"It's close. Just follow Tilghman east until you can branch off onto Broadway. Follow that for a mile or two, and it's on your left."

Ben folded it up, stuck it in his pocket, and said, "Thanks."

"Anything else? You thirsty?"

"I'm always thirsty. Whiskey. Bottom shelf. Gimme a shot."

A few seconds later, Ben had a tempting shot sitting on the bar in front of him, and he made it vanish.

"Another?"

"Yeah. Hey, how many people live around here?"

"I don't know. A lot. Why?"

Ben held out a hand, and the bartender tipped his head and waited while Ben shot the second one down.

"Ah, that's good. Because I feel like telling somebody, and you're as damn good as anyone else."

"Thanks. I think. Tell me what?"

"About a goddamn witch."

"A witch, huh? What, like some ugly old thing that—"

"No. This one's gorgeous. Long blond hair. Pretty face. Dresses like some Hollywood star."

Ben slid the glass closer to the young man.

"Another."

He got his third delivered and held it up.

"So, um, what about this gorgeous witch?"

Ben looked past the barkeep toward the mirror and his own reflection looking back over rows of clean liquor bottles. Seconds passed.

"Really, what about her?"

Ben sank his third and set the glass down softly.

He curled a finger toward the man, who leaned in closer.

Barely loud enough to be heard, Ben whispered, "I think I still love her."

*   *   *

Jack had rushed around his house to get ready, hoping to get to the restaurant before anyone else. A quick shower and shave, then his best clothes and only tie, and he was almost ready. The ring was easy to find. He took it out nearly every day, sometimes dropping to one knee and imagining how it would be.

With the ring in his pocket, he'd sped out of his neighborhood and arrived early at the restaurant. He'd looked it over from the outside for a while, searched for and didn't find Lin's car, then tried to guess where she might park. He parked there and went straight inside.

"Just one today?" said the hostess.

"Uh, yeah. For now. How about up there?"

Jack pointed up to the balcony.

"Of course. Follow me."

She led him along the bar toward the stairs, and Jack kept his eyes mostly on the entrance and the bar, which was almost deserted, as they climbed to the second level.

"Here you go," she said and laid a menu on the nearest table.

256

"If you don't mind, that one looks better."

He pointed to a table near the railing overlooking the bar, one that was partially blocked by a thick column.

"Of course."

She followed him to his preferred table and placed the menu and silverware there for him.

"Your server will be out soon."

She turned and passed the server as she left.

"What can I get you?"

"Nothing, miss, I'm not ready to order yet. Just a few more minutes, alright? But in the meantime, could you bring me a shot of whiskey on ice? Thanks."

"Right away."

She left, and Jack devoted only a few seconds to watching her walk away, then he turned back to his surveillance of the bar.

He looked back down and saw the entrance door still swinging itself closed and Lin walking toward the bar. She wore a short black skirt and black top, black stockings and high heels, and her hair spilled all over her shoulders from under a simple blue beret.

He could barely breathe, watching her taking long, graceful strides as if she owned the place.

His hand was in his pocket, holding the ring box, as he watched her settle onto a bar stool and calmly look around the room. She didn't look up, but he'd moved so that the column mostly blocked him, and the railing covered the rest.

While he was staring, still holding his breath, she turned her head and looked up at the balcony. Jack spun around, hiding himself and his smile, and he let his breath rush out and resume a normal pace.

Still smiling, and shaking his head, he said to himself, "My God . . ."

Chapter 45 – Party of the Blind

"My God, I don't want to be here," Lin said to herself as she strode into the bar with her heels clicking in the quiet, almost empty room.

She found her favorite spot—a bar stool right near the exit to the patio and with a view of the entire bar, including the front door. If Ben somehow managed to show up, she'd have a clear view of his grand entrance.

"What'll you have?" asked the young bartender as he looked at more than just Lin's eyes.

Without looking at him, she said, "A gin and tonic, please."

"Happy to get that for you."

She still hadn't look at him.

"Anything to eat?"

"No, just the drink. Thanks."

He smirked and went for her drink. A few seconds later, he set it in front of her.

"Here you go. Can I—"

"I'm good. Thanks."

He frowned and went off to talk with another customer.

The bar hadn't yet begun to fill up, and she had solitude to enjoy her strong drink. While sipping, she turned her eyes toward the young man who'd brought her drink, and he happened to look her way at the same time.

She quickly looked away and scoffed.

When the front door swung out, she snapped her eyes there instead.

It wasn't Ben. Dr. Grayson walked in and looked around the room before seeing Lin. He plastered on a big smile, then walked over and took a barstool next to her.

"Hi, Lin. Glad you made it. You look fantastic."

"Hi, Doctor, and thanks, it's good to get out of the house. Nomad isn't always the best company."

"What's wrong with him? Is he getting to be too much to handle?"

"No, nothing like that. He's a big baby. It's just nice to mingle with people sometimes too."

She sighed and started looking around the room before she'd finished her answer.

"We missed you all week. It's good to have you back. Are you recovered from the vacation or still a little tired?"

"Just a little tired. It was a good trip, though."

She groaned right after her response, then took a big swallow of her drink.

"I'll be honest with you, Lin, I just got the impression today that you could use an evening out and have a few laughs. You know, if there's ever anything bothering you, I'm always there for you."

She paused and stared at him for a few seconds, then looked away before answering.

"Thanks. It's just life in general, you know? There are always things going on. It's good to be back home."

*   *   *

Jack pried his eyes off of Lin only long enough to frown at the guy who'd sat on a stool beside her. He couldn't hear a word that they said, but he could see the way the guy looked at her, and he was sneaking peeks whenever she looked away.

He kept watching the scene, even when he heard, "Here's your drink."

"Thanks."

"Not ready to order just yet?"

"No, uh, soon. Probably."

He fumbled his hand around on the table until he found it.

Both Lin and her friend looked toward the entrance and a few seconds later, several more people walked over and joined them. Some sat at the bar, and some stood around Lin.

"Good. Talk to them instead, you jerk."

He ignored Lin and her co-workers long enough to raise the drink and sip some of it. Leaning over to one side, he fished the small box from his pocket and set it on the table.

"Soon," he said to it. "When everyone she knows is here to watch me ask her."

*   *   *

She nodded occasionally as Dr. Grayson continued to drone on, and she broke it up with a quick look in her purse. The only contents were a wad of cash and the usual things a woman might keep there.

No pepper spray. No cuffs.

"Huh," she said, smiling at the open purse.

"Uh, what's that, Lin?"

"Nothing, Dr. Grayson. Go on."

"Well, like I was telling you, ever since . . ."

The doctor's voice and all of the other conversations around her began to blur together into an unrecognizable, monotonous hum like from a field packed with buzzing insects.

Lin groaned and closed her eyes, then covered one ear with a palm cool and wet from her drink.

She had a brief thought of her mayhem, and infinity unrolled to every horizon. She heard the conversations trail off all at once, as if everyone that was speaking had just finished a sentence. It was like a huge coincidence.

She immediately began breathing naturally, and the world returned to normal. Dr. Grayson had been in the middle of a sentence.

She opened her eyes, which were pointed down at her drink, and said, "Oh my God. I have to really—"

"What's that, Lin? Oh my God, what?"

"Nothing, Doctor. Please, continue."

He stared at her for a second, his eyes big behind his glasses, which he pushed up along his nose.

"I, uh, can't. I . . . I kind of lost my train of thought there, Lin. Whew, that's not like me. What was I saying? Something about too many rabbits in my yard, maybe?"

"Yeah, I think that was it. Why do you think there are so many rabbits this year?"

"Oh. Yeah, that's right. The rabbits. So, Lin, the thing is that . . ."

Dr. Grayson's voice had again become an insect's unintelligible whining as Lin stared past him, her breaths even and strong.

*　　*　　*

Jack took another quick peek over the railing, and he snapped his head back around when Lin glanced up. But he'd looked long enough to know that more people had joined the party.

"Getting close!" he said, grinning.

"Close to what?" said the server, who had walked up unobserved by Jack. "Close to ordering, you mean?"

"Oh, no, something else. Just a few more minutes, please. I'll be ready to order soon. Thank you."

"Sure. I'll stop back in a few."

Holding a menu up next to the column, and allowing only enough room for one eye to peer through, he counted about twenty standing around Lin.

He held his cold whiskey glass still on the table while his hand shook, his heart pounded, and his eyes were locked on the small, very special box beside his drink.

*　　*　　*

261

Ben's truck rattled and backfired after he'd rumbled it into the upscale restaurant's parking lot. With a hot exhaust pipe still shaking, much like the whiskey in his belly, Ben sat at the wheel and rubbed his face. He looked around in every direction, for what he didn't know. That place was his only clue—a name on a take-out menu left in Lin's room—and maybe it was a dead end.

"Gotta be something flashy. Witch like that."

No witch cars were obvious, so he clenched his jaw and grabbed the handle to open his door. But he froze there, in the truck's dim overhead light.

"Could I even say that? I never say it. Not to anyone."

With the mirror tipped to bounce his eyes back at him, he saw the snarling face struggling to practice saying the words.

"I can't," he told the sullen face.

The face stared back, still angry but insistent too.

"Do it, damn it. Say it."

A hard wipe across his face dispelled some of the scowl.

"I'm . . . I'm sorry."

The reflected face's eyes seemed to take on a bit more sparkle.

"Bullshit. You don't like saying that. Just this once, goddammit, then never again."

He stepped out of the truck and ground out his cigarette. A convulsion of anger exploded inside him, the only thing that could prepare him, and he kicked the door shut, leaving another dent.

"Hey, a dent from Pennsylvania. That's kind of cool."

He straightened out his black t-shirt and crossed his arms from the cold, and he headed for the door.

* * *

"I think it's because my neighborhood banned the use of chemical weedkillers. I bet all the grass tastes better now. I don't know, though, because I haven't actually tried it myself."

"That's kind of funny, Doctor."

"Thanks! Anyhoo, that's probably why they're all moving in. We have thousands of them. I mean thousands, Lin."

"That's a lot of rabbits, Doctor. Where do they all—"

"Excuse me. May I buy you a drink?"

Lin turned her head slowly to see an attractive younger guy smiling at her and standing close.

"Thanks, I already have a drink."

"Then, the next one is on me."

"No, it's not on you. Thanks, but no thanks."

She turned back to her conversation and struggled to keep her mayhem from erupting.

"Okay. No offense, I hope. If you change your mind, I'm right over there," he said and pointed across the room to a table with two other guys who were both waving and smiling.

"Nice. Another John and Tommy."

"Huh?"

"Nothing. Thanks for the offer."

*   *   *

Jack watched the entire scene from the balcony with his fists clenched but at the same time, he was nodding and smiling at her. She didn't give that intruder the time of day. But he knew that he shouldn't be mad at the guy. She looked so incredible with her long hair falling over her shoulders, quietly enjoying her drink, and politely listening to the jerk next to her.

After Lin's suitor had retreated, Jack took another look around and saw that the party size had expanded.

He checked his watch, laughed once, and quickly downed most of his drink.

*   *   *

Lin sipped her gin and tonic, which was mostly gin, thanks to her infatuated bartender, and looked around the room. Almost every one of her coworkers had arrived, and word had gotten out to some of her few friends too. The room was filling up, mostly with people she knew. All of the people there cared about her, but she didn't want to see any of them. She had her entire life to sort out. Not one of them could help.

She'd beaten back the feeling of annoyance, and she felt only a calm disinterest in the whole scene.

This is what normal people do, she reminded herself. They get together and talk about mundane bits and pieces of their lives that don't add up to anything. They don't see the magic all around them. They're absolutely blind.

"You were saying? About all my rabbits?"

"Oh, yeah. Um, I was wondering where so many rabbits lived, that's all."

"Heck, they can burrow in just about anywhere. I've seen nests in the weeds up against fence posts, under the leaves of hostas, and sometimes—"

"Oops, pardon me. I'm really sorry!"

A twenty-something girl had bumped Lin's elbow, causing her drink to spill onto the bar. Lin stared down at the spreading puddle and bit her lip before looking back up.

"That's okay. Don't worry about it. It was almost gone anyway."

"Really sorry!" she said and merged back into the crowd that had begun to fill the bar.

The bartender got busy wiping up the drink and said, "Can I get you another? On the house?"

"Sure. Thanks."

"Anything else?"

"No. Nothing else. Oh, wait."

He leaned to look at her eyes and kept his eyebrows up.

"Make it a double."

He smirked and walked away to mix her drink, and she returned her attention to Dr. Grayson. He had just started picking up where he'd left off when Lin's eyes were drawn to the front door. A large shape had appeared behind the glass, and the door had begun to swing open slowly.

*   *   *

Jack had been watching everything and sighed with relief that it wasn't some other amorous guy that had spilled Lin's drink. He did notice, though, that she'd begun looking toward the front door. The crowd around her was excitedly talking and gesturing, and only Lin remained perfectly still, looking toward something he couldn't see.

"Sir, I can take your order now, if you're ready."

"Thanks, yes. That would be good. Sorry it took so long."

"That's okay. What would you like?"

*   *   *

The door swung open, and Ben's large frame filled the doorway. He took a few steps inside and stopped to look the place over.

Lin watched with no visible reaction. Her hand rested calmly around her fresh drink, and she only waited for him to see her.

"Had to happen," she said, then looked inside to see her mayhem swirling just beneath her surface. Ready.

"Huh?"

"Nothing, Doctor."

Dr. Grayson was about to ask again when he saw that Lin was looking past him, and he turned to see what had caught her attention.

With a puzzled expression, he said, "Lin, what's wrong?"

She didn't answer. She only controlled her breaths with complete authority.

Dr. Grayson turned back around.

"Lin, what's going on?"

*   *   *

265

Jack snugged his tie up to his collar then smoothed it down. With the server at the table and waiting patiently, he let go of the ring in his pocket and picked up the menu for one final scan.

"Could you bring me another shot of whiskey on the rocks? And I'll have a burger, well done, with fries. Oh, I might move down to the bar in a few minutes. Could I get the food brought down there?"

*   *   *

Ben's weary eyes separated Lin from the crowd, and he froze for only a moment. After taking a deep breath and letting it out, he walked in her direction, ignoring anyone in his path. Most people got out of his way.

Lin remained on her stool and took another sip of her drink. She checked again and found her mayhem where she knew she'd always find it. Her hold on her intent was unbreakable.

"Here, Ben?"

"What, Lin?" said Dr. Grayson. "What?"

She ignored him.

Lin felt her mayhem about to erupt, and she stared at Ben calmly, knowing that he didn't have a chance in hell.

He stopped six feet from her. Lin stood, and even the droning, buzzing insects all around seemed to swarm to some other field.

She felt the calm, dangerous determination in her green eyes just waiting for her command.

And she saw the anger in Ben's.

*   *   *

"Of course, that would be fine. I'll bring the drink over, and wherever you end up, I'll see that you get your food. Anything else?"

Jack tipped his head toward the bar and said, "Yeah. I want her to say yes."

He showed her the ring. The server raised up on her toes and looked over the railing.

"Her? The blonde?"

Before he'd finished nodding, she began to straighten his tie. She finished, then touched his cheek gently.

"If she says no . . . ask me."

She gave him a smile, then turned to walk away while writing his order. He watched her departure for only a few seconds.

After lifting his glass to finish his drink, Jack looked down, and his heart nearly stopped. The giant, violent man from St. Simons Island stood within striking distance of Lin.

Chapter 46 – A Life Ending

On that lonely Georgia road, with a fugitive convict's meaty hands squeezing her throat, and another watching and mocking her about it, Lin had found exactly how to raise her mayhem. She'd told Gabby later that she'd never lose it again. That it would always be there for her. And it was there for her in that Allentown restaurant.

Believing that Ben would soon strike, Lin found the magic in her breath. She became what her mayhem demanded of her. She opened the door to infinity in every direction. She was at the center of the calm surface of reality, a world built upon limitless layers of magic.

She'd learned that when she crossed into the realm of magic, when her intent took her there, that time stopped. Reality stopped. Reality appeared as a calm surface. No waves. Not even a ripple. No need to hurry.

She focused on Ben and noticed more than anger displayed on his face. She saw fear, of course, but also a full measure of sadness and confusion. She saw adoration too.

But she knew well enough the effects of her power. Adoration was often the result, like with John and Tommy and even the soothing of Jack's fears. It wasn't real. Ben's anger, his attempted murder of her . . . those were real.

She no longer needed to catch and hold a breath to begin, but she did it anyway. She found it hard to resist the heavenly feeling of lingering on the cusp of magic.

She drew in a deep breath and kept it. The air in her lungs was rich with magic, and it spread rapidly throughout her. She felt more alive with every moment until she felt she'd burst out of her body's limits. A soft green glow lit up her eyes.

Then, Lin understood. She *was* infinite. Her body and the rest of the real world were only finite. How she longed for the freedom of infinity. So did everyone else, she knew, whether they realized it or not.

Every desire, every dream that anyone had—that was their hunger for the infinite.

With every indescribable feeling they had from art, or religion, or love—they were being touched by infinity, tempted by it, drawn to it.

But Lin could find infinity and become one with it.

And from there, God, the things she could do . . .

*   *   *

Jack stood at the railing with his forearms grinding into it and gazed down on the scene. His mouth froze open, and his eyes didn't dare to blink. He could only stare at the big man from St. Simons Island looming over Lin and about to attack her.

He looked quickly at the stairs, saw how far away they were, then snarled and turned back to the scene at the bar.

"No, no, no . . ."

He gripped the railing tight.

He took a deep breath, gathering it up for the biggest scream of his life, and . . .

. . . he saw Lin's eyes close halfway and begin to glow a bright green.

*   *   *

Lin paused at the top of a towering hill, feeling those sweet, agonizingly slow moments before she dropped in a free fall. She savored the anticipation, knowing that the big crash was coming and it would send out that monstrous, unstoppable wave. That it was inevitable.

She teetered on the edge, blissfully near the point of no return, with magic filling every part of her and longing to break free.

She looked into Ben's sad, scared eyes. He appeared ready to speak, but he couldn't. She wouldn't let him.

She exhaled sharply, and an inescapable wave of magic rose up.

She was a boat grounded on a sand bar, and a strong current from the endless sea of magic broke her loose and held her. The wave rushed out from her in every direction, washing through Ben and anyone else close enough.

*   *   *

Jack froze on the balcony above, his face twisted and his breaths strained as he witnessed something that no one could explain, not even Lin.

Lin stood in the center of a large group crowded around her near the bar. She and the big man from the Island were motionless among the chattering faces. Her eyes closed halfway, and they lit up with a bright, green glow. And from Jack's distance, it looked as though she took a breath, held it briefly, then sighed comfortably.

His heart skipped a beat when he saw a wave rush out from her in every direction. But the wave didn't move anything. Instead, it passed through everything within twenty-five feet of her, and every person touched by the wave seemed to dissolve where they stood—they became unfocused.

After the wave had passed, all appeared normal again.

Jack shook and opened his mouth to try again at a scream as he lost the grip on his glass, and it began to fall to the concrete floor below.

*   *   *

Lin got swept along with the wave as it passed through Ben, allowing it to carry her into his very narrow space between reality and magic. She found just barely enough room to squeeze herself in.

She felt a silent scream of surprise from him, and then terror had him in its grasp. That's how it had worked thirty years ago, she observed. Back then, she'd had no control. But this time, she completely owned her mayhem. Ben had no chance at all.

Her first task was to keep him silent. She'd decided that it was too late for regrets or confessions. Or even a silent shriek.

Knowing that time had essentially stopped, she studied the narrow space where she'd inserted herself. In that space, Ben's spirit connected to his body in the real world. She didn't know how she was able to be there, but it felt completely natural.

She sensed all of the countless places where Ben connected to his body. They had fallen under her control, and his body would do anything she intended. Leaving him standing upright would be good enough.

Lin existed between two layers—Ben's body in the world of reality and his spirit in the world of magic. And beyond Ben's spirit, she could see endless, convulsing, unexplainable magic.

From that narrow space, she focused on the mystery of all that magic, and she tried to comprehend what it might be. As she watched its constant writhing, currents, and gyrations, her thoughts began to scatter, and her senses began to overlap. She felt the same odd confusion that used to hit her before she'd black out. Chaos rippled through her.

She had barely enough judgment left to look away. To lose herself in that magic would lead to madness. She could feel it. She had work to do. Ben could never be allowed to hurt anyone again.

Focusing again on Ben's body, she saw something that caught her by surprise. That surface, the calm surface of reality, was *not* completely still. It moved but oh, so slowly. Its motion was impossibly slow. If she hadn't been taking her time, she never would have noticed.

While gazing into that surface, Lin began to see that it, too, was magic. She laughed at seeing that it was all magic. Reality was nothing more than dreadfully slow, completely organized, and predictable magic.

She turned her focus to Ben's spirit and saw that it was a special kind of magic, infused with a brighter light than the magic all around it.

That must be life, she thought. Some kind of life force held together a portion of the boundless magic, and the world knew it as Ben.

Satisfied that she'd investigated the magic well enough, Lin decided it was time for justice. Time to eliminate one more bit of evil in the world. She turned her attention to the task at hand.

Well, she thought, soon the world will know a different Ben. A Ben that will never be able to hurt anyone again like he'd tried to hurt her. Like he'd planned to do right that second. It was time to stop Ben for good. Should she make it quick? Or slow? Where to begin . . .

It took her some time to scan his spirit completely, and her plans ground to a halt.

It bewildered her to see areas near the middle that didn't shine as brightly as the rest. The more she looked, the more distinction she could perceive. Parts of Ben's spirit appeared to be dead or dying. Darkness competed with the light and by the sight of it, the darkness would win.

With a closer look, she got struck by memories of her encounter with him over thirty years earlier. That feeling that she'd had, the memory that was like a nightmare, was of her squeezing Ben in some way, trying to stop him from attacking her. Ben's darkness looked so familiar . . .

The realization exploded and rocked Lin to her core. She knew with no doubt that she'd done that to Ben. He'd been damaged by her mayhem for over thirty years!

Her revelation humbled and saddened her. She felt no guilt because she knew her intention had never been to hurt him, but she knew that it wasn't fair. Her mayhem hadn't fought fairly. She carried the responsibility for the wounding of his spirit, which led to his wasted, pointless life.

But she could also see more darkness there, not just what she'd caused. The other damage looked older and more settled in, like it must have been done to him years before she'd ever met him. Ben's wounding had begun early in his life, and it wasn't all Lin's work. But the damage she had inflicted pushed him beyond some boundary to a point where his spirit likely had no ability left to overcome the darkness.

She no longer felt a need to hurt Ben in any way. He'd tried to kill her, but he'd never be able to. Her mayhem would never let him. And without any further thought, she knew that helping to repair that damage was the right thing to do. Gabby would be proud, she thought.

She focused her magic on those dark regions of Ben's spirit. She felt the magic flowing through her, much like she'd done with Jack but with a different purpose, and she directed it all to the damage, filling each dark area, a little at a time, with fresh light. With fresh magic.

To Lin, it was a painfully slow process, seeking out every tiny area of damage and making sure that all darkness had been chased away. Several times, she stopped to look it over and found more that needed attention.

Finally, Ben's spirit had a new, consistent brightness in every area. She could still feel that he had a bit of anger, though it was drastically less than before. But other feelings had become noticeable too.

Ben had a feeling of calm, of disbelief, even. And a feeling of gratitude. If he hadn't been so weakened by the encounter, there would be fear there too. But at that moment, he felt mostly the peace of being balanced, healthy, and complete.

Lin retreated back to herself, relieved that she hadn't hurt the big man.

She ended her mayhem and let time resume.

Ben stood weakly for a moment, then slowly began to drop.

Across the room, Jack's glass hit the concrete with a loud crash.

Ben slumped to the floor and leaned up against the bar, staring but not seeing. Tears flowed in two thin streams down his cheeks, but he also had the faintest trace of a smile.

She'd made Ben whole again.

The crowd around Lin all stopped talking and turned to look at her. All of the smiling faces gawked at her adoringly.

"Oh, boy. Should have known."

It was time to leave.

She grabbed her things and began walking purposefully toward the door. There was no need to run. She was in no danger.

After the wave had passed and the man from the Island had gone down, Jack stood speechless and shaking. He saw Lin walking toward the exit, and he hurried down the stairs to meet her at the door.

"Jack, I didn't know you were here."

"I, uh, just got here. Lin, I—"

"Come on. We have to go, Jack."

"Are you okay? He didn't hurt you, did he?"

"No, I'm fine. And so is he. More than fine, I think, but we should get out of here."

* * *

They jostled through the crowd and stood outside in the windy Pennsylvania air. Lin took Jack's hand, and they began the walk to her car. Her heels clicked on the parking lot pavement, and her hair trailed her like a flag.

Jack alternated looks at Lin and where he was walking while she looked only toward her Temt8tion. He held the ring in his pocket but said nothing.

She unlocked the car doors, and they got in, but Lin didn't start the engine right away. She sat there a long moment, looking at the restaurant entrance and feeling Jack's eyes on her.

"Lin, I—"

"Jack, just a moment, okay? I need to think a minute."

She felt the power and magic of her mayhem inside, knowing that it would always be there for her.

And knowing what she'd just caused in everyone she knew, she also understood that she could no longer be anyone but Lin Finity.

Lin's old life had just come to an end.

Chapter 47 – Lin's Horizon

Lin brought the motor to life with a deep rumble. She watched as her friends and coworkers began swarming out of the restaurant and coming after her. They all smiled and chatted with each other, and she knew that their adoration of her would never end. They'd all be like John and Tommy. Forever.

"Jack, where were you?"

"I was at home, getting ready, then I—"

"No. In there."

"Um, I just, uh, ran up to the balcony."

"So, not close."

She maneuvered the car around the restaurant, past the entrance jammed with the infatuated crowd, and headed for Broadway. Before turning onto the road, she put the car in park and turned to Jack.

"Jack, I can't explain anything to you. About who I am. Even about what I am. Or about where I'm going."

"You don't have to explain anything to me. I love you, Lin. No matter what. Wherever you're going, I want to go too. Take me. Just take me, alright?"

Lin looked away and sighed.

"It's not possible after what I just did. They'll all be like John and Tommy forever."

"What? What do you mean about—"

"My life here is over."

"What? Why? Can't we try? We're good for each other, aren't we?"

"Please, Jack. Maybe I'll be able to explain someday. I just know that I have to leave."

Jack's chin dropped to his chest.

She looked back at his clothes and smiled.

"Jack, you're all dressed up. What's the occasion?"

"Oh, nothing," he said without picking up his head. "I was just hoping I could be something more than a carpenter, that's all."

"You are, Jack. So much more."

He sighed but kept his head down.

"You really are some kind of cowboy. Don't ever forget it."

They shared a last smile, though Jack still hadn't looked up to see Lin's.

"Jack, please don't make this any harder for me."

She turned away and clicked to unlock the doors.

Jack's eyes were red, and his face had lost all expression. He said nothing as he got out of the car, and Lin continued to look straight ahead until he'd stepped out.

She turned to watch the door slam, and she said, too softly for him to hear, "Broken hearts or broken bones, my Cowboy."

She turned right and began driving southwest along Broadway, toward the cloud-covered sunset, but she stopped after a couple of car lengths. She didn't put the car in park. She only sat and looked in the rearview mirror at the life that she had to leave behind.

Jack had walked out to the sidewalk and stood motionless, watching her leave. He looked ragged. A scarecrow tossed by the wind.

From the restaurant parking lot, another figure walked out to the sidewalk and stood beside Jack. The northeast wind blew her long, black hair around her face, hiding her identity. The car's brake lights reflected off of her mirrored sunglasses, giving her an unreal appearance against the reality behind her.

Lin scoffed at recognizing her tight faded jeans and black boots.

It was the girl from lunch in Jacksonville. But Lin had moved beyond seeking explanations.

She remembered not wanting to leave Jack. Or Nomad. Or the rest of her life. But all of her doubts were peeling away, and her heart pounded.

Her mayhem began to rise as her gaze dropped from the mirror and focused straight ahead.

Through parted clouds, Lin's horizon blazed with the light of a thousand suns.

She flicked back her long blond hair, and a look of uncompromising determination set in her glowing green eyes.

She floored the gas, and the car sped over the road with every hood light lit.

Behind her, Lin's past faded into night.

Before her, infinity beckoned . . .

Chapter 48 – The Real Gabby

"Lin, I've never asked much from you, have I?"

Not a word had been spoken as Lin raced her Temt8tion west, hours after the sun had fled from the night. Gabby's voice cut through the midnight silence. Infinity still called to her, but the heat of the moment, the fever that she'd felt when leaving her life, had started to settle. Her eyes had returned to a normal green, but magic stirred just below the surface, forever ready to rise up if needed.

She felt ready to contemplate her life.

After pulling off of the highway into a rest area, Lin accepted yet again the impossibility of Gabby finding a way to join her if the need was great, no matter where or when.

"No, Gabby, you really haven't. All you've ever asked of me is that I choose to be good. You've been an amazing friend."

"Thank you. I've hoped to be a good friend too. But now, I *must* ask something of you, Lin."

"Anything, Gabby. What is it?"

She turned to look at Gabby.

Gabby turned toward her and looked into her eyes.

In a serene yet commanding voice that spoke to Lin's soul, Gabby said, "It's time for you to remember who I am."

"It's what? I . . ."

Lin's thoughts slowed and came to a stop. She couldn't remember who had just spoken to her. She could only stare at the calm figure with long brown hair as her mouth moving slowly, unable to form words.

A chill began in her neck and quickly spread. She fought to continue staring into the unblinking gaze as tremors rolled through her entire body like flowing electricity. Her heart raced, and heat swelled behind her eyes, driving tears down her cheeks. Her body shook while the eyes of the figure beside her calmly stared, and she looked away to focus on her trembling hands twisting the hem of her skirt.

Lin's vision turned inward, viewing memories lined up like a multitude of dark rooms. The memories stretched from the present moment in the car, back in time across more than three decades, back to the moment her mayhem had first erupted.

"No, please, I can't go there again!"

That dark room, that first incomplete memory, became filled with light. Lin saw that she'd just left Ray after her mayhem had destroyed him. She saw the weakness, the confusion, and the insanity that had besieged her after what she had just done. She'd had no strength left to do anything but crawl into that safe box that she'd avoided during all of the years of abuse. Using her mayhem had broken her.

Before she could fall into darkness, Gabby arrived. Gabby held her close and allowed her to turn away from the unexplainable events she'd witnessed. From the unexplainable person she'd just become.

"Oh, God. After I destroyed Uncle Ray . . . you were there."

In the same memory, Lin saw Gabby transform into a private companion. A hidden influence in her life. She'd carried Gabby within her since that day.

She saw her father saying her name over and over, and she saw that he'd been far away, too far for her to answer. She'd felt safe in Gabby's embrace.

Other rooms of memories began to light up.

"And that day with Ben. You held me, even then."

She saw the day she fought Ben at the big truck, and she saw Gabby still holding her, reminding her to be kind. And she had been somewhat kind. Her mayhem could have wrecked Ben completely.

"God. Everything I've been through . . ."

And countless more memories: every joy, every sadness, every regret; every feeling of love, of being lost, of being afraid; of growing up, becoming a woman, and finding her way in the world. And every time she'd used her mayhem. Gabby had been with her through all of it. Embracing her when she'd felt too weak, encouraging her when she'd felt hopeless, always gently nudging her toward good.

". . . you were always with me!"

On down time's line, Lin traveled through more than thirty years of memories, all newly lighted with the knowledge of the real Gabby. Every feeling and thought, every mistake and triumph, all the ways her life had been guided. All were rebuilt in truth.

"Always holding me, encouraging me to be good. Through everything!"

Finally, the last memory had arrived—the present day, sitting in the car after she'd left her life behind.

The chills had stopped, and the storms behind her eyes had calmed. The cloud of confusion that had always kept Gabby obscured, and never subject to any real scrutiny, burned away like a morning mist.

Lin knew the real Gabby.

Just as she had that fateful day at age fifteen.

She took a deep breath, let it out slowly, and turned to look straight into Gabby's eyes.

"I remember who you really are. Not just my best friend," she said as she wiped the tears from her cheeks with one hand.

"Hello, Gabriel."

Gabriel reached out and took Lin's other hand.

"Hello, Lin. It's good to be a real part of your life once more."

Lin fought back more tears as she looked into Gabriel's eyes. After a pause and several measured breaths, she laughed softly and wiped under her eyes.

"Thank you . . . for so much. I can't even imagine such goodness. Or such patience. For more than thirty years?"

Lin laughed through her tears, and Gabriel laughed with her.

"It's been only a few grains of sand, Lin. I've always been happy to be with you."

"But why did I have to forget you? Who you really are?"

"Who I really am became tangled with all you'd experienced. To remember me completely, you would have had to remember and accept everything else. It was too much for you until now. It would be too much for anyone. You needed to put your mayhem, your feelings of guilt, and the truth about me into that box, the box where you refused to hide yourself. You needed to continue with your life."

"Why now?"

"Your choice with Ben. You could have acted out of vengeance. Or your own view of justice. Instead, you chose to heal. You made that choice because you've become strong enough. It takes strength to command such a power, as you do, and still act with kindness."

"What would have happened to me if I'd never gotten strong enough?"

"You would have carried your mysteries to the grave. And you wouldn't have been the first. Or last."

Lin paused and continued to look into Gabriel's eyes. She saw only peace and love—love for her, and love for all of life.

She felt more tears pressing to be released—she saw her best friend and a being that she couldn't begin to comprehend.

"Gabby . . . oh, can I still call you Gabby?"

Gabriel smiled.

"Yes, of course. I'm used to it by now."

Again, they laughed as friends.

"Gabby, it didn't even feel like a choice with Ben. I saw the damage I'd inflicted and other damage from his past. I felt his pain and that he felt lost. I saw his unfulfilled life and all the misery he'd brought to himself and everyone around him. Deep inside, he cried. It was simply the right thing to do."

"Yes, Lin. You did the right thing, and that's why we're here today. On that day when you were fifteen, I was sent to protect you and inspire you to choose good. I arrived when your power first showed itself. It's a rare thing and when it does happen, when someone claims that ability, it is noticed. It's important."

"I can't really be that important, can I?"

"Yes, Lin, you're more important than you can possibly imagine, and we've only begun."

Lin accepted Gabriel's last statement without question. She released Gabriel's hand and turned to look out over the steering wheel, and she gently brushed her hair back over her shoulders.

A look of calm joined the determination in Lin's green eyes, and she and Gabriel continued the journey.

What happens next?

Find out with a FREE download of the Novella:

Lin Finity in Holding On

One memorable scene between Book 1 & Book 2.
Many powerful memories as recalled by Lin Finity.

https://dl.bookfunnel.com/xf2d4mkgoj

In the brief time after *Lin Finity and Her Mayhem Rising* and before *Lin Finity and the Words Unspoken*, Lin sits in her car with her best friend, Gabby. Lin has left her life behind and after racing west for hours, a growing uneasiness compelled her to stop. She'd mastered her mayhem and had finally shown that she was strong enough to face the realities of her life. So, Gabriel became real again and restored all of her memories of them together for the last thirty-plus years.

As Lin and Gabriel talk in her Temt8tion, in a deserted rest area under a bright midnight moon, she recounts the milestones of her life: her childhood in Pennsylvania and St. Simons Island; the time when her mayhem first erupted; the day she met Jack; the day she fell in love with Nomad; even the traumatic moment when Gabriel arrived.

Relive these pivotal times in Lin's life with her, and see how she became the first in twenty centuries to possess the unstoppable power of her mayhem. Find out how she became Lin Finity and began living a life like few have before or ever will again.

(OVER)

EDWARD ALLEN KARR
LIN FINITY IN
HOLDING ON
FRINGES OF INFINITY NOVELLA

After the Novella comes Book 2:

Lin Finity and the Words Unspoken

A DEADLY SCROLL bearing the Words of God.
An EVIL MANIAC seeking one who can read it.
LIN FINITY - Beautiful, Powerful . . . and Hunted.

Running from the trail of her mayhem, Lin has left her old life behind. But not for long. She's ready to face her future, and there's much more magic to learn. With Gabriel's help.

The Shield has been waiting for centuries for anyone with enough power to read the Scroll. If Lin won't come willingly, the diabolical group will try to force her. Everyone is in danger: her boyfriend Jack, her new friend Lee…even her dog Nomad. Lin must survive their onslaught and read the Scroll and not let it destroy her.

Along the way, her romance with Jack heats up, she discovers the truth of her daughter's illness, and she learns the Words of God. As they were understood by the Scroll's creator long ago.

WORDS that came UNSPOKEN.
WORDS Lin should have left UNSPOKEN.

(OVER)

EDWARD ALLEN KARR
LIN FINITY AND THE WORDS UNSPOKEN
FRINGES OF INFINITY BOOK TWO

About the Author

Edward Allen Karr is the pen name of Edward Sechkar—easier to pronounce and hopefully, easier to remember too. I was born, raised, and continue to reside in Ohio, USA. After many years of pursuing a variety of careers, ranging from working an automotive assembly line to designing space flight experiments that have been in use on the Space Station, I've realized that there is other, more practical work to be done: telling stories.

Visit my website:
www.LakesideLetters.com

On Facebook:
https://www.facebook.com/profile.php?id=100011967855880

On Instagram:
https://www.instagram.com/edward_sechkar/